"It's the start of a whole new year..."

"Hmm," Rick said as he tugged the duvet over them. "In all the drama I forgot about that. We're off to an interesting start."

"Yes, very interesting." She realized something else...she wasn't cold anymore. But she snuggled closer just the same. "Care to make it even more interesting?" she murmured, equal parts thrilled and alarmed to see his eyes darken.

Rick grinned. "I'm a storm chaser. I'm always game for more," he said and stroked her cheek. "Are you sure, though?"

"Oh, Rick..." Jenna studied his handsome face. "I'm going to regret a lot of things about this night. But none of them are you."

He shifted close enough that their bare legs tangled. And when she leaned in for one of his steamy kisses, he met her more than halfway.

No hint of shyness, no reluctance. Her hands were on his back, on his sides, exploring.

His free hand cupped her breast, and all was right with the world.

Dear Reader,

New Year's Eve is a great holiday. No gifts are demanded, it's practically illegal not to have a drink, it feels fantastic to forget what went wrong the past year and believe that the coming year is going to be your best one *ever*.

What is never supposed to happen, not even as a joke, is to find your fiancé in the hallway *kissing* his former college girlfriend at the stroke of midnight.

It doesn't just suck for Jenna Delaney, who has come with her betrothed to the same James Bond costume party in downtown Boston for the fifth year in a row. It's also a pretty major kick in the heart to Rick Sinclair, the boyfriend of the woman kissing Jenna's fiancé. Especially since Rick was going to propose at midnight.

The odds of Jenna and Rick getting snowed in together at a very swanky "smart" apartment in the heart of Boston are slim, and the chance that their heartbreak could turn into something better is off the charts. But love finds a way.

I hope you'll find Jenna and Rick as funny, bright and sexy as I did, and that you'll look for the next books in the Three Wicked Nights trilogy. All three heroes were best friends at MIT, and the smart apartment... the *really smart* apartment...belongs to their friend Sam, who's asked the guys to test the surprising tricks and treats they'll discover during their very wicked nights in Boston.

I'd love to hear from you! You can catch me as @Jo_Leigh on Twitter and at jomk.tumblr.com on Tumblr!

Jo Leigh

One Breathless Night

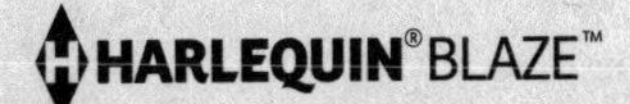

ISBN-13: 978-0-373-79864-3

One Breathless Night

Hard Knocks

This edition published by arrangement with Harlequin Books S.A.

For questions and comments about the quality of this book, please contact us at CustomerService@Harlequin.com.

Printed in U.S.A.

CONTENTS

Jo Leigh is from Los Angeles and always thought she'd end up living in Manhattan. So how did she end up in Utah in a tiny town with a terrible internet connection, being bossed around by a houseful of rescued cats and dogs? What the heck, she says, predictability is boring. Jo has written more than forty-five novels for Harlequin. Visit her website at joleigh.com or contact her at joleigh@joleigh.com.

Books by Jo Leigh

HARLEQUIN BLAZE

Ms. Match
Sexy Ms. Takes
Shiver
Hotshot
Lying in Bed
All the Right Moves

It's Trading Men

Choose Me
Have Me
Want Me
Seduce Me
Dare Me
Intrigue Me

Cosmopolitan Red-Hot Reads from Harlequin

Definitely Naughty

To get the inside scoop on Harlequin Blaze and its talented writers, be sure to check out BlazeAuthors.com.

All backlist available in ebook format.

Visit the Author Profile page at Harlequin.com for more titles.

ONE BREATHLESS NIGHT

Jo Leigh

1

"GUESS HOW MANY James Bonds there are in this room right now." Jenna Delaney tugged up her neckline as she watched the Bonds interact. Some were short, some rotund, some blond; quite a few had the beginnings of beer bellies. But they were all clearly dressed as the one and only Double O Seven.

Jenna and her friend Mindy were stationed perfectly: close enough to the New Year's Eve buffet table that they could nibble all they wanted, yet still have a great view of the reunion suite. "Ten? Twelve?" Mindy shook her head. "I give up. How many are there?"

"They're all Bonds," Jenna said. "Every single man here. All they had to do for their costume was rent a tux. That's it. Unless they already owned one, which would have made it even easier. Meanwhile I, silly fool that I am, shelled out big bucks for Mimco bloodred lipstick, OPI blackish-purplish nail polish that's the perfect shade but hideous, a necklace that looks like a noose, nearly cried putting my hair up in this awful twist and I'm wearing a dress that is far too revealing, just to match the outfit Vesper Lynd wore in *Casino Royale*."

"You looked all that stuff up, didn't you?"

"Of course I did. All the Bond girls have their own wikis." Jenna took her cosplay as seriously as she did her job teaching middle school English.

"Bless your heart," Mindy said, lifting a brie-covered

cracker to her mouth. “I stole my costume from the men’s playbook. None of it’s new. I put it together using stuff from my own closet.”

Jenna eyed her friend’s black blouse and slacks. “That’s supposed to be a costume?”

Mindy nodded as she chewed.

“So what are you? A background extra?”

“Don’t be silly. I’m Judi Dench’s ‘M.’”

Jenna turned to face her now. “But she wasn’t a redhead.”

Mindy grinned wickedly. “I’m M in disguise.”

Jenna laughed.

“For what it’s worth, *you* look sensational.” Mindy looked her up and down, and then zeroed in on her neckline. “Well, you would if you’d quit trying to hide your breasts.”

“What are you talking about?”

“You’ve been tugging on your top all night. You’re not showing off that much, you Victorian prude, you. Look around. There are women here who are barely clothed, for God’s sake. It’s a James Bond–themed party.” Mindy reached over and tugged down Jenna’s top an inch. “It’s called a plunging neckline for a reason. Why didn’t you just come as Miss Moneypenny?”

Jenna clutched her bodice. “I have. Three times, as you well know.”

“Right. Because we come here *every freaking year*. There are things to do all over Boston. I mean, it’s New Year’s Eve and First Night, yet every year, we get stuck coming to the same old party. It’s criminal, all that we’re missing. It’s not being disloyal to their alma mater if we want to see other things, too.”

They were Jenna’s fiancé and Mindy’s husband, both graduates of Boston University. “You have a very good point.” Jenna picked up what looked to be a salmon puff.

"It's time to expand our repertoire. Just…Payton has the whole routine down—"

"Tough." Mindy might not look like M, but right now she sure sounded like her. "I like you guys a lot, but I've had it. No more parties where we have to play dress-up. If the guys miss our skimpy outfits, they can wear them."

Jenna laughed until she realized her hand was still covering her décolletage. It wasn't as if her boobs were big enough to cause a stir. And she never used to be a prude. But then she'd started teaching twelve-year-olds. And dating Payton. Not that he made her a prude, but they did go to a lot of functions for his ultraconservative accounting firm, and she had learned to dress and act the part. She let her hand drop and straightened her back. "Okay, next year, you make the plans. I'm sure Payton will get on board."

Mindy raised one eyebrow. "And if he doesn't?"

"He will. Where are they, anyway?"

Mindy made a face. "Probably tucked in a corner somewhere discussing the newest thrilling tax requirements."

Zane, Mindy's husband, had not only gone to BU two years ahead of Payton, but he was also an accountant at the same firm. Jenna liked the couple a lot but they really only saw each other at events like these. They lived in a different suburb, and both Mindy and Jenna worked full-time.

"Have you seen *him*?" Mindy nodded toward a tall, dark-haired man standing at the other end of the buffet.

"Who? Oh. I hadn't, no. But I… He's…good-looking."

Mindy nabbed a chocolate-dipped strawberry, now that they'd moved the few steps over to the dessert section. "Good-looking? That's like saying the Mona Lisa is a nice painting."

"Okay, fine. He's gorgeous," Jenna said. "Honestly, I stopped listening to you the moment I saw him."

"You're forgiven. I mean, he actually looks like James Bond. Better than Daniel Craig, if you ask me."

Jenna nodded, even though she knew Mindy wasn't looking. "He must be a swimmer. Right? That's a swimmer's body."

"I don't know. I think runner. No. *Martial arts*," she said, her voice lowering an octave.

"Hmm. Quite possibly," Jenna said in a British accent.

Mindy laughed. "I'm sending him a telepathic message to take off his jacket."

"While you're at it, you might as well ask him to take everything else off, too."

"That seems greedy."

Jenna was giggling now. "Oh, damn, he's with someone."

"So are we."

"Of course we are. I'm just window-shopping. Ah, his girlfriend's beautiful."

"I never did like blondes." Mindy eyed Jenna for a second. "You'd look good with him," she said. Then she started loading a plate with petits fours.

Jenna laughed. She scooped up a bite-size brownie, while scoping out the rest of the goodies, ignoring everything that wasn't chocolate.

'He looks…dangerous," Mindy said. "If only he'd take off that damn jacket. Let us see what he's got under the hood."

Jenna looked up from the buffet table and stared at her friend, who was unashamedly checking out the guy.

"I wouldn't be surprised if he was hiding a Walther PPK."

Almost choking on the brownie, Jenna cleared her throat and said, "I thought that sentence would end in a completely different way."

Mindy's eyes lit up as she turned to Jenna. "I take back the Victorian comment. And give you extra points for the classiest way of subverting the 'is that a gun in your pocket' joke I've ever heard."

"That's me. Classy as—oh, crap, he's coming closer."

Mindy bumped her shoulder. "Don't look him straight in the eye."

Jenna nodded absently at Mindy, more interested in the gorgeous dress the guy's date was wearing than in him. A few seconds later, she realized what her friend had said. Her gaze flew back to Danger Bond. "Damn it, I just looked him in the eye. He caught me. Stop saying things."

"Jenna?" Mindy poked her in the shoulder. *"Jenna."*

"Yes, what? Hello?"

"Payton," Mindy said, a little too brightly. "Zane. Thank goodness you guys are back. We were beginning to think you'd asked some Bond girls if you could do their taxes."

"Ha," Mindy's husband said, without the least bit of humor. "I never get tired of accountant jokes."

Mindy waved dismissively before she accepted her double Scotch from him. Jenna's gaze caught on her wedding ring set. The rings were Vera Wang. Diamond and sapphires on white gold. God knew how expensive they'd been.

Then she looked down at her own engagement ring. She and Payton had picked it out together. The lovely three-quarter-carat princess cut on platinum had been a perfect choice. The money they'd saved by being careful was socked away in their new-house account. The wedding was set for the following June—if they didn't postpone it yet again.

Regardless, by then she'd have paid off the balance of her student loans and they'd have a significant amount for a down payment in Easton, a very nice suburb equidistant to both their jobs. There was a reason they'd decided to have the wedding in his parents' gorgeous backyard. It was very important to both of them to enter the next phase of their lives debt-free.

She took her White Russian from Payton, and gave him a kiss. "You should eat. Everything's very good."

"I'm grateful you went to the trouble of tasting it for us. In this place, it's impossible to tell the villains from the heroes."

"You're welcome."

Payton pressed a quick kiss to her forehead, and then went to get a plate. But he didn't make it that far. The beautiful blonde with Danger Bond gasped when she caught sight of him. "Payton?"

"Oh, for God's sake… Faith! You never come to these."

She was even more beautiful when she smiled. "I didn't know you did," she said, putting her plate down and giving him a really big hug. Jenna and Mindy raised their eyebrows at each other.

It lasted just a few seconds too long, that hug. It was so unlike Payton that Jenna barely noticed when Danger Bond joined them.

Faith stepped back. "This is Rick. My boyfriend. We're in Boston because of him."

Payton introduced himself. Jenna watched the two men shake hands. Evidently Faith was partial to good-looking guys with dark hair. Jenna sighed at her foolishness. It was an alumni New Year's extravaganza. People were consuming great food and lots of alcohol. So they hugged. It didn't mean anything. Even so, she moved right up against Payton's side.

Payton put his arm around her. "Jenna, this is Faith Quentin. We were friends in college." They shook hands, and Faith gave her a quick head-to-toe. It made Jenna feel superior when she didn't check out Faith in return. No one but Mindy needed to know that she'd already scrutinized the woman.

Danger Bond held out his hand, too. "I went to school across the Charles River, but Faith lets me come here, anyway. Rick Sinclair."

His smile was great close up, genuine but at odds with

his steely jaw and piercing blue eyes. It occurred to her, as Payton finished the introductions with Mindy and Zane, that the college across the river from Boston U was MIT.

"So you stuck with journalism." Payton smiled at Faith. Or maybe he'd been smiling all along.

"I did. I'm very lucky. Journalism has—wait. How did you know?"

"I—" Payton seemed startled. He recovered quickly, so no one noticed. Except Jenna. She saw the telltale tic that meant he was flustered. "I must've read something in the alumni magazine," he said easily. "If I remember correctly, you won a National Magazine Award."

Jenna blinked. Either he'd followed Faith's career or he'd read his alumni magazine cover to cover, something Jenna could have sworn he didn't do.

"Damn straight she did." Rick pulled Faith in for a quick hug. "She'd only been working for *Discover* for a year and a half. The NM award is the magazine equivalent to the Pulitzer."

Faith blushed and tossed her perfect blond hair behind her shoulder. "He's only bragging because he was a major part of the series."

"Really?" Zane, who'd lost no time filling his plate, rejoined the circle. "What was it about?"

Payton hadn't gotten his dinner yet. He should have been starving. Jenna was about to point out that he was drinking on an empty stomach, but when Faith said, "Climate change and the formation of supercells," Payton looked as if he'd never heard anything more fascinating.

When Payton asked her what part Rick had played, Jenna gave up. If he wanted to wake up to a hangover, that was his business.

Seemingly taking her fiancé's curiosity in stride, Rick said, "I'm a meteorologist at the National Severe Storms Laboratory."

Faith gave Rick a look. A couple's look. "More like a professional storm chaser who also happens to hold several advanced degrees."

That certainly got Jenna's attention. "Storm chasing. Well, that sounds terrifying and dangerous."

Rick shrugged. "It can be dangerous, but it's also an incredible rush. I don't think I caught what you do?"

"She's a teacher," Payton said. Another thing he rarely did. Speaking for her wasn't really necessary. "Middle school English. At a very good school in Scituate."

Jenna stared up at him. It was clear by his tone and the reference to South Shore, which was a good school but not like Thorndyke Road or Amigos, that he was trying to glam up her job. He wasn't even the least bit convincing. But that he'd thought she needed glamorizing squeezed her heart. What was it with him tonight? Maybe he'd already had a second whiskey before he'd come back to join her.

Faith gave her a charming smile. Rick, however, looked at Payton for a bit before turning to her. "That's where all the real action is," he said. "What excites students in those formative years makes all the difference. I've wanted to study tornadoes since I was fourteen. Kids are so passionate at that age."

"They are," she said. "I've wanted to be a teacher since I was thirteen."

There was a pause then, just long enough for a change of subject. Mindy was being awfully quiet. It was Payton who broke the ice. "Oh, wow, I need to eat," he said. With his hand on his stomach, he turned to Jenna. "Can I get you anything?"

She shook her head. At least that was more like the Payton she knew. Then he surprised her with a kiss. Not the usual peck, either. There was a little bit of tongue and everything, right there in front of everyone. She ended it quickly. "Thanks, Mr. Bond," she said, hoping she'd hit the right teasing note.

Payton winked at her. "You're welcome." He faced the group again. "Okay, then," he said. "Great seeing you again, Faith. Will you be in town for a while?"

"A couple of days." Faith smiled at Rick, and then at Payton. "I'm sure we'll run in to each other again soon. Nice to meet you all."

The beautiful couple eventually blended into the crowd.

Once they were back to being a foursome, the men went to peruse the buffet table while Jenna sipped at her White Russian. She and Mindy were standing right next to the chocolate fountain, but she wasn't hungry.

Mindy bumped her shoulder and whispered, "Danger Bond defended your honor."

"What?" Jenna laughed. "No, he didn't."

"Okay, your profession. Still…it was nice."

Jenna forced another laugh, grateful Mindy hadn't mentioned Payton's weird behavior. She did, however, give Jenna a couple of questioning looks, especially when Faith and Rick walked past them again. Jenna smiled as if nothing at all was wrong. She wasn't jealous. Not really.

But she had to admit she was mystified by Payton's behavior. He hadn't mentioned they were engaged. He'd spent most of the brief encounter grinning at Faith. But maybe he'd just been caught off guard, seeing his old friend. Jenna could imagine herself fumbling if she'd run in to her college boyfriend, Martin, at a party. Of course that was a different thing entirely. She didn't think anything had gone on between Payton and Faith. At least he'd never said as much. Anyway, Faith would be an idiot to roam when she had Rick. He'd been completely charming.

Payton claimed a recently vacated spot at a bar-height table. She would've preferred to sit somewhere, but it was nice to be able to put her drink down.

"Now that I've looked around," Payton said, finishing off his whiskey, "I don't think there's a more beautiful Vesper Lynd in the whole hotel."

She smiled, knowing he'd have said that even if she'd thrown a sweater over a workday dress. "I honestly thought there wouldn't be so many Vespers." The words were just out of her mouth, as yet another one walked by. "I suppose it makes sense, though. The movie was relatively recent."

"None of them carry it off as well as you do."

Another compliment? Interesting. Payton normally kept his praise private. But then, he'd never kissed her like that in public, either. There was no reason why he shouldn't say those nice things in front of Zane and Mindy, and yet…

"And I've never seen your eyes look so alluring."

Okay, that was really over-the-top. What the hell was going on with him? Did it have to do with Faith? Were these guilt compliments? Or drunk utterings? Like her, he wasn't a big drinker.

One of the things she appreciated most about Payton was that he was predictable. It might not be an appealing trait for a lot of women, but for her it was. She loved him for his stability. For the fact that their future together would unfurl without a lot of bumps and tears. Still, *three* compliments in a row? "What did you and Zane talk about for so long when you went to the bar? Ways to woo a sure thing?"

All of them laughed and Payton's shoulders relaxed as he said, "I haven't seen George and Cora for a while. Did they say where they were headed?"

Mindy finally piped up. "They're dancing downstairs. We're going to meet them as soon as Zane's finished eating. Want to join us?"

Payton shook his head. "It's too loud and crowded down there. I'll probably stick around here."

Jenna's chest tightened again, which was ridiculous. He and Faith, they'd been friends. If they'd been more than that, Payton would have told her. She'd been a Wellesley girl. Martin had been her boyfriend for two years. There had been a few others, as well. Payton knew about them. Just as she knew about Payton's old girlfriends during his years before the two of them met. In all the time she and Payton had been together, jealousy had never been an issue. It had barely been a thought.

She checked her watch before she turned to Mindy. "It's ten thirty now. How about you two text if you decide to leave early, or we can meet by the second-floor elevator in an hour before the countdown begins?"

"I think it'll be easier to meet here," Payton said. "We already know where it is and from what I've heard, the reunion committee is doing something special at midnight here in this suite."

Mindy and Zane agreed before they left, but not before Mindy gave Jenna an odd smile.

"You know what, honey?" Jenna said, catching Payton's gaze. "Maybe next year, let's think about going somewhere different for First Night."

The way Payton looked at her, she might as well have asked if he wanted to go on a crime spree with her.

"Sure," he said unconvincingly. "Why not? We can talk about it. What say I try and slog my way over to the bar again? We've got plenty of time. As long as I'm back before midnight."

His expression, as eager as a she'd ever seen it, was all wrong. And why hadn't he asked her to go with him. She'd known him too long to be this surprised. As he made his way through the throng of New Year's Eve revelers, her heart sank.

Had they been coming to this reunion party every year because of Faith?

2

RICK'S CELL PHONE VIBRATED. Stopped, and then did it again. Some oaf plowed into his back and the only thing that kept him on his feet was the mass of writhing, frenetic party-goers in a banquet room so packed it made him wish he and Faith had never come to the reunion. But she'd asked, and he'd just been talking to his friend Sam, who'd wanted Rick to check out the prototype apartment in Boston, so it was a no-brainer. He wondered now if Faith's interest in attending the party had been a little more personal than she'd led him to believe. She sure had liked catching up with Payton. Anyway, it didn't matter. He and Faith had been having a good time. And it was only going to get better.

He pulled out his phone as Faith rubbed against him on the dance floor. It was a work call, and he couldn't afford not to take it. There was no use telling her, not with the music so loud, but he held the phone up until she noticed and nodded at him.

He was grateful for the call. He liked to dance, but the band was loud enough to wake the dead. It took a bit of maneuvering, but finally he found himself in an over-crowded hallway, where he spotted a sign pointing him toward the restrooms.

Once inside, it was quieter. Still, his ears rang despite the high-end plugs he took out and put in his pocket. Not the pocket that held tonight's surprise. The other one. Then he pressed speed dial.

"Happy New Year, you bastard." Even in the echoing bathroom with two hand driers running, his coworker's Jamaican-tinged taunt came in loud and clear.

"Antwan, if you just called to harass me, I'm going to program your iPod to play nothing but ABBA."

"You're the devil incarnate," Antwan said. "Here I am minding the weather of the world while you're out dancing the night away. But being that I'm a nice guy, I'm still going to tell you that downtown Boston is looking tricky around two in the morning. Big snow dump, so you and Faith should hightail it to that fancy apartment right quick after she says yes."

Rick reached inside his other pocket and pulled out the one-point-four-carat engagement ring he'd put there just before they'd left the apartment. "Thanks, man. Any other trouble spots?"

"Why do you care? You're still going to ask her to marry you, yes?"

"Yep. Right after we finish the kiss. It won't be like… you know."

The last time he'd planned to propose, he'd hidden the ring in his jeans pocket. It had been her birthday. They'd gone up in a hot air balloon, which had seemed like a great idea at the time. The first ten minutes of their special flight? Fantastic. After that? A complete snooze. For both of them. The mood was irretrievably lost somewhere over the Oliver Wildlife Preserve a year ago November.

Of course, if he'd really wanted to ask her the big question nothing would have stopped him, as Antwan had been quick to point out. But then his friend thought he was being an idiot to propose. Antwan liked Faith well enough, but he said he couldn't see the sparks. He was too damn romantic. A shared sense of humor, purpose and comfort would last long after the honeymoon was over.

"I'm sure nothing will stop you this time."

Rick's pulse quickened, which was just his excitement over finally doing the deed. "You got it. Anyway—"

"Hold your horses, Ricky. I'm not finished. Book your flight home for early Saturday morning. That's the only break I see before Boston gets hit by a series of wicked storms. Potentially record-breaking snowfall."

"Well, that's annoying. I made dinner reservations for tomorrow night—"

"Which you might be able to keep, but I wouldn't count on it."

"Damn. So, tomorrow night's a maybe, then we leave on Saturday…how early?"

"Before ten."

"Well, thanks a bunch."

"Yes, because I specifically created the polar vortex just to screw up your holiday."

"I knew it," Rick said.

Antwan laughed. "You're proposing, and it's New Year's Eve. At least you'll have a couple of nights. So make them count. Don't you two be glued to The Weather Channel, eh?"

Okay, now Antwan was being plain annoying. Rick and Faith had been living together for over three years and they always watched The Weather Channel before bed. Just one of the many things they had in common. She completely understood about his work and didn't even blink when he would hare off with his storm-chaser team at the first hint of a supercell. Hell, most of the time, she'd head out, too. Not as part of his team, but to do her own reporting thing.

She'd come to live in Norman to be near the National Weather Center. They'd met when she'd interviewed him, and he'd known right away that the two of them would be good together.

"Anyway," Antwan said, a grin clear in his voice, "what

are you doing talking to me in some toilet when you could be with your fiancée?

"She's not my fiancée yet. And how did you know I was in the bathroom?"

"Nothing says class like a flush in the background, my friend. I'll see you on Monday."

"Yeah. Thanks, buddy. Happy New Year."

After disconnecting, Rick looked at the diamond again. It was all clean lines and flawless beauty, just like Faith. She didn't really wear a lot of jewelry. Not that he'd seen. Which made sense. She was working out in their home gym every day that she wasn't on assignment, or swimming at the rec center. And when they went climbing or scuba diving, jewelry wasn't a good idea. But she'd wear an engagement ring. Probably.

He'd noticed one on Jenna's finger. He wondered why good old Payton hadn't mentioned she was his fiancée. The thought was cut short when a heavy hand landed on his shoulder. He spun around, dislodging the hand and ready to flatten the moron who'd touched him—until he got a whiff of the moron's breath.

"Don't do it," the drunk said, his voice moist and sloppy. He looked to be in his fifties or sixties and was listing to his right. "Just live with her. 'N' don't have kids. They'll drain you dry. Happy New Year."

The man entered one of the stalls as Rick slipped the ring in his pocket. He hadn't actually thought about marrying Faith, not until a couple of guys he worked with had started having kids. They were around his age and while he harassed them a lot, both of them seemed happier. From there the seed had been planted.

Besides, with Faith in his life, a future with kids didn't sound so bad. She was an adventure junkie like him. They both had a major interest in atmospheric studies. And she was just the kind of woman he needed. Independent. Driven.

Career-minded. Gorgeous. He'd never met a woman as easy to get along with. So yeah, even though Faith didn't want kids now, she'd probably change her mind down the road. He wasn't ready for them now, either. But he'd turned the first corner in his thinking. Sure, things would change. But they'd always looked forward to challenges.

Proposing to Faith was the logical next step. He wouldn't say that last part to her, though. She'd just laugh and tell him his entire life was illogical. And he'd have agreed.

As he washed his hands, he thought again about that guy Faith had hugged. It was full-body contact. If he hadn't seen it, he wouldn't have believed it. She was most definitely not the huggy type. When she was forced into one, she'd bear it and come away with her very convincing fake smile, but she'd never initiated more than a guy hug—one shoulder to another, a quick pat on the back—when there was a choice.

Maybe she'd felt obligated to plaster herself against him? Some old debt she had to pay? No. She'd been smiling as if she'd just spotted a rare left-moving supercell.

What the hell was he worried about? Faith wasn't interested in anything besides her work and, well, him. And Payton wasn't as good-looking. Rick turned to check himself out in the mirror over the sink just to make sure. Damn it, he couldn't tell. He looked more like a villain than Bond. Faith liked to call him dangerously sexy. Seriously, though, who named a guy Payton? Jesus. Still, weird name or not, he'd managed to get himself a hot fiancée.

The paper towels left something to be desired, but finally Rick couldn't put it off any longer. He reinserted his earplugs and went back to find Faith. They only had twenty minutes until midnight.

JENNA WAS ONCE again by herself. Payton had gone off with a fraternity brother to grab a final drink, and she had no expectations of seeing him until just before midnight.

If Jenna had had it her way, she and Payton would have left with Mindy and Zane. They'd very rationally decided to go home so they wouldn't be caught up in the mess of drunken crazy people trying to get on the train for the suburbs.

Instead, Jenna had walked too far in heels that were too high, and somehow managed to end up right in front of the dessert table again. She'd never fit in her wedding dress if she kept this up.

Oh, screw it.

She chose a chocolate-stacked, delicious-looking thing. For God's sake, it had a brownie bottom, a cheesecake center and chocolate-mousse top. It would take a stronger woman than herself to walk away.

She'd just taken her second bite when Danger Bond entered the room. His gaze swept directly over to where she was standing. Of course.

Faith joined him seconds later and Jenna spun around. Now she was facing a blank wall. Nothing suspicious there.

Good grief, why had Payton left her here? Why hadn't they gone home already? She was tired and cranky. And she needed to put down her plate. Walk away from temptation. There was still coffee left, decaf even. But, naturally, there was no convenient tray nearby. The closest was by Faith and Rick, and since she wasn't going anywhere near them, Jenna walked all the way across the suite, where she found a big tray next to a pretty decent unpopulated corner.

All was well until she looked over at her favorite couple…

But they weren't where she'd last seen them. Instead, they were right in front of her. Well, not directly, but close enough to prevent a casual escape.

A deep cleansing breath made it possible to scan the room for Payton, but she couldn't seem to cut off her thoughts about Rick. Or Faith, if she was honest. She wasn't wearing an engagement ring. She'd called Rick her boyfriend. Those came and went, as she well knew, but surely Rick was a keeper. A beautiful woman like Faith could have anyone she wanted. A hunky storm chaser was far more in her league than an accountant.

Damn. Jenna was worried about Faith, but that was idiotic because Payton would never leave her. The two of them had their whole future planned out. They already had names picked out for their first child.

What was wrong with her? It had to be the alcohol. She'd had two White Russians, and Payton was bringing her a third. Even in college she was always on the hunt for caffeine, not booze. At least they were taking a train back home, but by the time they reached their stop, one of them had to be sober to drive Payton's car to their place.

Faith was on the move, and Jenna watched her until she left the suite. Then Rick headed for the buffet so Jenna was free to move out of the corner. When her gaze caught on a clock near the door, she stopped in her tracks. Payton had been gone more than a while. Maybe drinking on an empty stomach had caught up with him? How awful to feel sick when this place was packed to the rafters. She hoped he was okay. And wasn't still at the bar.

That thought made her queasy… Double damn it, because her first thought had been that Faith might be going to the bar and the two of them would run into each other. This night needed to end already. She didn't give one damn about New Year's. Or First Night. Next year, she wasn't coming close to this hotel. Maybe she'd stay home and watch a movie and eat popcorn. Yeah, that sounded great.

She kept her eye on the door for the next five minutes, but the only thing of interest was Rick leaving the suite. Two more minutes of pacing, and then she was really worried. She called Payton's cell phone. Again. And again, but it went straight to voice mail.

She'd have to go find him. The suite was packed but

she made it out the door quickly. And then she saw Rick. Alone. Staring down the hallway with a rapt expression.

Jenna followed his gaze. The hallway was busy with people, so at first, she only had a terrible feeling about what had made him stop in his tracks, but then she got the confirmation. A space in the crowd had opened up. As if to frame the last thing on earth she wanted to see. Payton and Faith were hugging so tightly Jenna forgot how to breathe.

But it got worse. Jesus, how could it get so much worse?

When they parted, it was only to take a half step back. Just enough room for Jenna to notice that Payton looked… happy. A different kind of happy. Nothing she'd seen in all their years together.

So happy he'd forgotten her.

"What the…?" She jumped and found Rick was inches away from her. He glanced at her, and then his gaze went back to the couple down the hall. He looked stunned.

"They're just friends," she said to him. "He said that several times. Friends."

He seemed surprised to see himself next to her, but he was quick to go back to watching Faith and Payton. "That's what she told me, too."

Payton continued to beam, even as he put their drinks on the closest surface, which happened to be a railing too narrow to properly hold the glasses, but he obviously didn't give a shit about the drinks or her because he was talking a mile a minute, making another woman laugh, making her put her hand—both hands—over her heart. He spoke extravagantly, with lots of arm waving, although none of it in Jenna's direction.

She'd known him five years, and not at all.

"Who the hell does he think he is?"

Rather than watch the train wreck down the hall she turned to Rick. He looked ready to pound Payton into a puddle, and she thought that was a fine idea.

"For one thing, he's my fiancé."

He turned to her, and took a moment. "Look, I don't want to cause a scene or anything, but I swear to God if he touches her again…"

"I know. I mean, I don't know. I've never seen him like this. Normally, he's…nice. He hasn't spared me a glance since your…girlfriend tried to absorb him into her skin."

Rick shook his head. "You saw that, too, huh?" He sighed, loudly. "I have a goddamn ring in my pocket. I feel like the world's biggest idiot."

As tight as her stomach was, the implication of what he'd just said made it tighter. "We need to do something. Now. There are only a couple of minutes left."

"Do something? Like knock his block off?"

She shrugged. "It's too crowded to take a swing up here. You could hit anyone."

"My aim's really good."

"Umm, has she ever done this before?" Jenna asked.

"Hell, no. Goddamn it, she'd been so casual asking to come to this reunion. Like it was no big deal."

"I know. I mean, maybe they discovered they're long lost…siblings?"

Rick gave her a look that made her last hope vanish. "You ever touched your brother like that?" He was practically growling in a very Danger Bond way. It was sexy as hell.

Oh, God.

Something had to be wrong with her brain. Had she really just gotten weak-kneed over the man who wanted to beat up her fiancé? Alcohol was the only answer, even though she felt as sober as a…sober person. "I don't know. Maybe you could hit him one time. One time wouldn't be too much."

Rick retrieved something from his pocket, and for a moment Jenna was afraid it would be a gun or a knife.

It wasn't either, although she had the feeling he would have been handy with both. It turned out to be the ring, of course, and it was stunning. "It's beautiful," she said.

"I thought so. I thought she'd think so, too. But then she met… Is he famous or something? Faith never said what he did for a living."

She sighed. "He's an accountant."

"You've got to be kidding."

"I can't seem to turn away. They just keep doing…" She moved her hand in a vague gesture.

Rick wasn't looking at her, though. He was tall enough to see over people's heads. "Shit. She's a well-respected journalist. She's won awards. She specializes in covering natural disasters."

"Like the one we're having now?" Jenna asked. The shock was wearing off a bit. More precisely, the shock was being shoved aside by a hurt that might be fatal.

"Yeah, except there's nothing natural about it," he said, as he put the ring back in his pocket. "Great way to bring in the New Year, huh?"

"I'm trying to think of one thing he could say right now that would fix this." If only they'd left with Mindy and Zane…

"Hey…" Rick put his hand on her arm. "You okay? You're looking awfully pale."

"I'm fine, thanks," she said, trying to breathe. "And by that I mean I'm not fine in any way. Although I doubt I'm going to faint."

"Ten…"

The number filled the air, so loud it hushed the huge crowd.

"Nine…"

"Shit," Rick said again. He took a step closer to Jenna. "If they—"

"Eight…"

"—even *try* to come back at the last second." He faced Jenna. "She hasn't even looked down this corridor. Not one look."

"Five, four…"

People shifted, the crowd seemed to part, giving her another clear shot of the happy couple for a few seconds. If Payton glanced to his right, he would see her standing next to Rick. But he only had eyes for Faith.

"For fuck's sake," Rick said. "All they'd needed to do was walk around a corner. We'd have never known why they'd missed the countdown."

"Maybe they planned…" They weren't kissing, but they might as well be.

On the count of three, Rick looked at Jenna again, and she'd never felt so much empathy for another person.

Trying as hard as she could not to cry, she moved right into Rick's personal space but she couldn't look away.

"One! Happy New Year!"

Payton leaned closer to Faith. So close there was only one thing it could lead to. One second after Payton's lips touched Faith's, Rick put his hand on the back of Jenna's neck and pulled her into their own midnight kiss.

The moment his mouth touched hers…*fireworks.*

3

RICK PULLED JENNA closer and kissed her again. He thrust into her mouth as the cacophony around them spurred him on. Even through his tux he could feel her fingers digging into him, her lips and tongue as fierce as weapons, the anger and the heat between them more dangerous by the second.

He hoped they were watching. That prick Payton needed to see what he'd lost. Never in his life had Rick experienced anything like this. In the back of his mind a voice whispered that none of it was real. Soon he would wake up, and the betrayal would have been a nightmare.

Jenna nipped his lower lip and broke that spell. It was real, all right. Revenge built on humiliation and pain, and he didn't give one damn.

He inhaled sharply as Jenna pressed against him, against his hardening cock. Good. Great. He pulsed back, but when his balls started to tighten, he pulled away. Not far. He had her by the shoulders and she looked...well, she looked beautiful, but wrecked.

Tears had smudged her makeup, and there was a very small nick in her lower lip. Even though her pupils were blown, he could see the desperation in them. Wanting, he knew, to turn back time. Trying to make some sense of this bizarre twist.

"You want to get out of here?"

She nodded immediately. "Anywhere else."

When he looked down the packed hallway, the lovebirds had finally stopped kissing and remembered who they'd come with. Payton looked stricken, which was a pity because Rick would've liked to have struck him first. Faith looked flat-out guilty.

Whether they'd actually spotted them, Rick couldn't be sure. But when the two of them began squeezing past people, pushing through the crowd, Rick took Jenna's hand and he bullied their way to the stairwell.

As the door shut behind them, he paused a moment. "I don't know if you saw, but they were headed toward us."

Her phone rang, and she pulled it out of her tiny purse. She shook her head and the sad smile she wore when she turned it off got to him. He much preferred the smile he'd seen at the buffet, when the world had still turned on the right axis. He doubted he'd see that anytime soon.

His phone rang, too. Like Jenna, he turned it off. Just for now? Maybe. He wasn't in a position to walk away from Faith. Their lives were connected. And as far as he knew, they'd only kissed. That pissed him off all over again.

"Come on, then," he said. They started down the steps. It wasn't the quickest getaway ever because a lot of other folks had had the same idea, but they weren't stalled often. Amazingly, when they made it to the coat check, the line moved along nicely.

Not quickly enough to distract Jenna from her thoughts, though. Her shoulders rose as if they could hide her. If he had a say, he'd keep her so busy for the next couple of hours that she wouldn't have time to look like that again. "You're from Boston. Where to?"

She blinked at him, coming out of her hurt, looking surprised to find him holding up her wool coat. "I don't know," she said, slipping her arms into the sleeves. "I rarely come downtown or to the harbor."

"That's okay." He hastily shrugged into his coat. "I know where there's a party."

Her hands shook as she slid on her gloves. He pulled on his own, and then took her hand. They hurried through the swarm of revelers, some still wearing the silly paper hats the hotel had provided. He wondered how many other hearts had been broken at the stroke of midnight.

The second they were out in the cold, Rick pulled her closer. It was freezing, and there was a huge line of people waiting for taxis, so the train it was. Luckily, it was just across the street.

Inside the terminal the mood was festive despite the terrible smell of overindulgence, but Jenna started shrinking again.

"All right," he said. "I'm whipping out a cliché, but only because when you mentioned you were a teacher, you lit up. What's your favorite book?"

The question appeared to win over her despair, and she surprised him with the smile he'd figured was a lost cause. "I do light up, don't I?" she said. "I know it's not glamorous, but I love turning the kids on to the magic of books. I honestly believe that being a reader changes lives for the better."

Oh, yeah. This was more like it. "I agree. But you're not getting out of answering my question."

"I get asked that a lot, but I never know what to say. I don't have a favorite. I learned how to read when I was four. My favorite back then was an alphabet book."

"How about when you were…fifteen. When the hormones kicked in."

Their train pulled up, and they scurried into the car, not even minding that they had to stand. "Let's see if I can remember. Um—" she lowered her lashes for a moment and he fought the urge to wipe away the traces of her tears "—okay, it was *All-American Girl* by Meg Cabot."

"Mine, too."

She laughed.

He wanted to kiss her. And punch Payton into next week.

The moment they'd reached Copley Square, something changed. The light that had sparkled in her seconds ago had dimmed. Rick led her to a shadowed corner. He stared into her sad, confused eyes as he shoved his gloves into his coat pocket. "I didn't mean to make you cry," he said and used his thumb to wipe the damp tracks from her cheeks.

She sniffed, but she didn't make a move. "It wasn't you. God, every time I think of how he—" A shudder shook her body. "I've already picked out my wedding dress."

"I have no idea what he was thinking. Anyone who could cheat on you is an idiot."

Jenna tried to smile. "If you were in my class you'd get an A for effort."

"Nah, I would've already flunked out." Rick grinned at her raised brows. "Too hot for teacher."

"Faith is the idiot," Jenna said with a soft laugh, and leaned closer.

Or maybe they both did. He wasn't going to kiss her, even though he wanted to. But he wouldn't object at all if she kissed him.

She brushed her lips across his and whispered, "Thank you."

He caught her elbows and pulled her even closer. She came willingly, her lips parted, her warm breath an invitation he couldn't refuse.

Everything else dimmed. The noise, the lights, the crowd. They were back to that space, that separate reality. From strangers to *this* in a single hour.

"Son of a bitch."

The man's voice was low and angry. "That's my spot

you're using. Don't you be messing up my spot with your nasty business."

Although he was big and held a large black case that would make an impressive weapon, he looked pissed off, not scary. "Sorry, man," Rick said. "Wouldn't dream of trespassing."

With his arm around Jenna, he walked them out to the edge of the flow of traffic. It must have been the right spot because the busker was pulling a sax from the case, which he left open for tips.

Jenna was frowning into her purse just as Rick pulled out his wallet. "Everything okay?" he asked.

She nodded. "Tiny purses don't hold much, especially cash on New Year's Eve.

"I've got it covered."

The music began, jazz, just loud enough and easy, that even the really drunk wouldn't have a problem with it. He left Jenna's side for a moment to drop a twenty into the case. When the busker paused, Rick said, "If you can play something to dance to, that'll double."

There was no way to tell if the saxophone player would go for it. But the moment Rick reached Jenna, the music segued perfectly into an old Gershwin song, "Embraceable You," which was one of the best slow-dancing songs ever.

Rick pulled Jenna close, already moving his feet to the music.

"What are you doing?"

"Dancing. In the subway. On New Year's Day."

"No, wait," Jenna said, her words riding a laugh. "I'm a terrible dancer."

"Nope. Sorry. That excuse is for other nights, other subway stations."

"That's fine, but I'd have to be a lot drunker than I am now. So let's just stop and listen to the nice man's saxophone."

Rick moved them into a shadow as other people stopped to listen. It was mostly an older crowd, but that was cool. No one was watching them, though, as he reached inside his coat pocket and brought out two miniature bottles of vodka. He snuck them into her peripheral vision and she barked out such a big laugh people did look. But Rick didn't care. "Drink up," he said.

"Seriously?"

He nodded. "I really want to dance with you."

"But we're—" Jenna looked around as if there were plainclothes cops on the lookout for tiny booze.

"You know what? It's fine." He smiled. "We can just go upstairs—"

She plucked one of the bottles from his hand seconds before it would have disappeared in his pocket. Grinning like crazy, she took off her gloves, opened the bottle, lifted it in a silent salute and chugged that sucker down like a pro.

Then she coughed for almost a minute.

By the time she lifted her arms in the traditional slow-dance posture, the song had ended. He decided he liked the new one just as much, even though he didn't recognize it.

They stayed low-key. There were no grand sweeping moves as they danced close, away from the people rushing by. Considering where they were and how many people surrounded them, he was startled that he could smell her. The ultrafeminine scent didn't surprise him in the least. It completely suited a woman like her. It was a weird thought that meant he might be drunker than he imagined.

The sounds of the trains made it hard to hear all the notes, but the crowd got bigger, and then some other folks started dancing.

He pointed it out to Jenna, and she just beamed. "I love this," she said, shouting to be heard.

"Me, too."

While it wasn't exactly a flash mob, the dancers and the

audience were making it difficult to pass through, which brought a cop around to break it up. Rick and Jenna exchanged smiles. She had beautiful shining eyes when she wasn't crying. No matter what happened next, or even tomorrow, Rick wanted to remember her exactly like this.

JENNA WALKED INTO the gorgeous Mandarin Oriental hotel, glad to have Rick's arm around her. It felt different, of course. She'd gotten used to Payton, and how they fit together. This was…unsettling. Because she felt comfortable. As if the difference suited her. Probably because she was tipsy. And pissed. And hurt down to her bones.

But that didn't explain how she'd felt when he'd kissed her. It was… No. She didn't want to think too much about it. Or the dancing, which had been like a scene from a romantic comedy.

Someone else's romance.

But it was the kissing that made her head spin. The last time she'd kissed anyone but Payton was almost five years ago.

No. She stopped herself again. Put on the brakes. Thinking was simply out of the question. It would only bring more tears, which hadn't helped thus far. And wouldn't be fair to Rick. He was being a sweetheart while still managing to look like Danger Bond.

His concern for her wasn't just because he was a nice guy. Clearly, taking care of her helped him avoid thinking about Faith and that diamond ring in his pocket. Not that she didn't appreciate his kindness, but they were both running as fast as they could to outpace the midnight that had come and gone.

"Isn't it late for a party?" she asked, glancing around the stunning lobby, tastefully decorated with white lights, red and white poinsettias and a Christmas tree that had to be fifteen feet tall. "Won't it be over?"

"Nope. They'll keep refreshing the buffet all night, until around five in the morning, when they'll bring out breakfast."

"I like this hotel," she said, trying for a more cheery disposition. "If breakfast includes waffles, I'm not leaving."

Rick led her straight to the elevator and two things popped into her head. Despite the unusual circumstance, he was still a stranger. And here she was blithely following his lead…to his room, for all she knew.

They stepped into a waiting car and as the door slid closed she asked, "Are you staying here?"

Rick smiled. "Nope. There really is a party."

"Oh, good." She stared at the flashing red numbers as they passed each floor. "Are we crashing it?"

"Is that a problem?" he asked, humor in his eyes.

Any other night? Yes. Tonight? Jenna shook her head. "None whatsoever."

With a wicked grin he leaned over, and she held her breath, certain he was about to kiss her. But the elevator stopped and as the door opened he straightened, leaving her breathless and disappointed. Why? It wasn't like her. Everything from midnight on wasn't *her.*

Sure, Rick was attractive. The second she and Mindy had seen him they'd both reverted to dreamy-eyed teens.

Thinking back to those lascivious jokes about Rick had her blushing as they walked toward the banquet room. Of course neither she nor her silliness had caused the night's events to unfold but how weird was it that things had ended up like this? "You okay?" he asked, and there was his arm again, around her shoulders, steadying her.

She nodded, finally accepting that nothing would feel like her regular life in the foreseeable future. It would either be too wonderful to be real, or a punch to the gut when she thought about Payton.

She wished she could be more like Rick. He was hurting, too, only he didn't appear to be dwelling on it.

He seemed to know exactly where the party was so maybe they weren't crashers at all. Alone for a minute while he checked their coats, her gaze swept the room as she hoped to see a banner or anything that would tell her who was hosting the party. And there it was, a banner made of rectangles, most of them dark gray, and the lowercase *i* in cardinal red.

Rick's alma mater. The suite was much larger than the Boston U room. And way more extravagant. The buffet was still stocked over an hour past midnight, and there were three bar stations, all staffed, none of them with horrible lines.

"Drink?" Rick asked. "Food?"

"Drink first," she said. "I need to be a little fuzzier than I am right now."

He nodded. "Yeah. Everything feels off for me, too. Like when you're in a car accident. Or a tornado."

"Yes." she said, sighing, though the tornado reference did make her smile a little. "Of course you get it…you should have been engaged right now, and I've hardly been there for you."

He shook his head. "Don't worry about me. Maybe I'll be loaded with regret tomorrow, but tonight I'm thinking I dodged a bullet."

"Really?" How could that be possible? A man didn't bring an engagement ring to a party without caring about the outcome. Or maybe men did. What did she know? She'd thought she'd never have to worry about Payton's commitment to her. Then again, she wasn't exactly a beacon of purity in this debacle. Kissing Rick the first time was forgivable, but all the kissing since? *Wanting* him to kiss her? If there could be any reconciliation at the end of this…thing, she'd have to own up to her own behavior, although she never would have been with Rick at all if Payton hadn't—

She forced herself to breathe, to blink away any tears. "Still," she said, "I'm very sorry. I hope there aren't too many regrets."

"I don't think it'll be too bad, although I've got a hell of a lot of questions."

She nodded as she realized they were already in line for drinks but she had no recollection of walking there. "Payton isn't… He's this steady man. He's always where he's supposed to be. Doesn't drink, except on special occasions, doesn't gamble, doesn't get high. He's a goddamn rock. Reliable in every way. Always where… Oh, I said that already. But honestly, he's the one I'd call if something like tonight happened to me."

Rick studied her for a long moment. "I'm not like him. Not that you couldn't call me to help out in a jam. But when I'm not working I'm most definitely not a rock. In fact, I climb them. I chase tornadoes and skydive, too. On the plus side, I try to be where I'm expected, I'm not much of a drinker, with the obvious exception of New Year's Eve. And you should probably know that punching Payton is still really high on my bucket list."

Jenna knew he was kidding, but if the circumstances called for a punch, she had no doubt he could pull it off, which was not just cool, but sexy as hell.

Yet another reminder that this was not her life.

4

IN BETWEEN SPOTTING Rick at the BU party and actually meeting him, Jenna's imagination had gone wild. Now that she'd spent time with him, it was clear she hadn't given him enough credit. He most definitely was a steely-eyed badass. But he'd also made her laugh, made her smile. Been there for her.

"Forget him," she said. "Forget Faith. What are we drinking?"

"Usually, I'm good for a beer or two, but tonight, I'm a Scotch man. And you?"

"White Russian. Heavy on the white. I'm a lightweight and I always go for the girlie drinks."

"I know plenty of guys who drink White Russians."

"Liar."

"Fine. I don't know them personally. But I'm sure I'm right."

She smiled. Again. A small miracle. "Why do I get the impression you say that a lot?"

"What, that I'm right?"

She nodded. "My guess is that you are. A lot."

"What makes you say that?" Rick was studying her again. It should have been intrusive and uncomfortable. It wasn't. "Except for the train wreck at midnight and the alarmingly amazing kissing, you don't know much about me."

"Uh, several advanced degrees?" she said. "That was a pretty big hint."

"I don't know that the two correlate, but I do have a habit of saying I'm right. How's that for obnoxious?"

"Oh, please. You're hot, brilliant and nice. Wait." The line moved. She didn't. "Are we talking about the same kiss?"

"What? I think I'm insulted."

"Oh, okay. Never mind. *That* kiss. Of course."

"If you need a refresher…"

What Jenna needed was that damn drink. Alarmingly amazing? Yes, that was a rather good description. She hurried a couple of feet to close the gap between her and the man in front of her. That was when she saw it was a cash bar and quickly felt around inside her purse for money.

When it was their turn she paid for the drinks. Rick let her easily, which she appreciated. Although what did it matter if he appeared to be nearly perfect? Yes, he had gorgeous blue eyes that threatened her undoing every time he looked at her, and the way he kissed made her forget her whole world had collapsed. And yes, he was being as nice and supportive as she could have hoped for, but…

"You know what?" she said. "You're right." She followed him to a small unoccupied table, where they sat across from each other. There were still people on the dance floor, despite having no band. She liked the piped-in music better than what she'd heard at the Bond thing. This was more her speed. Old-fashioned dance music. Like in the subway.

"What am I right about this time?" he asked.

"Oh." She'd forgotten why she'd been thinking. "No, no, you're right. It would have been the easiest thing for them to make sure we couldn't see them. But they were standing in the hallway right outside of the BU suite. As if they were so lost in each other that, that…" After taking a couple of big gulps, she put her drink down. "I would never."

"No," he said. "You wouldn't." He sipped his Scotch,

watched the dancers for a moment and then looked at her again. "Although, you do have a point. It's possible that they just lost their heads for a few minutes. That they'd had too much to drink, and things got out of hand."

"Is that normal for Faith?" Jenna said. "Does she just lose her head for a few minutes and kiss other men?"

"Not that I've ever seen."

She sighed. "Payton doesn't, either. Except he did, and from the way he looked at her, he didn't think of me at all. There was no other exit from that hotel suite. The first thing I saw was you, staring down the hallway. It was crowded, but it didn't take more than a couple of seconds for me to catch on." She winced at the memory. Her stomach did that twisted thing that made her feel like crawling in a hole and never coming out again. "I'm sorry. I'm trying to let it go, but… I had a trickster father and I don't want anything like that in my life."

"Trickster?"

"He's chock-full of mischief, my dad. He's always been a salesman, the kind that requires a lot of travel, but his real love was inventing things that were supposed to make gazillions of dollars. They never did. He knew how to charm the ladies, though. Lots of them. Including my mother. The only thing he couldn't do was take care of his responsibilities. My mom ended up having to work two jobs, sometimes three. She was exhausted all the time. I learned how to take care of myself. Which isn't a bad thing in itself. But…" She shrugged.

"Ah. That kind of trickster."

"I know, I'm a walking cliché, choosing Payton, who's the exact opposite of my father. But I don't care. I hated that my dad was gone so much. And that the only time I felt as if we were a family was when he came home. But that wasn't very often. The only time I felt really…"

She inhaled deeply, then decided to just tell the unvarnished truth. It wasn't as if she'd ever run in to Rick again. "The only time I felt really loved was when he was home. When we were all together."

"What about your mother?"

"She was a good mom, in her own way. She did the best she could. If she minded that he was away a lot, I never heard her complain. When he was home he was the center of her universe. I love my mom. I really do. But she just let him keep his head in the clouds, when he had a family to support."

Rick sipped on his drink, and Jenna felt foolish for that last outburst. She watched the couples on the dance floor, all around their age and older. It was nice, and she was able to calm down a bit.

"Do they live in Boston?" he asked, and her gaze went back to him. His blue eyes made her forget the question for a minute.

"Not anymore. They moved to Santa Fe four years ago. No, five. He still spends half his time on the road and she keeps accepting his crumbs. I know I shouldn't say any of this."

"Why not? I'm the ideal audience. The quintessential perfect stranger. In a blink I'll be gone."

"True."

"So, what's it like now, with them?"

She shrugged. Drank some more of her very strong White Russian. "It's okay. We're not close." Tears welled again. She blinked them back and then wiped away the one that had escaped. "Would you feel up to telling me about you and Faith?"

He did the staring thing again. She'd love to know what he saw, but she wouldn't ask. Finally, he nodded. "You know how we met? She was a freelance writer who specialized in the earth's atmosphere and climate change. I'd been in my job for a couple of years. After she interviewed me, we became friends. We went to the same gym, and we were both into mountain climbing, bikes, running. Sex was great, and we didn't get on each other's nerves. So she moved in with me.

"She knew I'd be working a lot, that I'm a storm chaser, and that all my friends were also into atmospheric studies. She went wherever the headlines took her so she was gone a lot herself. Every time we connected we were good together. There weren't any issues. We never actually talked about our relationship."

"What changed?"

"Hmm?"

"Something big must have changed for you to want to get married."

"You'd think. But I just figured we'd been together long enough and—" He shrugged. "Kids. The idea of having them. I want that. Not yet, though."

"So, you were putting down a deposit?"

He inhaled, and she wanted to take the words back.

"I'm so sorry," Jenna said. "Ignore that, please. I probably shouldn't have asked about her. Clearly, I'm no good for anything right now. Which is terrible, because you've been wonderful."

"Don't worry about it. You're dead-on. That's exactly what I was doing. But now I want to put some thought into what comes next. Faith and I get along. Always have. And yeah, I'll admit, with our chaotic lives, our relationship has been convenient."

He sighed and stared at the dancers. A song Jenna liked started, and for a few moments, neither she nor Rick said anything. His expression changed, though, from pensive to something darker.

"This wasn't the first time I tried to propose to Faith," he said. "Clearly I didn't try very hard. Hot-air balloons aren't great for proposals. But then, I thought New Year's Eve was a good idea." He shrugged. Took a drink.

Jenna's throat tightened as she stared at the small diamond ring on her left hand. She and Payton were nothing like Rick and Faith. Well, they were convenient, she supposed. He didn't live in California or work the night shift. But they had talked about their relationship. Each step had been carefully thought out. She'd been the one to decide that they wouldn't live together until they were married, but Payton had supported her fully. She loved him. He'd been exactly the kind of man she'd always wanted.

Though right now she had no idea what she wanted.

"That first kiss," Rick said, his smile so nice, she let go of the breath she'd been holding. "I mean us. That was unexpected."

"It was," she agreed. "Completely. To be honest, you literally took my breath away."

He was back to looking pensive. It was a damn good look on him. She imagined half the women in the room were undressing him in their thoughts.

But she worried she'd said the wrong thing. "Do you suppose payback somehow makes kissing more thrilling?"

"Thrilling, huh?" He didn't actually puff up like a sage grouse in heat, but his faint smile did look awfully smug. "Probably. Yeah. You think if I kissed you right now, it would be payback again?"

She finished her White Russian, feeling that buzz she'd been chasing. "Yeah. I think payback's going to be a big part of everything for a while."

"I've got no problem with that."

Jenna laughed, grateful she'd already swallowed. "You know what? I don't, either."

"Then we better get some food."

"I'm sorry, what? You're hungry? Now?"

"Not especially," he said. "But you just polished off a lot of booze. Have you had anything else to eat besides chocolate?"

How did he know about that? Had he been watching her earlier? God, she hoped not. She picked up her drink, remembering too late that she'd finished it. "You're probably right about eating," she said, gently putting the empty glass down. "Because I'm a little drunk."

He helped her up and they went to scope out their second buffet of the night. It was a very good buffet, especially when they zeroed in on the amazingly fresh crab and lobster. Just as Jenna was heading around the table to the oysters, an inebriated man in a beautiful suit stopped right in front of her, although he was looking over her shoulder.

"Rick? Is that you?"

"Hey, Paul. How you doing?"

Obviously, Rick wasn't especially happy to see Paul. The man was nice-looking, if you were into three-piece suits with just a hint of pocket square showing.

"Great," Paul said, his voice oily with booze and self-pity. "Just great. My wife left me last week. I thought it would be a good idea to come here instead of sitting home alone. Stupid. All I can think about is her and Dennis."

"I'm sorry to hear it, Paul." Rick slipped his arm around her so smoothly, she would have bet money that Paul hadn't even noticed. "Maybe this is just a separation—"

"Maybe nothing. She wants out. All she cares about now is my money and her dermatologist."

"Man, that sucks." Rick put a hand on Paul's shoulder. Steadied him a bit, and took him a few steps away from the food. "You have a place to stay tonight?"

"Got a room. Don't want to go until I know I'll crash until tomorrow. Why I came. Being alone is what sucks. The quiet. The…everything."

"I think you're gonna sleep just fine if you go up soon," Rick said. "Real soon. Okay?"

Paul nodded, but not at Rick. There was an older man heading for them. He appeared to be someone connected to the group, or the hotel, she wasn't sure which. But when he arrived, he smiled at Rick and then took over watcher's duty. "Real soon, it is," Paul mumbled.

"You think he'll be all right?" Jenna asked.

"Yeah," he said. "He knows a lot of people here, and he's a big donor. They're not gonna let him get into too much trouble."

"Does that mean you know a lot of people here, too?"

"Not necessarily. I'm trying to be as inconspicuous as possible. You about ready to go sit down?"

She put several oysters on her plate and nodded.

Rick shook his head and put some on his, as well.

They found another table. They were both drinking water and the food was delicious. Jenna liked that he wasn't hesitant to make yummy noises. It said a lot about him. He was comfortable in his own skin. She'd seen that all night, and she admired it a great deal.

Even though there wasn't a bite of chocolate on her plate, she enjoyed every last bit of her food. After quickly washing up in the ladies' room, she waited for Rick, who took her hand and pulled her onto the dance floor.

She didn't know the song. Or care. They didn't even dance, not for real. They just swayed back and forth, hardly moving their feet. She let her head rest on his shoulder. No, his chest. Rick was taller than Payton, and God, he smelled good.

"Payton loved me more," she said.

He stopped swaying. "What?"

She pulled back, far enough to look at him. "I always thought he loved me more. I wanted it that way. I never told anyone. But I wanted to have the upper hand."

"Because of your parents' relationship?"

"Yes," she said, surprised he'd made the connection so quickly. Obvious as the correlation seemed, it had taken her a while. She went back to swaying, and smelling his spicy cologne. It made her think of fall. Of leaves and grass and a storm brewing.

"I'm not in love with Faith," Rick said.

Jenna didn't lean back this time. She let him lead.

"I love her. Although I'm very disappointed and angry about what she did." His body had tensed, and Jenna gave his shoulder a light squeeze. He tightened his arm around her, bringing her breasts flush against his chest. "I guess I thought the more passionate, long-haul kind of love would happen eventually. And being friends wasn't a bad basis for a marriage."

"Fair enough," Jenna said, raising her voice, not her head. "But only if both parties agree." She felt a bit drowsy…from the music, she supposed, and Rick's warm body. "They both threw us under a bus tonight."

They kept on dancing their own slow way when the music changed and Katrina and the Waves started singing "Walking on Sunshine."

"Maybe you can salvage this thing," she said, tilting her head back to look at him. "You might want to check your messages. I mean, you're in Boston. You're probably going to be sleeping in the same hotel bed. Eventually."

"Well, that's one way of looking at things."

"And the other?"

He smiled his Danger Bond smile. "You and I go back to the apartment together."

RICK WAS ALMOST sorry they'd left the MIT suite. It was too easy to think without constant distractions. But he knew Jenna had to be exhausted, and not just because it was 2:00 a.m.

The lobby traffic had dwindled, because it seemed everyone was outside in the freezing cold waiting for transportation. The longest line by far was the queue for taxis and he could barely hear the piped-out Christmas carols for the sound of whistles.

The idea of hypothermia, mixed with the daunting proposition of checking his texts and calls, made him wish they'd stuck with booze instead of switching to shellfish. But he couldn't leave Boston without talking to Faith. "What do you think?" he asked. "Should we get in line?"

They were still inside the hotel near the front exit. Jenna had her cell phone out and from the number of tone notifications, Payton hadn't spent all of the last two hours kissing Faith.

"I've got nineteen texts and six voice mails, none of which I plan on reading. Well, maybe a couple, But my intention is to text him to let him know I've made other arrangements for the rest of the morning."

"Sounds about right. So, since I'm also just checking a few of Faith's texts, we should probably get in that insane line."

Jenna shivered preemptively. "Does that second bedroom have a heated blanket? Or a fireplace?"

"You'll be fine," he said. "I promise. Besides, the cab will be heated." With great reluctance, he turned on his phone. He had his own pile of unread, unheard messages. Checking the first three and the last three texts should give him all the information he needed. If Faith was truly stranded, he wasn't going to leave her here, even if it would make for the world's most awkward cab ride. He didn't want to think about the sleeping arrangements, but he'd do his best to make the night as comfortable as possible for the three of them. "I've got twelve texts and nine voice mails."

She took a step toward the exit, and then just stopped. "Huh. What if it's not all apologies?"

"What do you mean?"

"The way they looked at each other? Maybe they've reconnected with their soul mates. Maybe they're writing us to say goodbye."

"I doubt it. They chased after us, remember?"

"Right." She nodded as she led the way to the porte cochere.

The cold was like a sucker punch. Sadly, he'd learned a lot about that feeling tonight. But they found the end of the taxi line and he opened the first of the texts.

I'm so so sorry!

The second was straightforward and typed at 12:13 a.m.

Where are you?

At half past midnight the tone shifted.

I'm starting to get worried

It probably made him a horrible person, but instead of feeling guilty, he was glad. He swiped through until he found the last three texts. But the first of those was all he needed:

I'm with Payton and he's letting me stay at his place

He turned off the phone. Moved a whole quarter of an inch forward, trying to save not only their place without disturbing Jenna, but also gain some distance from the man behind them. Nothing was shady about the guy, but he got inside their personal space bubble. And as soon as Rick could, he moved his wallet to a safer inside pocket.

But all that was nothing, really. He looked over at Jenna. She was texting so he couldn't see her expression. Couldn't read her through her heavy woolen coat. Was she telling Payton to go to hell? Accepting his apologies?

When she did meet his gaze again, she'd put her phone back in her purse and donned her gloves. "We've hardly moved. At this rate, we'll still be in line next New Year's Eve."

She seemed fine. Subdued, but fine.

"We could take our chances with Uber." He'd used the services of the app-generated taxi service before, but not on a major holiday.

"That's true. I imagine we'd find a ride sooner that way. But I don't know. I think we should walk."

He laughed out loud, evidently annoying Mr. Oblivious behind them. Rick didn't care. What he should do was tell the inconsiderate bastard to just move. But first he said, "You're joking, right? The apartment isn't around the corner. It would be a challenge in the middle of spring, and, if you haven't realized, it's snowing."

Jenna shook her head. "What kind of a weather chaser are you? So it's cold out. We'll walk fast."

The man behind him snorted.

Rick tensed and turned on the guy, ready to teach him a thing or two about manners. But the guy was completely absorbed by something on his tablet, and not paying any attention to Rick or Jenna.

Stepping to the side to regain his equilibrium, Rick wasn't sure if he should laugh his ass off or find a therapist. Normally, it took a hell of a lot more than inconsiderate line movers to make him Hulk out. Perhaps he wasn't quite as Zen about Faith's midnight kiss as he'd thought.

Turning to Jenna, it also occurred to him that her impulse to walk to the financial district wasn't such a crazy idea. They both had a lot to process and he knew of no better way to unclutter his mind. "Okay. Let's go for it," he said. "We can always defrost when we get to the apartment."

Her expression changed from that self-contained cool to ready, willing and able. She started walking as fast as those stupidly high shoes would let her. And that was pretty darn fast. It actually took him a few seconds to catch up to her. When he did, she turned on him so sharply he nearly ran in to her.

She grabbed his lapels and yanked him even closer. "Whose stupid idea was this? It's freezing out here. We'll never make it to the corner, let alone your fancy-ass apartment."

He laughed, and then kissed her very cold lips. But that was just a peck while he unbuttoned his coat all the way down. The second the last button was undone, he pulled her against his body. Then he closed the coat, making them a warm cocoon. "Better?"

"Oh, yes," she mumbled against his collar. "How are you going to call Uber?" Adjusting her head so she wasn't smothering herself, she said, "Keep in mind, I'm not letting you go."

Unable to resist, he bent and maneuvered them a small but crucial distance. One that changed a gentle forehead kiss into a fiery, no-holds-barred stunner of a *kiss*.

Everything disappeared. The street, the cold, the whistles and the horns. There was just Jenna with her death grip on his tux, meeting his tongue thrusts with her parries until they were both dizzy with lust.

And then…

"You want to carry that inside, fella? This is a public street you're on."

He only opened one eye, just in case the voice was in his head. But no. It was one of Boston's finest.

He hated moving her away, but there was nothing to be done but to call Uber and freeze as they waited for their ride.

5

"YOU'RE NOT GOING to believe this apartment," Rick said. "Describing it as state-of-the-art doesn't begin to cover it. Maybe in four or five years the technology will be commonplace. At this point it's still a prototype."

"How did you get so lucky?" she asked, sliding closer to him as the Uber taxi, a very clean town car, took a turn. "Every room in the city must be booked tonight."

"I'm testing it out for my friend Sam, who designed it. We went to MIT together."

"Does Sam live there?"

Rick shook his head. "But I meant it when I said you'd be fine. The second bedroom is huge and it's got an en suite that, well, you'll have to experience for yourself."

"Oh," she said, scooting a few inches back to her side. "So it's definite, then. You'd prefer I take the second bedroom?"

"I want you to be comfortable," he said. "Whatever you choose."

Now that was part of the problem, wasn't it? Jenna had no idea what she wanted. Every time she thought about Payton the hurt hit her full-force. And then here was Rick, being so wonderful, his pretty eyes making all sorts of promises she didn't doubt he'd keep.

If she wanted him to.

They hadn't waited ten minutes before their cab arrived, and now they were on their way to Boston's financial district, where this magical apartment was located. She could hardly believe she'd agreed to go with him. The idea of running off with a strange man when no one knew where she'd be was about three floors higher than insane. Speaking of… "I hope you won't take this the wrong way, but I'm going to text my friend Ally as to our destination."

Even that would be tricky. Ally was her closest friend but Jenna wasn't anxious to explain the circumstances. Of course Ally would find out sooner or later. Unless things somehow worked out with Payton.

The thought stopped her. This wasn't the first time she'd considered the possibility, but his text messages hadn't helped. In fact, she wasn't considering anything, really. Not even the enormous risk she was taking by going to the apartment with Rick.

She realized he was staring at her and she pulled out her phone to find another text from Payton, a voice mail, as well. Both time-stamped between now and the last time she'd checked at the hotel. Was she making a huge mistake? Payton might deserve a chance for forgiveness even if she couldn't see it now. He'd never given her any indication that he was a cheater.

Well, of course he hadn't. That's why tonight had been such a shock. But that he had the *potential* for doing something so hurtful wasn't easily forgotten. Trust had been shattered, and entering into a marriage with a man she couldn't trust was unthinkable. If she stayed the night with Rick, Payton might not be the only one who needed forgiveness. Was that something she wanted?"

"What's wrong?" Rick asked, and she warmed at his concern.

"I'm getting sober."

"We're not far from the apartment. There's a great bottle of champagne in the fridge, plus a very well-stocked bar. In fact, I know I saw Kahlúa on the shelf, vodka in the freezer and cream in the fridge."

"That's oddly specific."

He grinned. "There are also cocktail onions, green olives, limes, lemons, Tabasco, celery and God knows what else. Everything the modern alcoholic needs at his fingertips."

"Good to know. But I'm also feeling pretty sure that while I have no desire to see Payton right now or go back to my place, I'm going to have to talk to him at some point."

Rick shifted a bit on the seat, giving her some room. It was dark and snowing outside their taxi, and she wished she had more than her cell phone, twenty dollars and a credit card on her. Like a toothbrush, some panties and makeup remover wouldn't have been unwelcome.

"We can turn this taxi around," Rick said, his voice soft enough she doubted the cabbie heard him. "Take you where you'd feel safer. It's fine. I'd understand."

"It's coming down pretty hard," she said, as the options played slowly in her head. Try to make it back to her place in Scituate? It wasn't too far, a twenty-five-minute drive if the weather was good and it wasn't rush hour. But with this snow? She was used to rough weather, she'd lived in Massachusetts all her life, and yet this snow felt colder. She could only see Rick's face when the light posts hit the window at a certain angle. She read Payton's last text.

I don't understand why you're not replying. I've apologized in every way possible. Honestly, it was nothing. A whim. A poor decision. Yet I don't know where you are, who you're with, what you're doing. For God's sake, Jenna, stop being ridiculous. Look, I don't blame you for being angry. But enough is enough.

Ridiculous.

Why was it every time she wasn't ready to throw in

the towel over an argument, her behavior was ridiculous. When he did the same thing, he'd chalk it up to his stubborn streak, the one that worked like a charm while buying cars or engagement rings.

The burn in her veins was very welcome. It made every decision from here on out easier.

"Tell you what," Rick said, surprising her. "Once we're inside, I'll pour us each a large glass of water accompanied by two aspirins. Maybe by candlelight, haven't decided yet. Then we'll reevaluate our options."

"And what about the storm?"

Rick's arm went around her shoulders. It was illogical to think he could instantly make her warmer, given the car's excellent heating and her heavy coat. But it happened nonetheless.

"Right. Yes. The storm. Which I know quite a bit about. So, no, if we don't zip you home now, it's going to be difficult to get anywhere for the next few days."

He kept his expression neutral. Mostly.

She took hold of his elegant tuxedo lapels and pulled him into a kiss.

NORMALLY, HE'D WANT to show off the apartment first thing because it was spectacular, but there was more at stake than his excitement over the pad's whiz-bang gadgets. It was enough that the fireplace in the living room was already ablaze when they walked in. That the subdued lighting and soothing music had appeared without him having to touch a single switch. Everywhere Jenna looked, there would be something beautiful, from the modern industrial kitchen to the wall above the fireplace, which was showing live scenes from downtown Boston complete with a scroll describing the current weather.

"That's not a TV," she said as she undid her coat.

"You're right," he said. "And it gets better. But first, water. Then champagne? Or a cocktail?"

"Just the water, thanks," she said. "With aspirin. That was a great idea. Do you mind if I finish going through my texts at the table?"

"Not at all. But I think you might be more comfortable on the couch. It'll warm you up faster. If you'd like me to disappear for a while…"

"You've already seen me crying with makeup all over my face." The way she looked at him made him still. He hoped he hadn't pushed too hard. Finally, she shook her head. "You don't have to leave. But I want to give you your privacy, as well."

"I'll be in the kitchen or my bedroom." He pointed to a door across from the large living room. "The bathroom's there," he said. "The second bedroom is through the door on the right."

"Got it, thanks. This place is huge. It must cost a fortune."

"Just about," he said. "Or it will when Sam works out all the bugs. We're only the third people who've stayed in it. At the end of our stay, we fill out a survey, which is very specific and long. Totally worth every moment spent. Then Sam will make adjustments, and there will be at least two more test runs. All old friends from our MIT days."

"Lucky them. Hell, lucky me."

He smiled, then quickly filled two glasses with water and retrieved the aspirin from the bathroom. Jenna had taken his advice and she looked comfortable on the sofa. She was already reading her texts so he moved as quietly as possible when he set down the water and pills, plus a box of tissues just in case.

He made a stop in the bedroom to get out of his tux. He was sorry Jenna didn't have her own things with her, but they'd get by. He put on some jeans and a long-sleeved Henley, and then returned to the kitchen.

After he took his own aspirin, he settled on a stool at one of the high counters, his back to Jenna. The wet bar was nearby, but he wanted to be sober when he read the rest of the texts from Faith. This wasn't going to be easy for him. Or her. Now that he was thinking clearly, he was worried about her. Despite everything, they'd been friends for a long time, and he wanted to know she was safe.

He'd already read the first three texts, so he began with number four.

More apologies followed, then the subject circled back to worry. She wanted to know if he was in the hotel. If he'd left. Did he know where Jenna was, because Payton was worried.

That one pissed him off. But when he read the next text—This is just cruel—his gut clenched.

The hell with sobriety, he wanted a Scotch. Because she was right. It had been cruel. He'd been hurt. Humiliated.

Leaving without telling her where he'd be going, well, shit, what had she expected? But he should've texted her the address of the apartment. It wasn't as if she hadn't been there, but he'd made the arrangements, and of course, Faith had no reason to think they weren't going home together. Even if he'd said outright that he'd rather she didn't come back.

She'd done a hurtful thing in a very public way on a stupidly significant night, but he was reasonably sure she'd done them both a favor. Marriage would have been a mistake.

From the living room, Rick heard Jenna sniffle. And there might have been a sob in there, too.

Wondering if Faith was doing the same thing out there somewhere sent him scrolling to the latest message. If she needed him, he wouldn't desert her.

I'm heading to Payton's guest room. Please let me know you're all right. I'm assuming you'll send me the apartment address when you sober up.

The next text gave him Payton's phone number and that made him sad, as well.

He immediately texted her that he was fine and gave her the address. It was snowing hard. She wouldn't be popping up anytime soon. Then he typed:

I'm sorry, too. I shouldn't have left like that. We'll talk.

He could have said more, but he wanted the rest to be in person. Texts were great for a lot of things, but telling Faith he'd be moving out wasn't one of them.

As he waited for a response, which might never come, he went to the living room to see if Jenna was all right. It was easy to see that she wasn't, though he'd already known she'd been crying.

At this point he'd said everything there was to say without getting in her business. If she asked, he'd try to find her transportation to wherever she lived, but he doubted she'd be able to get there. But then, with Faith staying with Payton, perhaps it was a good thing Jenna was here.

Jenna, her eyes red and her face flushed, looked up at him. "This is awful. He doesn't understand that everything's changed. He thinks I'm the one being ridiculous because he's apologized and I'm still upset." She sniffed and picked up another tissue from the box. There was a pile of them on her lap. "Sorry. You've got your own things to deal with." She held up the box. "Want one?"

He smiled and shook his head. God, how he wanted to comfort her.

"I'm going to take you up on that offer of the second bedroom."

Perfectly understandable, and he'd already guessed the night might go like this, but damn if he wasn't disappointed. That comforting thing tended to work both ways.

"No problem. I have something clean for you to sleep in.

I was thinking of having another drink before bed. Would you like one? The pantry is full of teas and hot chocolate."

She perked up a bit. "I'd love some hot chocolate, but you don't have to make it for me."

"I'm making myself one. It's simple enough to make two."

She nodded. Winced at the tissues on her lap.

"Hang tight," he said. "I'll be right back."

Rick went to the kitchen and found a smallish pot. Then he put some milk on to heat. After he made sure the fire was low, he looked back at the sofa, at Jenna's profile. Even with her red-rimmed eyes and her sad smile she was beautiful. He wanted her more than he should have. Not that he begrudged her the second bedroom. In fact, it was probably the best thing to do, but he'd have liked more.

Kissing Jenna had startled him. The way she fit in his arms, the taste of her, her lips, her style, the soft moans of pleasure that made him ache to know what she'd sound like in bed.

But she wanted to be alone and he'd give her that. And a paper bag for her tissues.

"Thanks," she said. "Again. For everything."

"No problem. The drinks are coming soon. I'll go grab that T-shirt for you. I can bring you your mug in the bedroom when it's ready. Or…"

"No. That's okay. I mean, yes, I'd like to borrow a T-shirt, but I wasn't planning on going to bed for a while."

"Oh. That's good. Great. I'll just—" He pointed to the kitchen as he moved in that direction.

After a quick check on the milk, he went into his bedroom. His suitcase, along with Faith's, were still in the closet. Payton, he felt sure, was supplying her with whatever she'd need for the night.

After zipping away Faith's things, he grabbed his T-shirt

from the National Weather Center. Lucky he had an extra. Curse of being a storm chaser.

Jenna had the tissue box and her used tissues in hand as she stood. "I'll go put these in the—" She tilted her head toward the second bedroom.

"Yeah," he said. "There's a trash can in the en suite." He headed to the kitchen where the milk was close to boiling, so he poured in the powder from two packages. Godiva chocolate. He imagined Jenna would like it.

He hoped she'd meant it, about staying up. It was nearly three thirty and she'd been through the wringer. It wouldn't surprise him if she crashed right there on the couch in the middle of drinking her hot cocoa. But he wanted to talk with her more. Even if she all she wanted to do was vent, though Rick hoped they could move on to other subjects. He liked her wit, her strength. Her life had just taken a turn that could result in repercussions for years to come, but she wasn't about to take Payton's crap in order to save face, or to get that wedding band around her finger and hope she'd change him later.

Maybe that was why his situation with Faith seemed so easy to handle. Comparatively, he'd gotten off easily. Now that some of the shock and hurt had eased, he knew that Faith and he would be friends again, although the idea to look for a new apartment had started to take root. It would be good for both of them to feel free to see other people.

After adding a hit of peppermint schnapps to his drink, he saw Jenna enter the great room. She'd let her hair down and it fell to her shoulders in gentle waves. Her face was far less puffy, but the closer she got, the more he could tell her sadness hadn't abated.

"Just poured you a cup," he said, and then held up the bottle of schnapps. "Peppermint?"

"No, thanks. I have a lot to think about, and liquor won't help."

"It might help you sleep."

"I'm still wired, but once the adrenaline stops making me want to scream, I'll probably fade like a punctured balloon."

"Well, then, why don't we go back to the couch. I'm almost an impartial observer. As close as you're going to find tonight. Feel free to say what you like. I promise not to repeat a word." He put the schnapps down and picked up the T-shirt. "It's the most comfortable one I own."

"What is that?" she asked, looking at the shirt. Her voice was a bit higher. Lighter. "An eye?" She took the shirt, unfolded it and put it up against his chest. "A tornado inside an eye. That's very clever. I guess there are lots of people who love storm chasing."

"Yep. Lots." His voice, on the other hand, had gotten lower. And his mouth had gone dry. She'd washed the smudged makeup off her face and even this close her skin was flawless. Smooth as silk. Her light floral scent teased his nostrils and messed with his already foggy brain. But he wasn't going to move.

"'Certified storm watcher,'" she read on the bottom of the shirt, which was exactly where he didn't want her to look. He wasn't hard. That would have been pretty scary, actually. He was thirty-four, for God's sake. But he was definitely starting to thicken.

"I don't know about this," she said, her full lips curving up at the corners. "Someone might mistake me for an actual storm watcher."

"And that would be so terrible? You disrespecting my profession?"

Jenna blinked at him, saw he was teasing and laughed. "No. Just a little too busy having my very own earthquake. Everything seems to be falling to pieces around me."

He studied her a moment. Despite the comment she wasn't the sad woman who'd walked out of the bedroom.

"Well, lucky for you no one will see you wearing the T-shirt but me."

She blinked again.

"Somehow that did not come out how I meant it," he said and put the shirt over her arm, picked up both mugs and gave her his most innocent smile.

When they were both seated, he found the remote and turned off the living-room feed. After pressing two more buttons, he put the remote away and waited for Jenna's reactions. What Sam had done in this room alone was right up there with the most innovative tech he'd ever seen.

"The walls."

He grinned. "They're changing colors. And if you listen..."

"The music has changed, too. It's very soothing. But it's not trying to lure me to sleep. Just to relax."

"Yeah, that's... You caught on way faster than I did. But you're right. Each seat on the end of this sectional turns into a recliner, except they're both massage chairs. Better than any I've tried before."

"If you keep telling me stuff like that, I'm never going to leave."

"I can't do it justice, but okay, that huge fridge in the kitchen? It knows when it's run out of something. Not every single thing you'd put in there, but all the normal stuff like soda or beer or eggs. Even stuff in the freezer. Anyway, the fridge orders the replacements. You can add or take off anything you want. If you order before ten in the morning, you'll have your delivery by five that evening."

"This is crazy. I've heard about smart houses, but that was just to turn off the lights, or water the lawn on time. I could sit here all day and watch the walls change colors. I want to say it's like a lava lamp, but it's not. It's the walls, the ceilings."

"If it's dark, you can see the night sky on the ceiling."

"Does it keep refilling my cocoa?"

"Nope. But I will."

She smiled at him. "With a place like this, why would anyone want to leave?"

"I don't know. I guess for me, being alone, even with every gadget here, would get lonely after a while. I like good company."

"Bummer for you that you're stuck with me tonight."

He stood up to start the second batch of cocoa, but he stopped in front of Jenna first. "I'm really glad that you're here. And I'm glad we're going to be snowed in. Even if it is just for a day or so."

The smile brought on by the pretty walls was replaced by one just for him. "If my world had to fall apart, anyway, there's no one I'd rather be with."

6

Of course she couldn't sleep. As soon as she'd slipped under the covers and closed her eyes the first image that came to mind was of Payton and Faith kissing. Although, on the plus side, the second was a snapshot of Jenna punching him in the jaw. It had helped relax her some.

After rearranging her pillow for the tenth time, she turned on her side and stared between the slanted blinds covering the window. The snow hadn't let up. If anything, it was coming down heavier now. Maybe that was why she'd found the room a bit chilly. Though snuggled under the covers it was nice and cozy.

She rolled over to face the wall and forced herself to close her eyes. She really was exhausted. Sleep should have been the easiest thing in the world but as the minutes ticked by, her mind refused to settle. She wasn't only obsessing about Payton, either. Her thoughts had been straying to Rick with alarming frequency.

He'd been great out there on the couch. After distracting her with descriptions of the apartment's many wonders, he'd listened patiently as she'd gone through all five stages of grief in about half an hour. She must have sounded like a lunatic.

He really was ridiculously handsome. Those blue eyes of his were made to mesmerize. She'd found herself staring. And staring. She'd looked away, sure. Only to notice how long and elegant his fingers were, how large his hands. His touch, she thought, would feel amazing on bare skin.

And kissing her like he had at the party, then at Copley Square, and on the street, in the taxi…

Jesus.

Okay, she was entirely too sober for this torture.

She started to flip over again when she heard her phone. The phone she thought she'd turned off. Heart thudding, she slipped out from the covers. It was Payton, of course—she didn't have to look to know that. And it wasn't a text. Even though she'd texted that they would talk tomorrow.

Maybe she just needed to say her piece, get it over with so she could finally sleep. Hoping like hell it wasn't a mistake, she grabbed the cell phone before the call was sent to voice mail. "Hello?"

"Jenna. Thank God." His voice shook. "Where are you?" he asked, managing to sound worried, relieved and exasperated all at once.

Sitting on the edge of the bed, she'd grabbed some tissue from the box she'd left on the nightstand. But the frustration in his tone reminded her that he thought she was being *ridiculous*. So no, she doubted she would be shedding any tears. "Why are you calling, Payton? I was very clear about waiting until tomorrow."

"I've been worried sick. How could you expect me to wait? Running off without a word, not answering my calls. This isn't at all like you."

Unbelievable. Could he even hear himself? "Well, I guess we both stepped out of character tonight."

His sigh came through loud and heartfelt. "I'm sorry about what happened with Faith. I really and truly am. But I swear to you, it meant nothing. It wasn't planned… it just happened."

"It just happened," she murmured, another piece of her heart splintering off.

"You know what I mean."

Sadly, she thought she did. Basically, Payton, who took pride in his steady, orderly life, his well-planned future, hadn't been able to control himself around Faith. Astonished at how calm she felt, Jenna remained completely quiet while he began another round of apologies.

"I have a question," she said, cutting him off. "We've been going to the BU party for five years. It was your reunion and why go anywhere else when there was a great buffet and dancing and all the perfectly logical reasons you basically insisted we go to that party every New Year's Eve." She forced herself to slow down, made sure he wouldn't hear her quickened breathing. "Were you hoping to see Faith?"

His hesitation was the last straw. She felt numb and cold at the same time. The silence might've lasted only a matter of seconds, but it told her everything. No matter what he said now, the evidence was in.

"No, of course not," he said. "Naturally, I thought it would've been nice to see her and catch up but—but no, we've enjoyed the party every year. You told me so yourself…" He kept talking, but Jenna stopped listening.

Nothing he could say would ever erase those few moments of damning silence.

One option was to hang up. Turn off the phone. But in spite of everything, she didn't want to hurt him any more than she had to. There was no joy in ending their relationship.

Payton was a great guy. Just not the right great guy. Even if they did manage to stay friends, so many changes lay ahead of her. For one thing she'd have to return her wedding dress, which was a shame. It was gorgeous. And the engagement ring. But those were just two of the hundreds of things that were irrevocably changed by a hesitation. No, that wasn't true. The hesitation was simply the tipping point.

God, she was sad. Her lover, her fiancé, her closest friend went on to explain, to rationalize the kiss, the reason he'd never mentioned Faith before. He made promises he'd most likely keep, but he couldn't change the fact that in the moment of his hesitation, she'd seen the two of them so clearly.

Payton had been the man Jenna wanted. He would be home every night. They'd never be too far apart. He wouldn't travel on business. When they finally bought a home of their own, he would take care of the maintenance. Handle their savings beautifully.

But she would never truly trust him again.

Five *years* he'd looked for Faith.

He'd followed her career, her life.

And Payton had never, not once, looked at Jenna the way he looked at Faith.

Jenna squeezed her eyes shut. She knew what she had to do. Call off the wedding.

Not over the phone, though. She'd arrange to see him tomorrow or the day after, depending on how raw she still felt. How wicked the weather was.

When he asked again where she was, she assured him she was fine, physically at least. There was no need to tell him about Rick, except that he'd made sure she was safe. But it took a while for Payton to hear her. To believe her.

By the time she hung up, she was exhausted. And cold. Freezing, actually. The room's temperature had dropped considerably. She looked around for a switch, a knob or a dial to turn the heat up. But she hadn't found one when she'd searched earlier and she couldn't find anything now.

She slipped back into bed and pulled the blanket up to her chin. Her teeth chattered. Was this a symptom of a broken heart? Because it was broken, no two ways about it.

And it really was freezing. The stupid apartment must've short-circuited. Was Rick having the same trouble?

Every thought was bracketed by shivering and when that didn't stop, she added cursing. Out loud. This wasn't like her at all. But nothing helped her feet warm up. Or the rest of her, for that matter. How was she supposed to get any sleep?

She threw back the covers and got up so quickly she had to hold on to the padded headboard for a few dizzy seconds. Then she tugged down her borrowed T-shirt and headed across the living room. Lights in the floor tile showed her the way. Precisely. Every step lit up the second her cold foot touched the tile. The one she left went dark.

Rick had pointed them out earlier but she'd forgotten. She jumped two tiles, then three, then straddled two tiles, which both lit up. Evidently, the floor was a lot smarter than the heating system.

She didn't stop until she was at Rick's door. He probably wasn't asleep yet. Besides, he'd told her that if she needed anything at all, she shouldn't hesitate to ask for it.

She hesitated.

Until the goose bumps on her arms sprouted their own goose bumps. When her first gentle knock got no response, she knocked again. Harder. She didn't want to walk in without permission. Too much potential for seeing yet another thing she couldn't unsee. The third knock did the trick.

"Come on in."

His voice sounded low and gravelly, and once she opened the door, he made quite a picture sitting up in his bed. Perfectly dimmed lights had switched on from the ceiling. The light was soft enough to sleep through, but bright enough that she could see the way his hair spiked, how he was trying to blink himself awake. And that he wasn't wearing a stitch.

"Jenna. You all right?"

Her teeth still chattered. His room didn't feel a whole lot warmer than hers. "Go back to sleep," she said, regretting that last knock. She should've known better. "I'm sorry I woke you."

"Don't go. Please."

With her back to him, she said, "The heat in my room doesn't seem to be working."

"The heat? Well, that should have been taken care of automatically."

She glanced back at him, and then quickly turned away again. "You'd think so, but I'm freezing."

"Why aren't you looking at me?"

"You're naked."

He laughed. "I've got pajama bottoms on. If it'll make you more comfortable, I'll put the top on, too."

"No, no. Of course not, just— All I need to know is where the controls are."

"I'll go have a look."

"Really, you don't need to get up..." She finally turned. Looking at him in that movie-star light quieted some of the louder warning signs in her head. He didn't have six-pack abs, but his chest was lean and firm with just the right amount of dark hair. When he ran his hand through the mess on his head she saw his bicep bulge to perfection. Then she saw his face. His utterly bemused expression.

"You are," she said, "a very nice man."

"Excuse me?"

"I mean it. You've been nothing but nice since the whole surreal incident began."

"Great. You woke me up to tell me I'm *nice*. The ultimate death knell." He covered a yawn and then rubbed his eyes. "I suppose you're going to tell me I have a great personality, too."

"Now that you mention it." She shivered again, her extremities still Popsicles, and she guessed her nipples were extremities. Because damn, they were hard and cold. Good thing her arms were now across her chest with her hands tucked under her armpits. Although, the pose pulled up the T-shirt far enough that he could see the entire front of her scarlet bikini panties.

"Honestly, it's not that cold. But I can see you're shivering." He patted the mattress next to him. "Come on. Get in. I won't bite. I'm way too nice for that."

This wasn't what she'd come looking for, but she was in no mood to argue. Walking across the very large bedroom suite, this one as exquisitely decorated as her bedroom, only warmer, she started to relax. She could feel it in her jaw, her shoulders.

"I can't sleep when my feet are cold," she admitted. "You sure you don't mind me stealing all the heat?"

"I don't mind at all," he said, holding up the covers for her.

She crawled in beside him. Shaking as much from adrenaline as cold. She was getting into a virtual stranger's bed. Oh, who was she kidding? If he turned out to be Mr. Hyde instead of Dr. Jekyll, fine. At least she'd die in comfort.

The relief of the warm bed couldn't be praised highly enough, though she had yet to stop shivering. When her thoughts flashed back to the phone call, another chill swept through her.

Her gaze connected with the man looking at her from his pillow. How could Rick seem safe and familiar after meeting him only hours ago? She managed a smile and inched closer, lured by the heat coming from his body. And by his eyes. Those damn hypnotic blue eyes of his could land her in real trouble if she didn't pull herself together.

"I'm not drunk anymore," she told him.

"Okay," he said, looking slightly amused.

"So, I didn't say you were nice because I was hammered. I'm not."

"I believe you. Neither am I, even though I had the schnapps in my drink."

"I probably should've had some in mine, too."

"I can get you—"

"No." She caught his arm before he could get up.

"How about more hot cocoa? To help get you warm."

The way he was staring into her eyes, she'd bet anything he had just thought of a more personal approach to stop her shivering. A muscle running along his forearm tensed beneath her palm. The jitters had already started in her stomach, and she withdrew her hand. "I'm really glad we talked out there on the couch. I'm just sorry it was so one-sided."

"I'm not. You have more at stake than I do."

"Not really," she said, somewhat confused. "We both had—it doesn't matter. I don't want to talk about what happened anymore. For me, anyway. If you need to vent, I'm happy to listen."

"No, I've done all the processing I need to do." He seemed so sure, so…unaffected. "Unload all you want. Don't worry about me."

"Nope. I'm really done." She smiled. "I realized today is the start of a whole new year for both of us. I think it's safe to say, at least for me, a whole new life."

"Huh," he said, turning his body to face hers. "In all the drama I forgot about that. You're right. We're off to an interesting start, that's for sure."

"Yes, very interesting." She realized something else—she wasn't cold anymore. Not even a little. But she moved closer just the same. "Care to make it even more interesting?" she asked, equal parts thrilled and alarmed to see his eyes darken.

Rick grinned. "I'm a storm chaser. I'm always game

for more interesting," he said and stroked her cheek. "Are you sure, though?"

"I am."

"I don't want to do anything you'd regret."

"Oh, Rick..." Jenna smiled into his handsome face. "I'm going to regret a lot of things about this trip. But none of them are you."

He shifted close enough that their pillows and legs touched.

And when she leaned in for one of his amazing kisses, he met her more than halfway.

RICK WASN'T one hundred percent sure he wasn't dreaming. He'd signed off on all things carnal half an hour after they'd reached the apartment. To have her in his arms? In his bed?

His dreams were never this good.

He pictured her as she'd stood in his doorway, her hair tousled, her hands tucked under her arms. Her nipples so hard he thought he saw the big eye on the front of the T-shirt blink. He'd never be able to wear that one again. Not just that particular T-shirt, but all of its identical twins.

Now he could feel those puckered nipples against his chest while one long leg wrapped itself over his thigh. Damn, if he had to choose between a category-five tornado and being here? The tornado would just have to chase itself.

"I didn't even ask," she said, breathing hard, not taking her mouth too far away.

"About?"

"I don't have a condom with me."

He laughed. "I've got it covered."

She kissed him again, and then started laughing herself. He was the one who had to pull away this time.

"What?"

"Pun," she said.

"Pun? Uh, I have enough blood in my brain to do basic math and spell my name. You're going to need to explain."

"It's nothing. Really."

"What am I missing?" he asked. They were still in the kissing position. His erection was well on its way to full hardness. The back of her foot continued to brush against his thigh, almost reaching his butt. He had no idea what she'd meant.

"It's so stupid now," she said. "It won't be funny anymore."

He nodded, done with it, and proceeded to kiss her three ways to Sunday, but it occurred to him her laugh had sounded nervous, self-conscious. So he pulled back.

Jenna blinked. "Why did you stop?"

He could see her under the muted ceiling lights, and hoped the flush on her face was from arousal than embarrassment. Or from having second thoughts. "Tell me the pun."

"Really? Now?"

"Come on."

"I asked if you had a condom. You said you had it covered..." She trailed off with a sigh.

"Ah, now I get it." Smiling, he brushed the hair away from her cheek, aching to do so much more. "You still okay with this? We could just cuddle for a while."

"That's a very nice offer and an appealing idea, but, um, you know how you were kissing me so hard it made my toes curl?"

"Yes, I remember that very vividly."

"You thinking of picking up where you left off?"

"I am."

Her cockeyed grin made him hum.

"You're playing a dangerous game, Mr.... Oh, my God. I don't remember your last name and we're having sex."

"Well, we were close."

"Did you tell me before? Because I don't recall. What's your last name?"

"Sinclair."

"Oh," she said, her voice dipping at least an octave. "Okay."

"Are we good now?"

Before she could complete her nod he kissed her again—he couldn't have held back if the world were coming to an end. And she kissed him in return. No hint of shyness, no reluctance. Her hands were on his back, on his sides, exploring. His free hand had immediately cupped her breast, and all was right with the world.

But…that breast was still covered. He needed to reach under that damn T-shirt and find out what she felt like in his palm.

He groaned as he gently squeezed her soft flesh, her puckered nub poking at him, begging him to do more than squeeze. He wasn't about to argue. As hard as it was to leave her lips, he slid under the covers and pulled up her T-shirt as far as he could. Jenna did the rest.

He'd have to pace himself. First of all, he hadn't shaved since before the party. Second of all, Jenna was perfect. She had the most perfect lips and the perfect breasts.

As his tongue swirled and teased, Jenna made sounds. She'd moaned before. In the taxi. Thirty seconds ago. But this was a whole new skill set. It wasn't just sounds, but words. Kind of.

"Oh, gaaah," she said, her voice still in that low range that made him crazy. "Do that a—hhh—there. Right…" Her hand went to the back of his head, making sure he didn't move. Though he doubted she realized how tightly she was pressing.

When he finally sucked that pointy nip, he hit the jackpot. She thrust her hips forward and her pantie-covered crotch met his very hard cock.

He wasn't quiet, either. The way he was thrusting and she was thrusting, he wasn't going to need a condom. He'd come right in his pajama bottoms.

And that was not the plan.

"Too soon," he said, trying to catch his breath and push back her surprisingly strong grip on his head.

"Too soon?" She moved her hand away. "Sorry, sorry."

He looked up as she looked down. "Sorry? There's nothing… I was too close to coming. Believe me, you've got nothing to be sorry for."

"Oh, thank goodness."

He smiled. He couldn't help it. She just charmed the living daylights out of him. When he'd thought of doing this back in the taxi and when they'd first arrived, he'd imagined hot, sweaty, angry sex, not this. He wasn't delusional. They both had a lot of things to go through, especially Jenna. But right now, she looked happy.

And now that he wasn't as close to coming as before, he could give all his attention to her other nipple.

He was, after all, a hell of a nice guy.

7

THIS WASN'T WHAT she'd imagined when she'd set out from the second bedroom. All she'd wanted was warmth. It hadn't occurred to her that the warmth needed to come from the inside.

Rick bent his head to kiss her between her breasts, but she didn't want him so far away. Not yet.

Moving gently, she ran her hand over his head, and that got his attention. "Can you come up here for a minute?"

"Of course." He didn't ask her why, he just shimmied up until they were eye-to-eye, lip-to-lip.

"Just so you know, I loved what you were doing, but I wanted you…closer." For some reason, she'd whispered. Probably for the same reason she'd asked him to come up.

"Believe me," he whispered back, "if I could be in two places at once—"

She grinned. "We'd both be exhausted."

"True. But it'd be worth it."

"Seeing as how you're here now, I was hoping for a kiss. Or two."

He didn't hesitate, but he also didn't rush. First, his hand went to her hair, fingertips gliding through, brushing her scalp with perfect tingle-inducing pressure. "You're very beautiful," he said, his voice soft and his breath against her lips still sweet with chocolate and peppermint.

With his other hand, he brushed her cheek with one

finger, and then did the same to her bottom lip. When he got to the middle, Jenna touched the tip with her tongue.

The way he inhaled and blinked, it was as if she'd given him something wonderful.

Then he kissed her. Softly. A brush of lips, a sigh. She felt his smile and she matched it with her own. The second kiss was a little harder, but instead of a third, he wrapped her in his arms, rearranging them both in the nicest way.

She felt his erection against her thigh, while her head rested on his shoulder. Well, no, she was lower than that because she could hear his heartbeat. It was so close to perfect, she couldn't help but close her eyes and feel safe. Warm and safe.

After a bit, his hand skimmed over her back. No rhythm or rhyme to it, just stroking her shoulder blades, skimming the back of her neck, moving down her spine all the way to her waist. It felt like heaven—he knew to apply just the right amount of pressure so she didn't have to worry about feeling ticklish.

He did that for a few minutes, both hands wandering, lazy and comforting, until he touched the band of her panties.

Using his fingertips once again, he snuck underneath about an inch. But that inch changed the game. The air she breathed suddenly felt electrified. The fingers on her scalp made her moan. His cock against her thigh pulsed and her priorities shifted from one breath to the next.

She smiled on his chest, directly above his heart.

His soft chuckle was just loud enough to hear, and strong enough to jiggle her lips.

Body language. Only, not the regular kind.

She'd been remiss, not using her hands at all. One arm was trapped, but she held the other close, fisted under her chin.

Okay, that was the regular kind of body language. No wonder he was only using his fingertips.

Releasing the fist made her sigh, made him inhale and hold his breath. She ran her palm across the top of his chest, then stroked down, mapping his coordinates, getting a feel for the terrain.

The more she explored his trim body, the lower his fingers moved inside her panties.

God, she wanted him. He'd been so patient, making sure each step he took was preapproved. Safe.

Now, though, she was ready and aching for Danger Bond.

As she skimmed her fingers over his chest, his nipple raised for her, which was very sexy. Her scalp massage stopped as she took hold of the little nub between her thumb and index finger. There was only one thing to do, and it meant leaning on her trapped arm, which had gone to sleep ages ago. Worth it, though, because when she licked that tiny male nipple, he groaned so loud and so low, she'd have thought he was dying.

Except, of course, for the way he squeezed her left butt cheek. His hands were large, and the squeeze made her gasp, but it didn't hurt.

Hardening her tongue, she flicked him. Just the way she liked it when she was on the receiving end.

Suddenly, he had her panties down as far as he could move them. It pained her to leave his chest, but there were places to go, things to tease him with.

Her hand moved down, followed by her tongue, to his tummy. His hips bucked when she brushed the underside of his cock with the back of her hand.

Without warning, he took her by the shoulders and pulled her up so he could see her, but it wasn't comfort he was seeking. Permission was granted by a nod and a gasp when he kissed her. Hard.

They were both moaning, moving. Her, trying to get off her damn panties, and him, reaching over until he was forced to break the kiss so he could get a condom.

It didn't take long to rearrange themselves. Being highly motivated, it was done before she knew it. He was on top, and that was exactly what she wanted. No frills, nothing to distract her from their connection. Not this time.

Good God, she was panting as though she'd run a mile and he wasn't even touching her yet.

They locked gazes as he pulled on the condom. Then his legs pressed her thighs wide. He bent forward and kissed her again; it was wet, sloppy, fierce and perfect. Balanced on one elbow, his hand went down between the two of them. "You ready?" he asked, his voice wrecked.

She raised her head and kissed him. In, out, then his teeth gently pulled her bottom lip while his hand slipped down to her landing strip, which he followed like a pro.

He pulled out of the kiss when his fingers dipped inside her. "God, you're—"

"Ready. Very ready."

His eyes widened, dark and hungry. "You want this?" He used the head of his cock to tease her, sliding it up and down her spread lips, but not pushing in, which she wanted very badly.

"Yes," she said, and it might have been louder than she'd intended.

"Me, too," he said, and entered her in one smooth glide.

"Oh, God." Her breath caught. "Do that again," she said, her own voice nearly unrecognizable. "More would be great."

He held himself up on his elbows. The muscles of his arms in bas-relief. She wanted to taste him, to feel him in every way she could.

Her leg went over his hip, her pelvis tilted up so he could go deeper. His hiss of pleasure made her moan.

"Touch yourself," he said, the words rushing out with a deep breath. His gaze was pure dark need now, and she knew he must be feeling the same thing. The briefest thought that she should have done it already swept through her, only to be replaced by sounds too urgent to be words.

Snaking her hand between them was a thrill all its own. Touching both of them, feeling his taut flesh with the back of her hand, their gazes still locked. "Close," she said. Finding her clitoris swollen and wet, she knew it would be seconds before she came, not minutes.

Rick moaned, his head dropping down to his chest for a long moment before he lifted it, his hips shifting into fifth gear.

She loved it, met his thrusts with her own. Wanting everything he could give her. The muscles tightened in her legs, her thighs, her arms.

He winced, shook his head. "Shit, I'm too far gone."

"Go," she said. "I'm right behind you."

He nodded once before his rhythm went to hell, and he was just pounding into her, and she was almost…almost.

She closed her eyes as it hit like a supernova, everything exploding at once. She'd had great sex before, but this was a whole new thing. Dangerous and new. She felt fearless, as if she could do anything, everything.

When the quaking settled into aftershocks, her throat felt raw from unremembered screams. No breath was quite enough. Dark spots still filled her vision and when she could finally see again…

It was fireworks.

Literally.

Fireworks above her. The sound was dim but unmistakable, and the sight made it even harder to breathe.

She pushed his chest, shocked he could still hold himself up. "Look up," she said, not having any idea if he heard her.

When he said, "Well, fuck," she laughed. He joined in as he fell like a log beside her.

"What the—"

She nodded. "I know. It's everywhere. Every wall. The whole ceiling."

"Magic," he said. He found her hand somehow and threaded his fingers between hers.

She met his gaze when they both turned to face each other at the same time. "Magic."

RICK SMELLED COFFEE. Part of him didn't want to move even his tiniest muscles, but damn if coffee didn't sound like the best thing ever. When he opened his eyes he realized coffee was nothing compared to the sight of Jenna snuggled up next to him. He didn't touch her, or move, yet she opened her eyes, too. They smiled at each other. "Morning," he said.

"Is it?"

He kissed the tip of her nose. "I'm not sure. The blackout blinds came down sometime after we fell asleep."

Instead of sunlight, the soft light coming from the walls and ceiling had gently woken them both. It beat the hell out of an alarm clock. Whatever time it was in the real world, it felt like morning. But he'd have to check.

Sam had warned him. The computer that ran the house was several steps above anything he'd be used to. It intuited programs based on sensory input. It could tell loud from soft, and now that he thought about it, could explain the fireworks. It also "listened" for changes in breathing and heart rates, which explained the perfect timing of the coffee.

Jenna sniffed.

"Yep," he said. "The apartment has made us coffee."

"Please tell me 'the apartment' isn't code for a lot of people watching us through invisible windows."

"No people involved. Just a computer genius. Anyway, fresh coffee is nice and all, but I had hoped it could also make us bacon and eggs."

"What? No dice?"

"Nope." He put an arm around her and pulled her closer. "This is better, though."

"I agree," she said, and smiled against his mouth right before he kissed her.

He took his time, trying to curb his excitement when her already hard nipples grazed his chest. She was so soft, so warm, so…

Jenna broke the kiss. "We really don't have any idea if it's morning, do we?"

"I can check my phone."

"I guess it doesn't matter." She started to settle and then lifted her head again. "Old habit, but I'm really curious."

He pulled away to reach for his cell phone sitting on the nightstand, and then remembered. "Time?" he said aloud.

The numbers flashed on the ceiling.

Jenna giggled. "Oh, my God. It's that late?"

"You anxious to leave?" He half expected to see a trace of regret in her eyes, but she looked fine. Just shook her head. So he kissed her again before he sat up. "There's a robe in the closet," he said. "Although the other bedroom should have one, too."

She blinked at him, her mouth agape in surprise.

"What?"

"There are robes in the closets?"

"You didn't see it in the closet?"

"I had no reason to open the closet, so no. Besides, you little sneak, you gave me a T-shirt so I thought that was it."

Rick laughed. "I wasn't trying to be sneaky, I swear. Had I thought of it, though…"

Jenna's eyes narrowed and then she grinned. "Go, on.

Get cleaned up. I'm going to steal your robe for now and taste that coffee for myself."

One more quick kiss and then he darted to the bathroom. There was a long mirror above the double-sink vanity. He touched it as he reached for his toothbrush and the news popped up, along with a local weather feed. In the two minutes it took to brush, he had confirmation that Jenna wasn't going anywhere today.

And he couldn't say that he was sorry. Antwan had been right about the big freeze, of course.

Jenna would have to stay at least until tomorrow morning, early.

He thought about it as he went back to the bedroom. Jenna wasn't there and he wanted her to be. But in the closet was another robe that she must've brought from the other room. He shrugged into it while staring at Faith's luggage. Odd how he hadn't given her a single thought this morning.

The scent of coffee pulled him into the kitchen, or maybe it was Jenna, her hair still sex-tossed, her trim body looking small in the thick white bathrobe. She'd already poured herself a cup and left a mug out for him.

As much as he wanted his morning jolt of caffeine, he wanted her more. He joined her and slipped his hand under her hair so his palm rested on the back of her neck, pulling her into a kiss. She tasted like coffee with a hint of mint. She also tasted like Jenna. God, how he wanted to take her straight back to that bed and not get up for a couple of weeks.

He heard her cup touch the slate countertop and then her hands went to his back. The temptation to sneak a feel underneath the bulky robe was strong.

"It's not freezing anymore," she said, just before she kissed his stubbly chin. He'd have to shave soon if he wanted to implement his plan of making out all day.

"What's not freezing?" He looked over her shoulder, to the weather report on the wall.

"The second bedroom. It's perfectly warm."

"Fixed itself, I imagine," he said, his gaze back on Jenna. "It had nothing to do with me." Though he suspected her sudden chill had had more to do with the emotional impact of what she'd been through, he said nothing. "I've pressed very few buttons in this apartment."

"You really didn't have anything to do with the fireworks?"

"Nope." A brief internal struggle ensued, where he debated kissing her again or getting his coffee and shaving. He went for the long-term goal and let her go. "I swear it wasn't me."

He plucked a packet of sugar from the coffee station. He could have had anything from stevia to honey to agave nectar. It was all there next to an impressive tea caddy, which was next to an espresso machine that looked more complicated than a jet's dashboard.

"Okay, I believe you. For now. Although from what I'm seeing on the magic TVs, I may get to know all the ins and outs of the apartment before I'm able to leave."

"I'm just hoping to learn your ins and outs," he said, sidling up to her again.

"No." Jenna winced while trying not to smile. "Don't use that line again. Ever. Although I'm flattered and pleased by the sentiment behind it."

He shook his head. "Guess I'm pretty rusty."

Jenna turned away to sip her coffee. "How long have you and Faith been together?"

That certainly changed the mood, but it was also inevitable. "Five years, give or take. It wasn't that formal with us. We were so much alike, we just fell into being a couple."

Jenna didn't say anything for a minute, then she asked,

"Do you think Payton is the first guy she—" Jenna shrugged. "Sorry, I guess it really doesn't matter."

"I don't know," he said, in all honesty. "I'd never had doubts about her. Obviously we had different views of the relationship." He drank some coffee then opened the fridge, checking out the contents. He didn't want to talk about Faith anymore.

There were eggs, of course, but the double-door Sub-Zero was packed with all kinds of odd stuff. He slid out the meat drawer looking for bacon. He found some, although he didn't recognize the brand, but mostly the drawer was full of white packages. He read the label on the top package. "Whoa." He stuck his head out from behind the fridge door. "You've got to see this."

"What's wagyu beef?" she asked, sidling up next to him, casually slinging her arm around his waist. She picked up another white package. "Free-range wild-boar tenderloin?"

"What a relief," he said. "That's the only kind of wild boar I eat." He joined in, picking up the last package in the meat compartment. "Chicken and poussin," he said, "with recipes taped to the back."

She didn't look. Instead, she was checking the middle shelf. "There are fresh truffles in here. And caviar."

"Damn good beer, too," Rick said, and then pointed to a tall, slim cabinet on the other side of the kitchen. "Wine fridge."

She looked at him, grinning as if they'd just broken into a big mansion in the Back Bay. "Just how rich does someone have to be to stay here?"

"Really, really rich, I imagine. Bill Gates rich? I don't know. Way richer than me." He put the package of chicken back. "Can you cook?"

"Real-person food, sure. I have no idea what one would do with poussin. In fact, I don't know what a poussin is.

And honestly? If I was rich enough to stay here, the last thing I'd want to do is cook."

Rick shrugged. "At least we won't get bored if we can't get out. What the hell. We'll become great chefs and get our own television show. Could be worse."

His phone ringing in the living room was a reality check. Jenna went to the counter to refill her coffee, but her smile had disappeared before she'd turned away. Obviously, she'd recognized Faith's ringtone. No surprise since there had been a lot of texting going on last night.

He went to the living room and caught the call before it could switch to voice mail.

"Hey," Faith said. "Are you still in Boston?"

"Yeah."

"You might be there for a while if you're not careful."

"Where are you?"

"Didn't you get my texts?"

"I missed a few." He sat down, and the fireplace clicked on and the weather feed appeared on the wall.

"Ah. Well, I'm on my way to Mexico City. There's been a major quake."

"How did you get a flight out?" Not that he was shocked she had. She'd actually hitched a ride from the United States Air Force once.

"I got lucky. I was able to catch the last flight out before Logan shut down. And, well, I was hoping you'd ship my things home."

He was about to answer, when she said, "Wait, what I wanted to say first was that I'm sorry. I was inexcusably stupid last night. And mean and rude. Nothing happened between Payton and me, but that kiss was… I don't know what I was thinking. Payton was from a long time ago, and I had no desire to pick up where we left off. But I really am sorry I screwed up our vacation. I know how hard it was for you to take time off. And yes, the weekend would have been ruined, anyway, what with me dashing off for this story. But I heard this quake was worse than the one in '85."

There came the first truly awkward silence between them that he could ever remember. He should have said something, but he was too shocked. Not by anything new, but a recognition of something he should have known all along and Faith had just confirmed.

Her apology was completely in keeping with their relationship. Everything between them was built on a base of convenience and the agreement that the work came first. He tried to remember why he'd thought marrying Faith was a good idea. At the moment, he couldn't come up with anything except that it felt like the next thing to do.

"I don't blame you for still being pissed," Faith said, ending the silence. "But I'd really appreciate it if you shipped my bag home."

Rick flinched. He wondered what she thought would happen in terms of their living arrangement. Or if she'd even considered it. "No problem."

"Thanks." She paused again. "Is Jenna with you?"

"Yes."

"I'm not asking if—"

"I know," he said, rubbing a hand down his face. It might've been nice if she'd sounded a little jealous. For old times' sake if nothing else.

"It's just that...well, I think you should let her know that nothing happened between me and Payton. He's a good man. That hasn't changed since I knew him in college. He's beside himself over the stupid kiss. He truly loves her. It would be a real shame if this mistake cost them their future together. So, maybe apologize for me? And if they haven't already spoken, you could give her a heads-up."

"I'll tell her."

"I'll call you when I can, but don't be surprised if it's in a few days. I heard communication is going to be tough. Anyway, I'm glad I got to talk to you. And please believe me. I'm so, so sorry."

"It's okay," he said, and he supposed it was. Shit, everyone they knew treated them like roommates who had sex. Convenient sex. Convenient kisses. Easy fun. No wonder he wasn't heartbroken. She'd never had his heart.

But that wasn't true for Jenna. She loved Payton. They had a real chance to get back together, to make a life with each other. The last thing he wanted for her was to have regrets about what they'd done, but there was nothing he could do now. Except tell her the truth. His foolish thoughts about spending the day together making out, eating, making love, cooking, having another night of fireworks. All that was out the frigid window.

Damn it.

But then again, it was the start of a new year. And he was entering it a little wiser and a little sadder.

8

RICK THOUGHT ABOUT changing the sheets, which was a completely idiotic use of his brain. The residual anger he'd felt since he'd seen Faith smiling up at Payton was turning into embarrassment. And feeling like that was also foolish, because Faith hadn't known about the ring. Had never known about his intermittent thoughts of marriage. What was that, anyway? Even if there was such a thing as a male biological clock, it hadn't ticked very loudly. The odds of Faith wanting to add children to her leave-in-a-minute lifestyle were slim.

The closest he could come to a solid guess as to why he'd wanted to get married wasn't flattering. Life with Faith had been simple. The least complicated relationship he'd ever had. By sheer luck he'd found a partner whose priorities were work first, adventure second, sex third. Marriage was probably on page twenty-seven, sandwiched between buying a motorcycle and learning to surf.

He'd wanted to freeze time. Guarantee smooth sailing for the rest of his life. He sighed, disappointed at his subconscious. Idiot.

Right now, though, Jenna was in the kitchen, undoubtedly wondering where he was and why he was taking so long. As he pulled on jeans and a sweatshirt, he made a plan for what to say to Jenna. There was no use delaying things. She deserved to know that nothing had happened between Faith and Payton, and that Payton wanted to patch things up.

Although delaying things had its own appeal.

Even though he knew their forced captivity wasn't going to last, the idea of kissing her, touching her—God, making love with her—filled him with more than just lust. He couldn't pinpoint what that feeling was. Given they'd known each other for all of ten minutes, it likely had something to do with their so-called shared trauma.

That wasn't fair. The situation was different for Jenna. He supposed for her it was a level-five trauma—complete devastation. He'd just have to suck it up and do the right thing because Jenna deserved that.

With a deep breath and a mental shove out the door, he found her on the couch, still in her robe.

She turned, even though he hadn't made much noise. Her smile slipped. "Oh. You're dressed." She tightened her belt, trying to be subtle about it, and then tugged the lapels together.

Well, that was just great. He'd managed to screw things up the minute he'd walked in the room.

He pasted on a pleasant smile as he joined her on the couch, keeping a good distance between them. One, he imagined, an Amish father would have approved of. There were two cups on the coffee table, not the same ones they'd been using, though. The remains of a dying marshmallow told the tale.

"I took a chance," she said. "If you'd rather have something else, you can save yours for later."

"No, cocoa's great. Thanks." He tried a slightly different smile, one that didn't feel completely fake, although he was pretty sure he'd missed that boat. He glanced around the room, hoping to get his head straight before saying anything, and saw… "Is that *While You Were Sleeping*?"

"Yes."

A few seconds dragged by before he realized that was her whole answer. "I liked that movie," he said. "And, I didn't know until now that there could be two simultaneous screens on the wall. That's the National Weather Center."

"I figured you'd want that on, with the storm and the polar vortex and all."

"That's nice. Very considerate. Thank you." He honestly was touched that she'd thought about it enough to figure out the complicated remote control, even though her expression had gone from confused to worried.

Damn. Another sign he needed to do the right thing here and not be a selfish jerk. Jenna had made it easier for him to check updates to see if there would be a big enough break between the storm and the vortex that would allow her to go home. He knew she lived in South Shore, but he had no idea what the snow-removal patterns were for the suburbs or Boston proper.

Jenna put her mug on the table, next to the one he hadn't touched. "Are you all right?"

Shit. "I'm okay, yeah. I'm fine."

"If there's anything you want to talk to me about, I'm happy to lend an ear. I know you were speaking with Faith, and, well, if you two are getting back together—"

"No, no. We're not. But, while I was in the bedroom, I put a pair of jeans on the bed. And a T-shirt. Don't laugh, but a pair of boxer briefs, too. I know the jeans will be too long, but you can just roll up the cuffs. Maybe put your things in the washing machine."

It took her a long time to respond. "Uh, okay," she said, looking bewildered.

He could end both of their torment right now by simply passing on what Faith had told him. Though if he did, and Jenna decided she wanted to forgive and forget with Payton, it would change everything.

And if that happened, Rick knew there was no way she wouldn't feel guilty as hell about having sex with him.

While he ached to touch her, to kiss her, doing anything remotely sexual before he told her that nothing had happened between Faith and Payton would make him one step below a slimy bastard.

The thing was if she felt guilty, the last thing she'd want to be was naked under a robe. She'd feel even worse about what they did, and damn it, he didn't want anything to tarnish his memory of making love with her.

It hadn't been a mistake for him. There had been fireworks. Magic. It didn't matter that as soon as the storm was over they'd never see each other again. She'd been the best part of this whole trip.

He closed his eyes for a second. Took a deep breath and considered gearing up and taking a walk outside. Anything to keep his mind free of sexual thoughts.

"Seriously," she said. "Something seems off. Is Faith coming here or something?"

"No. She's actually on her way to Mexico."

"Mexico?"

Thank God he'd found something to say that wasn't what he should be saying. He picked up his mug, not caring at all that it was lukewarm at best.

"There was a major earthquake in Mexico City. Really strong, with a lot of damage, even though the city has been trying hard to retrofit their buildings. Anyway, that's the kind of thing she covers. Major natural events. She was a junior reporter for the *Houston Press* when Katrina hit, and she did an amazing job on that. Personally, I think she should have gotten a Pulitzer, but she was too new, and you know, politics and all."

"You've known her a long time."

"Yep. We hit it off right away. See, that's the thing—I know Faith pretty well. That's why it's hard to understand what I was thinking buying an engagement ring. She doesn't want to settle down, and neither do I. We each have a go-bag ready at all times. During tornado season, which is getting less predictable, I go out every time clouds grow from dust whirls to organizing. I have to call the team together. Well, I say team—it's actually a bunch of interns I'm teaching. It's a lot of excitement over a short period of time. Most often, the storms pass, but… I'm just rambling. Sorry. You're not a student and you certainly don't need a lesson on tornado formations."

"But it's fascinating. Really. I'd love to know more. In fact, I'd love to set up a teleconference with the kids in my middle school, if that's something you do. They'd love it. Of course, you'd have to really make it clear to them they should not be chasing tornadoes."

"They should be prepared," he said. "Boston had a tornado in 2014."

"Yeah, it did. Although, not in Boston proper. Or my neck of the woods, but yes, a real tornado. I can tell you're a terrific teacher," she said, her voice softer and her smile sweeter. "So much passion."

She leaned in to kiss him, and it was all he could do not to jerk his head away. When her lips met his and the tip of her hot little tongue came out to sweep across the seam, his willpower took a hike.

For a few minutes, he didn't think of a blessed thing besides the kiss, the way she tasted like chocolate at first and then just her. Then he remembered what he had to do and guilt shot through him like an arrow. He backed off, trying to make it seem normal.

"All right. Now I'm sure something's off," she said, color rising to her cheeks as she prepared to stand up. "Whatever's going on between you and Faith is none of my business, except that it is, at least temporarily."

Damn it, if they weren't sitting so close on the couch

it would make things a lot easier, and yet his hand on her arm stopped her. Now wasn't the time to wimp out. "Nothing's going on between me and Faith."

"I'm sure you think that's true," she said. "But your behavior has changed since you spoke to her. If you think you two can still salvage your relationship I don't want to get in the way."

He started shaking his head before she finished. "The most I want is for Faith and I to remain friends, and if that doesn't work out, so be it." He wanted to leave it at that, change the subject. Keep Jenna to himself while they rode out the storm. "I'm very clear on that. You and Payton, on the other hand, you two can—"

"Remain friends?" she said, cutting him off. Her hands went to the thick robe lapels and she pushed them up again, covering more of her throat. "Maybe. But that's the most we'll ever be."

It was too late now to do anything but tell her everything, even if he never got to see that beautiful body of hers again. Or experience the closeness they'd shared. "According to Faith nothing happened after the kiss," he said, watching Jenna's reaction, which amounted to very little. "And I believe her."

"Yeah, I know. Payton told me the same thing."

"You talked to him?"

She nodded. "Last night."

Rick waited for her to elaborate, not that she owed him a blow-by-blow account, or anything at all for that matter. But the conversation with Payton had to have happened before she'd come to Rick's bed. Now her chills finally made a weird sort of sense.

"Wait, so you don't believe him?"

"I do. If I didn't I wouldn't want anything from him, especially not a friendship."

"So, knowing nothing happened—"

"Look, can we not talk about this?" She finally stood up. "Unless you've got something to tell me about you and Faith, I'd rather not dwell on it. We're here now, and look," she said, raising her left hand and wiggling her fingers, "both single, I was hoping to explore the hidden features of this magic apartment. Maybe starting with the shower?"

He stood up, too, moving close. But she was the one who leaned in for the kiss.

Was he being a weasel for not giving her some space to rethink her position with Payton? Was that any of his business? Or did he simply accept that she knew what she wanted, even if it was the end of an engagement. Jesus, he didn't want her to regret last night.

He met her halfway, pulling her close against him. And when her lips touched his, they surged into a searing kiss that brought up the temperature in the room at least five degrees. After he'd undone her robe and put both his arms around her bare flesh, the kiss managed to deepen. Or maybe it was the thought of all they could do in the shower that got him hard in record time. Finally, though, he had to pull back to get some air. But that didn't stop him from moving his hands down her back until he had a very decent hold of both butt cheeks. "My offer still stands."

"What are you talking about?"

It would be easy enough to lift her up and set her back on the couch. Do all the things he'd wanted to do since they'd stumbled into the kitchen for coffee. Like open that robe and make her come with his mouth before he did it again with his cock. "The whole thing of you wearing my underwear while we wash clothes."

"Oh, so now it's only your underwear?"

He grinned. "It's whatever you're comfortable in. Although I think you'd be missing a rare opportunity to wear boxer briefs during a polar vortex."

"So you're asking me to be mostly naked for science?"

"Is there a nobler cause?" he asked. "I don't think so."

She barked out a laugh. "Pretty much every cause is nobler than that."

"Yeah, well I'm just trying to be a nice guy."

Jenna laughed. "I so regret telling you that. But I have a better idea."

"What would that be?"

"I'm thinking we should go take a shower. Together. Naked. Wet. And most definitely not for science.'

"Oh, that is a good plan. We could go nuts with all the showerheads."

She pushed her hips forward, knowing exactly where she touched him.

"Completely mind-blowing," he said, walking her slightly toward his room. "There's music, too. In the shower." Another bump, and since he'd already started getting hard… "You can have any kind from country to… something else."

Jenna flexed her ass. Both cheeks at once. Jesus. How was a man supposed to think when she did stuff like that? "Uh, it also has heated towels. And colors and scenes like…you know." So much for her needing space. Or him being at all coherent.

Giving up, he finally pulled her right up against his poor hard cock, which was pressed so tight in his jeans he feared for his zipper.

Her eyebrows went up and her eyes widened, her smile so genuinely charming he could barely keep himself from dragging her to the bedroom.

"Although my idea trumped yours by a lot," she said, "I still like the way you think. You're not afraid to go off script. But you're logical, with good common sense, and always thinking ahead, i.e. washing my clothes. Although, you're a storm chaser, which is very illogical."

"Only kind of illogical. I literally wrote a book on safety

and storm chasing. Besides, it's a major rush. Kind of like kissing you," he said, surprised that it was true. Huh. Although realistically, he'd been monogamous for five years. It was the newness of being with her, that was all.

Jenna grinned. "If you'd kindly take your hands off my ass, we can get busy."

He smiled. She was definitely a better idea person than he was.

9

THANK GOODNESS HIS mood had lifted. She'd realized quickly that he'd gotten dressed for her benefit, and that his weird behavior was because he didn't want her to regret anything when the storm was over.

She knew that she'd have plenty to deal with regarding Payton, but that was for another day. When she wasn't in a smart apartment. When she no longer had the perfect distraction in the form of Rick Sinclair.

When she was with him, and that included times when they weren't having sex, she was completely present. Not thinking about the fact that she'd come here with only the clothes on her back. Thank God she'd never have to dress up like a Bond girl again. That she'd put up with it for five years? That would also be thoroughly examined another day, because she did not want to be that woman.

While he was busy with a call from his buddy Sam about the apartment, she decided to try on the clothes Rick had left out for her. The T-shirt was fine, but then she stepped into his Levi's. To her surprise she was able to zip them all the way up, given his waist was so trim. Taking a seat on the bed, she rolled up the hems. It wasn't very elegant. The hems were thick and they rubbed together when she walked. But that was all right. She wouldn't be wearing them much.

The boxer shorts, now they were going to be a lot of fun. There were at least three ways she could tease Rick with them. Right now, though, she wanted to peel out of his too-big clothes, then let him distract her some more.

Had she ever been as daring and playful as she was with Rick? Not that she could remember.

Of course the man she was with wasn't ordinary Rick Sinclair. Just like she wasn't ordinary Jenna. They were squarely in the middle of a first-time bubble. He could pretend to be anyone he wanted as long as it didn't hurt either of them. In fact, it wouldn't hurt her feelings if they both wanted to get a little more wicked. Maybe in the shower she could…she wasn't sure yet what she'd do, but she was open to suggestions.

Swishing her way to the full-length mirror, she grinned. The rolled up hems were uneven, but she didn't mind, which was also something new. At home she'd have had the measuring tape out, but here? No rules. Once she was out of the shower, she'd put on the clothes again. It would feel good to wear clothes, although being naked under the robe had been exciting. Maybe she would carry this side of herself back into her world. That would be interesting, but unlikely. For one thing, she wasn't going to be having this much sex. Or any sex, for that matter. Not right away, at least.

Her plan was to take a nice long break from men once she got home. Give a lot more thought to what she wanted. Who she wanted to be, with or without a husband. Why it was so important to her that she have the upper hand. As far as she could tell, she'd done everything she could not to be like her mother. She loved her mom, but she hated the relationship between her parents. Still, she didn't want her future to be reactionary. All that could ever amount to was a small life.

She took off the jeans and laid them out on the bed, then put the rest of her *après*-shower wardrobe with them. Later, she'd put her clothes in the washer. There was no way to tell when she might get the chance to go home.

It was a pity she and Rick hadn't met a long time ago. Although how could that have ever happened? Even if they had met, she'd never have gone out with a tornado chaser. God, how much she'd have missed.

Nope. No use going there. The object of the day was to keep her mind and body occupied. No time for soul searching or remorse. She'd found her line in the sand. Period.

She slipped on her robe, ready to go find Rick and drag him into the shower.

"Miss me?"

Jenna spun around to find him at the door, leaning against the frame. Even in the white robe, he looked like sin on legs. She had to admit that his looks were a part of what made this whole thing so otherworldly. He was out of her league in that department. Not that he seemed to mind.

"I did miss you," she said. "Everything okay with Sam?"

"Yep."

"Good. I believe we have a date with a hydra-headed shower?"

"Okay, first, I find it incredibly hot that you called the shower hydra." He narrowed his gaze as he pushed off the door. "I'd heard about English teachers being hot, but I never imagined you. Hydra-headed shower, indeed."

By the time he reached her, his eyes had darkened and his robe had opened completely, the tie dragging behind him. "May I take you on a tour of the facilities?"

"Yes," she said. "Please do."

He leaned in, but didn't kiss her until he'd undone her robe so they were flashing each other shamelessly. This was very high on her scale of erotic moments. The kiss, when it came, made her toes curl while he made sure all their visible naked parts touched.

Somehow, without seeming to look up, he led her through

the bathroom. The whole time his fingers ran through her hair just the way she liked it. He kissed her until she could scarcely breathe. And the way he used his tongue to tease and tempt, she became wet without touching water.

Magic.

Behind her, she heard music, soothing spa sounds, as well as the sound of gentle rain. They broke the kiss a few seconds later, and Rick pulled his cell phone out of his robe pocket.

"Are you really going to take another call now?"

"That would be very difficult," he said, "since this is a remote control."

"Oh. For the shower?"

"Come on. I'll show you."

The shower in this bathroom wasn't like the one in the second bedroom, which was all kinds of awesome in its own right. This one, though, was luxury to the max.

There was no door. Instead, there was a gorgeous curved tile entry. The tile changed from sea-green to teal in the outer edges, where they hung up their robes, to a beautiful lavender and pink as they walked through to the shower itself.

"Oh, my God," she whispered, spotting the rows of jets coming from three directions, the music getting a bit louder the closer they got to the heart of the system.

"Is the temperature all right for you? We can change it in a heartbeat."

She stuck her hand under the waterfall. "Perfect so far."

"Don't be shy." He pointed to a digital keypad next to a single sprayer that reminded her of a car wash. "You can change the temp or the flow to whatever suits you."

There was no way to tell but to dive in. She moved to the center, where every jet hit her, and it was so glorious she wanted to stay right there until school started on Monday. Maybe longer. Closing her eyes made it easier to immerse herself in the sensations. When she opened her eyes again they were no longer in the bathroom.

It was a jungle.

Everywhere she looked the jungle surrounded them, crawled up the walls to the canopy on the ceiling. She could barely make out the many showerheads, but Rick was perfectly clear.

With his hair wet and his body glistening, he approached her slowly. “Look at that smile. I think I’m jealous.”

“Of a shower?” Jenna laughed. “I’m a water baby, that’s all. I would swim every day if I could, then sit in a hot tub every night. At home, I spent a lot on an oxygenated showerhead. But this, holy cow, this is the mother ship.”

Grinning, he inclined his head. “Check out the amenities.”

She hadn’t even noticed the shelves filled with all manner of wonders. Everything from body scrubs to shampoos.

“I’ve never heard of any of them,” he said. “But then, I’m not a spa kind of guy.”

The first thing she picked up from the shelf was a body wash by Hermès. The next was Guerlain. “Uh, won’t your friend be pissed if we use these? I know they cost a fortune.”

“It’s okay. Promise.” He took a bottle off another shelf, poured what looked like liquid gold into his hands, and then walked behind her. Seconds later, he was washing her back, soaping her up with what felt like wet silk. When she had abandoned herself completely to pleasure, wet and warm as could be, he pressed his front against her back. Then he began at her neck and moved his large hands down.

She dropped her chin when he started on her breasts. Reaching behind her, she caught the back of his head and brought it to her shoulder. “I want to wash you,” she said.

“I’ll let you.”

"Okay, but I don't want to make love in here. I want to wait until we go back to bed."

"I'm good with that."

"Excellent," she said, then let him go. He moved down her abdomen, guiding her this way and that so he wasn't competing with the jets.

When he arrived at her landing strip he soaped that slowly, moving down farther until his fingers were inside her.

It didn't take but a minute for him to put his index finger on her now ripe clit.

"Remember," she said, turning her head so she'd hear him. "Not till we get to bed."

"I think you're forgetting that you, Ms. Jenna, don't have much of a refractory period at all."

"Oh, right," she said, nodding. "Go for it."

His chest shook with a laugh but not for long. Her hands were on his arms, lightly holding him, loving the feel of his muscles as he worked her into her own private lather.

Behind her, she could feel him. He was very hard, and very clever as long as he didn't take it too far. He thrust his soapy cock between her buttocks. She'd never been big on frottage before, but this was sexy as all get out. The jungle was alive around them, the rain full of tricks. But now all she could think of was his fingers, and how her body was tightening, preparing to blind her with a whole body orgasm. It was there. Rising, pulsing. "I'm close," she said.

"Good."

"Rick!"

"I'm here," he said. "Let go. I've got you."

In the dead center of what had to be a wet dream, she came apart. The only thing keeping her from turning into a quivering puddle was his arms. Lights flashed behind her eyelids and the room spun. She was gulping air, somehow not drowning. Probably because Rick was there, strong and steady, with his wicked fingers slipping away seconds before she became too sensitive.

Finally, after who knew how long, she stood on her own, anxious to feel his body under her own soapy hands. Instead of the Guerlain, she went to the men's shelf where… "Oh, my God, you have to see this."

He gave her a quizzical look, but his eyebrows rose when he read the label of the shower gel. It was called Bond No. 9.

"Do you like the scent?"

He uncapped the bottle, sniffed, and then handed it to her.

She inhaled deeply. "Mmm, I do," she said. It smelled of ginger and leather and something darker but also citrusy. It didn't matter, as long as he liked it. "Okay?"

"As a very good friend of mine once said, go for it."

She lathered up, and went to town. It was more amazing than she'd imagined. Especially because the whole time she was caressing every part she could reach, he was shampooing her hair.

Magic. Again.

Not the jungle, not the luxurious products, not any of it.

Just him.

Just Rick.

THEY'D ALMOST made it. Almost.

He thought he had better control of himself, but when she started to wash him below the belt, so to speak, the switch got flipped and he was a goner. She'd barely touched his cock with her handful of shower gel and he'd popped like a champagne cork.

It didn't matter. They had all night.

But for now, they were happily drained, done in by an overdose of pleasure. It was remarkably difficult to get dry despite the warm towels, then to make it all the way to the bed. He'd been worried about being away from his gym routine, but the hell with that. All he wanted was lying next to him, her hair dried and gorgeous, spread over his shoulder. They'd exchanged maybe ten words since leaving the shower.

He was glad for Sam, because this place just kept getting better, but unlike the superrich would-be clients, Rick had to go back to his apartment shower after this.

He'd always bought serviceable crap for the bathroom. He wasn't a pig or anything, but he bought his things from the neighborhood drugstore. He was tempted to go online right now and order some of that Bond stuff, but no. He'd do it later, when he wasn't so perfectly at peace.

He felt pretty certain that every time he used the gel it would remind him of Jenna. Of how lucky they'd been to meet each other, let alone to spend this kind of time together. To remember this New Year's Eve as the one where he'd met her instead of the one where he'd almost made a huge mistake with Faith was pretty great.

The walls had been changing colors ever since they'd slid between the sheets. They were soft, like the color of the wheat fields he'd walked past on his way to school when he was a boy, and the pale blue of the cloudless skies of summer. Odd. He hadn't thought about his hometown in ages, and he wasn't sure why he was now.

He ran his hand down the downy soft skin of her back. "I hate to be the bearer of bad tidings, but I had to change my flight plans. I'll be leaving early tomorrow morning. It's probably our only chance to get out before the really big storms come through."

"Oh. That's awful. I was hoping we'd get to stay until Sunday," she said.

"Me, too. But I have to get back to work. This is a very unusual winter. I usually hate the idea of being stuck inside for any length of time. I pretty much build my life around outdoor sports. But with you…"

"I wouldn't mind being trapped here." Jenna shifted a bit until she was able to meet his gaze.

"No. If I had my way, I'd keep us here through here through Monday. Just think. Two more nights…enough food for an army. That shower."

She moaned, and he felt himself react as if he hadn't just come thirty minutes ago. "I noticed the tubs are pretty spectacular. The one in my bathroom is a whirlpool. I've never seen one with more jets."

"Big enough for two?"

"Definitely. But I don't see how we'll ever get to use it." She ran her hand over his chest. "I've been trying to figure out why I'm more comfortable with you than I am with people I've known for years."

"Think it's shared trauma?" he asked, then wanted to bite his tongue for the mistake. Things had been nice and easy. The last thing he wanted to talk about was Payton or Faith.

"Some of it," she said, "sure. For all intents and purposes, we were in the same train wreck."

"Which doesn't quite explain that first kiss."

Her hand stopped. A few seconds later, she was playing with the sparse hair on his chest again. "Or the one from ten minutes ago," she said, making it sound almost like a question.

But when he thought about it… "You're right. I don't think I've—I don't know, everything feels different."

"It'll probably fade. We'll get back to our real lives, and then all the stuff that we've locked out will come crashing down around us."

He nodded. "I've got to find a new apartment."

"Ugh," she said. "I don't envy you that. I hate apartment shopping."

"Especially after staying here."

They both laughed a little, but feeling her against him was like a drug. "What about you?"

"You mean when I get back? Well, I've got school, of course, but at least I won't need to scramble. I prepared a week's worth of lesson plans right after Christmas. But it's always weird on the first day back after a long break. The kids will be humming with energy. Missing the freedom of Christmas vacation."

Everything about her in his arms was perfect. He had no reason at all to move a muscle, and yet he had no choice but to move them both until he could look her in the eyes.

"Hey," she murmured. "I was enjoying that."

He smiled. "I don't think you'll mind. At least, I hope not," he said, lowering his head so he could kiss her.

She moaned, and it was one of the good ones. He pulled her body close, the softness of the clean sheets yet another great sensation that couldn't top the feel of her skin, the flesh against flesh. Her foot rubbed up the front of his calf. His hand found the sweet spot on her scalp that made her sigh. They didn't speak, not for a long while.

"You seem to have found your second wind," Jenna said, as she ran her palm over the underside of his thickened cock.

"I don't know what's in the water in this place, but I haven't been this quick on the draw since my early twenties."

"What do you mean *the water*? I'm a little insulted. Here I was thinking it was me that made all the difference."

He stopped moving, stopped breathing for a moment as he realized she was right. "My mistake," he said. Then he turned over until he was almost covering her with his body. He met her gaze, trying hard to remember that moment in the hotel, the feel of her lips under his. How it had been a shock to his system. And when she'd parted her lips to let him inside?

He kissed her. And it happened again. Like a moment trapped in time. That same shock ran down his body, settled in an ache that only one thing could possibly assuage.

When he finally pulled back, it was light enough in the room for him to see into the mesmerizing dark of her eyes.

"You've still got it," she whispered.

"So have you," he whispered back.

10

Rick had just awoken at a god-awful hour and was buck-naked on his way to the kitchen for coffee when Antwan called to Skype. He thought about putting on a shirt and eyed the camera over the fireplace. With that wide angle he'd have to put on jeans, too. Instead, he grabbed the robe he'd left over the back of the couch when Jenna had lured him to the bedroom last night.

While he waited for Antwan's upper half to appear on the TV screen on the wall, Rick cleared the sleep from his voice and pushed a hand through his rumpled hair.

"I would have called you before now," Antwan said as he popped up, "but the bastard I work with ditched me for a woman."

It was only January 2. How had so much happened in the four days since Rick and Faith had left for Boston? "Well…"

"No." Antwan shook his head, which looked very large on the wall screen. For all the fierce weather they'd been having, the picture was crystal clear.

Rick could even see his desk in the background, which had unsurprisingly sprouted a large stack of files. "No… what?"

"I don't want to hear about how great everything is. Shit, man, look at you, more relaxed than I've ever seen you. But I suppose that'll happen after so many nights of shagging." Antwan's head jerked back. "Dude!"

Behind him, Rick heard a little squeak. He whipped around to see Jenna wearing one of his shirts, unbuttoned, and a mortified look on her face, backing out of the living room and disappearing with a soft whimper. So much for springing the news of his failed proposal slowly.

"That wasn't—" Antwan looked behind him, then leaned closer to his computer camera. "I can't wait to hear this story, man."

"I didn't propose," Rick said.

"Damn. I had it the other way 'round."

"I was going to ask her at the stroke of midnight— Wait, what did you mean, you had it the other way around?"

"You proposed, she laughed. You know, for the office pool. I think Wexler won."

"So everyone in my workplace, my home away from home, was betting that I'd make a fool of myself?"

"No. Not everyone," Antwan said with his big white grin. "Sorry, *bredda*, I wouldn't be joking but I can see you're not too broken up about it."

Rick sighed, not because of the pool. How could he when he'd won money on a few himself? But because in hindsight, he would've bet against himself, too. Shit.

"Go on. Tell me about it."

"Nothing to tell," Rick said. "Look, I know you aren't surprised. And frankly, I'm not, either. You were right all along. Faith and I are better friends than anything else."

"Hey…" Antwan shook his head. "I don't mean to rub it in. I shouldn't have mentioned the office pool."

Rick laughed. He wasn't offended. "How much did you lose?"

"I can still pay this month's rent." Antwan grinned and glanced toward the hall where Jenna had disappeared. "So, who's the hottie you been shagging?"

Rick stiffened, not liking the reference one bit. "Her name's Jenna," he said evenly, knowing his friend didn't mean anything. "And we've spent a very nice couple of days…well, nights together. This apartment is so dope, man, I can't even explain it."

Antwan read him loud and clear and just nodded. "You'll have to tell me about it when you get back. Actually, that's why I'm calling. Forget about your morning flight. The snow was a little bigger than we predicted."

Rick smiled, which he probably shouldn't have. He'd be missing a major change in the weather patterns.

"But Lester's pretty sure you'll be able to get out tonight. "

"How thoughtful of him," Rick said and Antwan laughed. Their boss was an okay guy most of the time, but he could also be a pain.

"I can tell him I never reached you if you want to stay longer."

"That's okay. I've been checking myself." Rick glanced over at the weather feed showing on the other side of the fireplace. "You're talking about the red-eye."

"Yep," Antwan said, "or a crowded flight tomorrow afternoon. You're not the only one stuck in that storm, my friend. But we can pull some strings."

"I'd rather leave tomorrow, but I need to talk to Jenna. Make sure she can get home before I leave."

"Where is she heading?"

"The suburbs," Rick said. "South Shore. I don't know what's going on with the roads, though. Do me a favor—text me the info on both flights?"

Antwan nodded. "Travel safe, *bredda*. If something changes, I'll give you a call."

"Good deal. Later."

The second he closed the connection with Antwan, Rick said, "It's safe to come out now."

He got up, wanting that coffee, but more important, to kiss Jenna.

"Give a girl a heads-up," she said, coming out of the bedroom wearing her robe over his shirt.

It made him laugh. "Sorry."

"I didn't even have the consolation of my first cup of coffee. It was terrible. Like a nightmare I had once where the only coffee anywhere was really bad decaf."

He shuddered dramatically, and then pulled her into his arms. "Would it be dangerous for me to stop you for a kiss?"

She met his gaze with a glower. "I wouldn't joke about that. I can be pretty mean before I get my first cup."

"I'll risk it." He made good on his promise, giving her a kiss tailor-made for Jenna and no one else. He'd learned a lot about her in the past couple of days, most of which had to do with what made her happy and what made her crazy happy. He'd save that kiss for later.

She looked a bit dazed when he finally let her up for air. "Sheesh, you took your time there, Sinclair."

"And you liked every second of it."

She grinned as she led him to the kitchen.

He wasn't surprised that he was smiling, too. He'd done a lot of that lately. "Did you hear the conversation?"

"What? Me? Eavesdrop? Never." She filled mugs for each of them.

"So, you heard that we'll have two weather breaks where we'll have a chance to get to our respective homes." Taking her free hand, he walked her to the couch. His first choice would have been back to bed, but he was afraid they'd get distracted. He didn't want Jenna to lose any opportunity to leave. He sat first and she joined him, leaving barely enough room to use her right arm.

After a deep inhale, Jenna shook her head. "I don't want to go. I want to live here forever. And I'd like it to remain this amazing fairy tale."

"You mean the part where we didn't have to work at

all?" It was hard to hang on to a smile. She was right. Since they'd arrived, life had been magical. But now, as he looked into her sad brown eyes, he wondered if she was thinking about her broken engagement, the future she'd have to rebuild. Was regret already erasing the magic they'd shared?

"Actually I was thinking of this part," she whispered and leaned in to kiss him.

The mugs were safely set aside before she dragged him down by his lapels. And the next time he looked up, an hour had passed.

JENNA PROMISED HERSELF she wouldn't pout any more than was absolutely necessary. Rick had to go back to Oklahoma, and she had to go home. Even now, he was finding out about flight opportunities. She hadn't planned to be gone at all. Some of her plants were probably desperate for hydration, but that was her only worry. Still, it hurt to know the party was over. "What are our two choices?"

"You could leave around six o'clock," he said, putting his phone next to him on the couch. "The roads to South Shore should be fine by then, and the next storm won't come until morning."

"And you?"

"If it's still available, I'd catch a red-eye at midnight."

It was still morning. They hadn't even had breakfast yet, but six o'clock seemed as if it were minutes away, not hours. There was so much she'd wanted to do. "What happens if you don't get the red-eye?"

"Then I stay until tomorrow afternoon."

"Just you?"

He gave her a look that she couldn't misinterpret. "I know how I'd vote," she said, itching to dissuade him from tonight's flight. "But let's try to be responsible and get you safely back home. I can get a ride anytime."

"I'm not crazy about this being-sensible nonsense. You're right, of course. But there's something else to consider. If we did stay here, we'd be helping Sam out by testing more features. Like that big whirlpool bathtub."

Jenna was already nodding. "Plus, we should have at least one more great meal."

"Four, if we can."

She reached for her coffee, but it was cold. There was a perfectly fine microwave that could zap it back to the right temp, or she could make a fresh pot. Maybe try another kind of coffee. "Oh, I found a waffle iron in the cabinet. How about I make waffles while you cook bacon. Sound good?"

"Sounds great."

Forty minutes and a pretty big mess in the kitchen later, they were still in their bathrobes, sitting at the dining room table. Of course there was real maple syrup, and the waffles were the old-fashioned kind, more dense and flat—her favorite.

Jenna put her fork down even though there was a perfect mouthful of waffle on the tines. "Did you ever check on the red-eye flight?"

His wince answered the questions. He whipped out his cell phone and went through the messages. "Antwan got me seats on both flights. We still have an hour to cancel before things get pricey."

She ignored the rest of her food, her appetite as gone as they would both be in just a few hours.

"We can still take that bath," Rick said.

"That's true," she said, wondering if this counted as a necessary time to pout.

"And there's…" His words fell somewhere short of his lips as he stared at her.

"Yes?"

"I didn't expect this. Since we got here, it's been—"

"Wonderful?" She knew she was putting herself out there, making a leap like that, but the way he looked at her made her warm from the inside out.

"Yeah. Wonderful." He kept looking at her. "So?"

"I don't know. Do you think we could still be in shock?" She blinked, and then stared right back. "I mean, from the moment we kissed it was like—I don't know. I didn't expect to—" She inhaled through her teeth. "That it would be forever seared in my memory. I remember how when I just let go, let it happen, it was as if we were alone in that hotel. But for that feeling to last all this time?"

Worry lines marred his forehead, and she couldn't figure out which thing she'd said that had caused them. "Please don't get the wrong idea, but I think I'm going to miss this apartment as much as I'll miss you."

He laughed and finally looked away. He wasn't worried anymore, which she realized would have been the true moment for a pout. But she smiled instead.

In fact, she probably needed to dial it down a whole bunch of notches. Once that door opened to the outside world, she'd have to face her real life. A life without truffles or Prendimé dark chocolate with almonds. That second one actually made her want to weep. She'd never tasted anything better.

Wait. There was one thing—kissing this gorgeous man while he still tasted like maple syrup.

HE WASN'T WORRIED about catching the red-eye. He'd make it to the airport just fine, sleep on the way home. Staying longer than he had to was unprofessional. Keeping Jenna here an extra night just because he wanted her company wasn't like him at all. He loved his job, his career, and he never missed a day if he didn't have to. If this was tornado season, he'd fly out the minute he could, but—

"What made you so interested in tornadoes?" Jenna

asked, her head cradled against his chest as she occupied herself by twirling his chest hair around her fingers.

After breakfast, they'd meant to clean up the kitchen, then take a bath in the whirlpool tub, but one kiss had led to another and they were still in bed, still catching their breath from yet another astonishing round of sex. He was propped up by a few pillows, his arm around her.

Soon they'd be returning to their regular lives, and his life was all about tornadoes, so the question wasn't a surprise. Yet it wasn't an easy one for him to answer.

The short version was the one he told most everyone. It consisted of two words: Tornado Alley. But he wasn't sure he wanted to make light of what he knew now was his calling. Hell, she'd probably get a kick out of what had happened to him.

He'd never told Antwan, and he never told the storm chasers he was in charge of. His father knew, of course, and so did Faith, but he hadn't told her until they'd been living together for two years.

"Rick? Is that too complicated for your sex-addled brain?"

He smiled, although she couldn't see. "Smart-ass," he said, giving her shoulder a little squeeze. "Do you want the short version, or the long?"

"Long, of course."

"Why?"

She looked up at him, her finger hovering a quarter of an inch from his right nipple. "Come on. You know I'm interested in learning new things. And you're definitely something new."

He'd have been disappointed if she'd answered any other way. "Okay, but you have to understand, I don't tell many people what really happened to me. Can I trust you to keep it a secret?"

"Not for a minute. I'll probably call the Boston papers as soon as I get home."

"Okay," he said, nodding. "Just checking."

She pinched him. Not hard, and not in any supersensitive place, but she got his attention.

"All right," he said. "Jeez. I'll tell you. Everything."

She gave him a look before settling down.

"I was fourteen years old," he began, "and I lived in the most boring town in Oklahoma, right in the middle of Tornado Alley. Which, when you think about it, could explain everything."

"A lot of people live in the middle of Tornado Alley and I bet they aren't all storm chasers."

"Excellent point." He smiled. With Jenna, the short version would never have cut it. "Anyway, I was kind of a mix of jock and nerd, heavy on the nerd, and I didn't have the kinds of friends that you might expect a kid to have in a small town. My closest friend had moved to Texas when I was six, so I spent a lot of time alone, playing 'Mortal Kombat' and dreaming about becoming an FBI agent like Fox Mulder.

"My mom had died when I was ten. It was cancer and really quick. At the time I was furious that we didn't have more warning, but now I realize how lucky she was. She hardly suffered at all.

"My dad's a pediatrician. He worked long hours back then, and I don't think he was prepared to take care of the house and me. Mom had done most everything. To be fair, though, I always knew I could talk to him and that he wanted what was best for me. We didn't have a tornado shelter or anything. We hadn't ever had a tornado where we lived, so most people didn't. Although, I doubt anything could have stopped what happened.

"It was June. I was off for the summer and one morning I woke up in my attic bedroom to the sound of a thousand trains coming straight at me. I couldn't scream or anything, it all happened too fast. I just gripped my twin mattress as hard as I could, and the next thing I knew, it was eerie and quiet and noisy as hell all at the same time. The world was spinning faster than any carnival ride and I was sure I was gonna die any second. I didn't know where I was, or what was happening. I might have passed out, no way to know, but there were a few seconds, maybe a minute, where I realized I was in the tornado. Me and my mattress."

Jenna had brought her head up and was staring at him with huge horror-filled eyes. He bent and kissed her nose.

"You can't stop there. Go on."

He smiled and rubbed her arm. "Shit was flying by me so fast it was like this crazy dream. I saw a refrigerator, the sign from Wallander's farm and a tree. A big tree. Something hit the other side of the mattress hard. Turned out I'd nearly missed being impaled by a chunk of fence.

"The next thing I knew, I was being wheeled out of my dad's office, which still had a roof on it, and into an ambulance. The paramedics kept me breathing on a trip that was evidently epic. Half the roads to the closest standing hospital had been shredded. Everyone made a hell of a fuss when I told them what had happened. My father had actually seen me flying away, never thought he'd see me again. Not alive.

"I was hurt, though, pretty bad. Compound fractures in one arm and one leg, three cracked ribs and one doozy of a cut on the back of my head. For a long time after, every time I fell asleep, I was in that tornado again."

"How horrible."

"You'd think so, but it was just the opposite. It was the most exciting thing that had ever happened to me. To anyone I'd ever known. The rush was so intense, I'd have done it again in a heartbeat, even knowing the odds."

"Wow. That's..."

"Weird," he said. "I know. But before you ask, there were no flying monkeys or wicked witches."

Jenna sat up. She pulled the duvet over to cover her bottom half, but left her top half bare. God, her breasts were beautiful.

"No, you goof. It's extraordinary. A real life-altering event."

"Yep. It definitely did that. It's one of those things that no one can understand. Like, I could try to imagine what it feels like to win the Super Bowl, but I'll never know. Or stand on the moon. There aren't many people who survive being picked up like that, and the few who do, don't remember any of it."

"Do you all meet once a year or something?"

He shook his head. "Nope. But I think about it every time I go out chasing. Sometimes I'll tell bits and pieces to students and journalists, but rarely, and I make the story about someone else."

"Why?"

"Honestly, sometimes it's hard to keep to myself. But it's tricky. Reckless kids, amateur storm chasers, a lot people would only focus on the high, view it as an awesome once-in-a-lifetime experience they want a taste of. They don't understand the incredible danger involved or that I'm extremely lucky to have survived. I don't want anyone to get hurt trying to catch a ride."

"That makes sense, but holy cow, Rick. I'm just… I mean, being swept up in a tornado!"

"Don't tell me you're catching the bug."

"Me? Oh, hell, no. I don't even ride roller coasters," she said with such conviction he laughed. "But I can see how it shaped your life. God, no wonder you chase them. How could you not?"

Again, she'd floored him by her insight and her ability to appreciate something that extended beyond her own world. He'd admit it. He'd been somewhat reluctant to tell her the story because he was afraid she wouldn't get it and he'd be disappointed. "One thing for sure. I'll never forget what it was like to fly. To tear up the sky. I could barely breathe, but the atmospheric pressure wasn't what stole my breath away."

"I can't even imagine," she said. "I mean, how are you going to top that, right?"

The air left his lungs and his thoughts stopped. Once again, Jenna had hit the nail on the head. He couldn't top it. Although God knows, he sure kept trying.

He made up his mind right then and there. "I'm not leaving tonight," he said. "I'll catch tomorrow's flight. If you'll stay with me. What do you say?"

She kissed him first, and then smiled. "What do you think?"

11

Jenna had always liked her apartment. It was small, a bit pricey, but she'd been lucky. The place was close to school and had practically fallen into her lap. Her friend Ally had given her a heads-up about the vacancy three years ago.

Another great thing about the place? Rent included snow removal. She'd arrived home late Sunday evening and almost wept with gratitude when she saw that a nice clear path led right up to her front stairs. She was even able to pick up her mail with no problem. Outside the complex, huge piles of dirty snow left by the plows sat everywhere. Boston had been hit hard, and so had most of the suburbs.

Jenna supposed she and Rick should consider themselves fortunate. He'd grabbed the last seat on that afternoon flight out of Logan. And she'd managed to make it home in a little more than two hours.

Halfway to her bedroom, Jenna stopped to check if the small potted fern sitting on the counter needed water, and in just those few seconds she totally forgot why she was going to her bedroom in the first place. For heaven's sake, it was only Tuesday. And this wasn't the first time she'd blanked like that.

Rick.

Thoughts of him, the memory of his touch, how urgently she wanted to remember every last detail. If all that nonsense didn't stop, she'd have to pick up her long-abandoned journal. She wondered if teenage girls even kept those anymore. No, they just put everything out there on Facebook and Twitter.

Not her. She wanted to write about the crucial details. The way he used his eyebrows. With one lift, a certain kind of lift, he could make her bust out laughing. When he furrowed his brows he looked positively Byronic, and made her embarrassingly hot.

Oh, God. She really was the ultimate sap.

Dear Diary.

Ugh. Somebody shoot her now.

On the plus side, it didn't matter at all what she wrote about him. From this moment on, he was more fiction than fact. He certainly wasn't going to be a part of her future.

Ah, it was laundry. No wonder she'd done her best to forget that. But there was the basket, ready with clothes in it. She should have washed them straightaway, but yesterday she'd been in a daze, and today had gone by in a flash. She needed to go back to her routine, like preparing her meals the same way she prepared her lesson plans. It would be a little tricky because Payton had been woven into the fabric of her life, but her motivation was strong. And lists and routines made her happy.

But oh, how she missed that magical apartment.

Although her dinner tonight was going to be just as sumptuous as any meal she'd had at the smart apartment. She'd defrosted meatballs she'd made three weeks ago, so she'd heat those along with some bottled marinara sauce. She'd even bought whole wheat Italian sub rolls and decent mozzarella cheese.

Yeah. No difference at all.

It was already dark out at five thirty. The temptation to do the same thing as yesterday—crawl into bed at around six o'clock and fantasize about Rick until she fell asleep—was strong, but no. ROWE was exactly what she needed to get on with her new life.

Routine, order, work, exercise.

Maybe use her journal to examine what had happened with Payton. If she hadn't realized subconsciously that Payton wasn't the right man for her, breaking up with him would have been infinitely more painful.

As she picked up the laundry basket, her gaze caught on a framed picture of herself and Payton from the long weekend they'd spent in New York. Not for the first time, she needed a moment to regain her bearings after discovering another piece of their lives that had been scattered around the apartment.

She'd started a box for the obvious things. Since he wouldn't be spending the night there again, everything in his drawer had been simple. Same with the closet and the bathroom. Then things had become a little more difficult.

Books he'd left here versus books he'd given her. CDs that had found a place in her collection. The TV shows he'd marked for saving on her DVR, some of which she'd found herself enjoying even though it hadn't started out that way. And some of them a joy to delete.

The phone rang, bringing her out of her reverie, but before she took the call, she put the photo of her and Payton facedown, wishing she had pictures of her and Rick together. Then she went to find her cell phone.

It was her mother. Oh, yeah. This would be an interesting conversation.

"Hi, Mom," she said, leaving the basket on top of the washing machine before she went to the kitchen. She'd stored half a bottle of pinot in the fridge and half of that went into her glass.

"Happy New Year, honey. I haven't heard from you since before you left for your party."

Jenna sat in the comfy chair, the overstuffed beast that didn't go with anything else in her mix of shaker and craftsman furnishings. Bless its ugly patchwork, the damn thing hugged her the moment she leaned back. "Ah, well, since I can't figure out a way to ease into this, I'll just go with the facts. The wedding's off."

There was a long silence. A really long one. That Jenna wasn't going to interrupt. At least it gave her time to enjoy her wine.

"What on earth happened?" Her mother sounded calm enough, though Jenna knew it was a precarious perch.

"He kissed another woman at midnight."

"Well, honey, that's..."

"Don't even bother finding a way to forgive that because there's more."

"Oh, God. I don't know if you'll be able to get the full deposit back on the dress. Or the banquet room."

"Not the salient bits, Mom. Truly."

"Okay, right," she said, her voice sad. She liked Payton.

"Look, the particulars don't matter. He wasn't the man I thought he was, and I'm not willing to settle. The end."

"You've been with him a long time. You told me he was exactly who you were looking for."

Jenna held back a sigh. It wasn't as if she wanted to keep secrets from her mother, but they were complete opposites when it came to men...no, to their definition of happiness. Jenna wasn't ever going to be that woman stuck at home with no idea when or if her husband was coming home. Uncertain every month if the bills would be paid, if her children would have everything they needed to be whole, happy and successful. "I made a mistake," she said. "I'm grateful it happened before the wedding. It's much less complicated now."

"You can really shut the door on Payton that easily? I mean, you were in love with him. That's a very complex feeling and doesn't have much to do with logic or reason."

"I get that, Mom. I do. It hurts. Of course it hurts. But it isn't crippling, which is a sign that I didn't love him as much as I could have. I appreciate your concern, but I'm okay. I promise."

"That's good."

Jenna was about to say goodbye when her mom asked, "And you just came home?"

"No. I wasn't able to get out of Boston before the big storm hit. I stayed in the city with a friend." Jenna wasn't going to talk about Rick. Or their one glorious, magical weekend together. She'd keep their brief fairy-tale romance close to her heart. Maybe forever. But as wonderful and charming and yes, nice, Jenna thought with a smile, Rick had been, she was very clear that he wasn't a forever kind of guy. At least not for someone like her. And she'd made peace with that. Well, it was more a work in progress, but that was okay.

"Good. It's nice that you have girlfriends in the city."

Rick was definitely not a girlfriend, but he'd been just the ticket. "Yeah, it was nice. But now that I'm home, I've got so much to catch up on."

"Don't be hard on yourself. You're still in mourning over Payton. It's such a shame. I suppose knowing he'd slept with this other woman…that would be too much to bear."

A sharp pang in her chest came with the surprise that although he hadn't slept with Faith, it hurt her as if he had. "I was just working out what to do about the pictures. Of Payton and me. Or us with other friends. There are a lot of photos. I don't feel the need to rip them apart or cross out his face. I did spend a number of years caring about him."

"That's true," her mother said. "If you want my opinion, I say take all the pictures and put them in a box. Put that somewhere you never look. Eventually, you'll find them again, and they'll either bring you joy or not."

"Oh, that's very clever. Thank you."

"You're welcome."

It struck Jenna that the whole conversation had been about her. She wished she could think of something to ask her mother, but there was only the usual. "Was Dad there for New Year's Eve?"

"No, he couldn't make it in time. But we were together by voice. It was lovely."

What it was, was typical. Her father rarely made it home for holidays. Or parties. Or birthdays. Or recitals. "I'm glad you enjoyed yourself."

"I saw some beautiful fireworks with my friends from work. I had a lovely time. I'm sorry you didn't. Although you sound awfully good for someone whose life has just done a one-eighty."

"I'm fine. Honestly."

"I believe you. But, if you don't mind one more opinion from me, maybe it's a good time to look at that requirements-for-a-husband list of yours. See if maybe there's room for some flexibility."

She was never going to be as flexible as her mother. Not when it came to a husband. But for now, she said. "I'll think about it. Thanks, Mom. I've got to go eat something or I'll really get drunk on this glass of wine. Talk to you soon?"

"Anytime, sweetheart. Anytime."

Jenna hung up, but she didn't rush to the kitchen. Or to the laundry. She thought about Rick and wondered what she would have done without him.

HE FINISHED HIS beer and used his hand to crumple the can, something he never did anymore. For years, he'd done it while yelling like an idiot, but now he only did it to see if he still could.

Instead of grabbing another one, he examined the contents of his fridge. Beer, another kind of beer, Chinese food leftovers, pizza still in the box, milk and a half-dozen organic apples. The milk won the toss. He grabbed the Raisin Bran from the cupboard, along with a bowl and a spoon, then settled at the table. He ate while he finished reading an abstract from the *Journal of Meteorology and Climatology*, then checked the time.

Jenna would be home now. She'd had to stay after school for a parent-teacher thing, but she'd said she'd be home by nine.

Considering what he'd learned about her evenings over this past week, he'd bet she'd be finished with her chores by the time he packed three boxes. Not books, though. He'd need to go through those carefully, so tonight he'd gather his summer clothes and the spring workout equipment that was currently stored in the gym closet.

After he finished his cereal he grabbed an apple, then took a look at the living room. The open-plan two-bedroom apartment he and Faith shared was tidy, but not really clean. Only some of the furniture matched, but that was because the pieces had been purchased for practicality instead of decor. Good ol' Ikea. The pictures on the walls were shots of nature or sporting events. In fact, all the pictures on all the walls were like that, and he was pretty sure the lion's share were Faith's.

In all the years he'd lived with her he never noticed that their place looked like a big dorm room. One step up from a storage shed. The books they had were mostly nonfiction and mirrored their professions. They'd gone in together on the big-ticket items in the living room, like the fifty-inch LED television.

Without having to look, he knew that their cupboards held a lot more protein powders and supplements than food.

And the gym, well, that said a lot about them both. He tossed the apple core in the trash, and then started with the closet. Their exercise room took up the entire second bedroom, except for a small desk where Faith worked when she wasn't on the road.

Damn, they had a lot of stuff. A top-of-the-line Bowflex, free weights, kettlebells, balance balls, a yoga station, the Pilates bench, a treadmill and an elliptical machine. The problem was that they'd gone in together on most of it.

When she got back from Mexico, they'd have to discuss the division problem in depth. And that meant he had to do more than drop hints about him moving out. She'd been slammed with the Mexico assignment, the communication between them had sucked and he'd thought he'd wait until she got home to even start looking for apartments.

But he didn't want to wait. He wasn't sure why it felt so important to leave soon, but there it was. She'd be in Mexico for at least another week, which would hopefully give them time to talk and him the opportunity to make the move. He didn't want Faith to feel bad about any of this.

He put in his earbuds and listened to his iPod on shuffle as he packed three boxes. It went quickly, but he was highly motivated. The first thing he did after packing was make a green drink. He turned on the gas fireplace in the living room and settled on the couch before he dialed Jenna's number.

She answered on the second ring. "How many boxes tonight?"

"Three. How did the parent-teacher thing go?"

She sighed. "Why is it never anyone's fault but mine when their kids misbehave? According to the survey I've conducted over the past several years, based on my own experiences plus the bitching in the teacher's lounge, every single child in America is an angel who never does anything wrong. Ever."

"Well, yeah. I guess you didn't read the fine print on your contract. You've got some nerve making angels weep when you give them homework and expect it to be turned in when it's due."

"You're right. I'm to blame."

"I miss you," he said, unapologetic about changing the subject.

"I know," she said. "Me, too. It's been a little over a week and it feels like a month. What time did you get home from work?"

"Around seven."

"Wow, early for you. Did you find an apartment?"

"How could I? I've been too busy working, packing and talking to you. Every night," he said, which was the sad truth and damn ridiculous when he thought about it. But Jenna's laughter was a balm, better for him than any green drink.

"Well, you're doing a good service because I needed this call," she said. "Especially after my conversation with Payton."

Oh, shit. "Wait." Rick had known this could happen once things returned to normal. They'd talk, reconcile. "Tonight was the parent thing."

"Lunch. We met at Applebee's. He wasn't happy. He didn't bring any of my things, even though I'd asked him. When I gave him all his stuff back, I felt terrible. He was really hurt and confused, and kept telling me he hadn't done anything except kiss her."

"I can spare him a little sympathy," he said, more relieved than he had a right to be. "I'd hate to lose you, too."

A moment of awkward silence had him shaking his head. He could've worded that better. So, what now? Did he explain he'd been speaking in general terms, or…?

"Thank you for the compliment. That was very sweet," Jenna said. "Payton's a nice man and someday he'll understand this is for the best, but right now he can't see that he'd settled for me. He just can't."

"Not to be obnoxious, but I doubt he *settled* for you."

Another few moments of silence. "We went to that stupid Bond-themed reunion five years in a row."

"Okay."

"That same night, well, after you and I went to the apartment, I asked him if it was because he'd been hoping to see Faith."

"Okay." Surely the guy hadn't been stupid enough to admit it.

"He said no, but only after he'd hesitated. And I knew, right then, that's exactly what he'd hoped for. But he settled for me. And I don't want that. I want someone who loves me. Who can't stop thinking about me. Who won't shut up about me. I know, it's pie in the sky, but that's it. That's the truth."

"You deserve that," Rick said, knowing that wasn't all she wanted. Jenna wanted someone steady and predictable, which put him out of the running, and that was okay. That was why this thing between them could be fun and casual. Hell, if he'd learned anything with Faith it was to keep it real. Not make more of a relationship than he should. "I mean it, you do."

"Thank you," she said. She'd be blushing now. Those lovely pale cheeks a delicate pink.

Christ, he had to stop thinking about her that way. "I'm checking out two apartments tomorrow."

"That's right. I was going to ask you about your wish list."

"What wish list? You mean about what I want in my new place?"

"Yeah. Like, for me, it would be a balcony that has the right amount of sun in the spring and summer."

"For tanning?"

"No, silly. I'm always this pale. I grow vegetables. For eating."

"That must be a large balcony."

"Nope. I do vertical planting. Some hydroponics and clever stacking. I love eating things I've grown. My summer salads are really delicious, but that's just me. What do you need to have?"

"A second bedroom for a workout room. Good internet. Big master suite. A real wood-burning fireplace would be nice. I've got a gas one here, and it's just not the same."

"A whole room for working out? No wonder you're so buff."

"I'm a little obsessive about keeping in shape. Not just for my ego, but for work. I have to be in good shape to do my job.

"I certainly approve of the results."

He sighed. "I want to see you again." The silence lasted longer than he'd hoped.

"I've been thinking that, too," she said softly. "And trying not to."

"What if we don't try not to? What if we do something about it?" he asked, dead serious.

"Oh. Gosh. I guess we can find a weekend that works. Decide who's doing the traveling."

He grinned. He'd been so afraid she hadn't wanted what he wanted. "Okay. Let's do that."

"Maybe discuss it after you've moved?"

It made sense. He couldn't get away from work now, anyway. "Good. Excellent."

"You know what?" she said. "I won't even mind that we won't have a magic apartment to stay in."

"Yeah," he said, remembering her in his arms. The smart apartment gadgets hadn't meant a thing when they were making love. Not one thing. "Guess we'll have to bring the magic with us."

12

THE SCHOOL AUDITORIUM was packed with sixth graders for the annual sex-education talk. Their teachers were there, as well, although none of them wanted to be. But it was a mandatory talk, not nearly as good as it should be, and exactly, word for word, the same speech the school nurse gave every year.

Jenna, along with five other teachers, was standing in the back of the room, theoretically making sure none of the students started something. Like playing ear-shattering ringtones on their phones, passing around porn, drawing porn, talking, laughing, throwing things, texting, sexting, making out…the list was as almost as long as the speech.

Jenna had always been in favor of banning cell phones on school property. Of course, the rule was for the students, not the teachers. Still, she'd made a habit of only checking her messages at lunch and after class. Well, she *had* made that a habit.

For the past couple of weeks, her phone had taken residence in the pocket of one of her pairs of skinny jeans, like the ones she wore today with a gray pullover sweater and a darker gray blazer. She'd actually bought two more pairs of black and dark blue jeans that could hold her cell phone, and that didn't break the dress code.

Because of Rick.

Last night, she'd told him that she wasn't looking forward to the mind-numbingly dry address by their nurse.

Perhaps if the woman wasn't so horrible at public speaking, Jenna would gladly have paid attention. But Mrs. Epperson spoke in a monotone. A slow, slow monotone that would cure anyone's insomnia, guaranteed.

So he'd said he'd text her sometime during the talk.

As she waited, Jenna stood with Ally. They'd hit it off the first day Jenna had joined the staff at South Shore Middle School. Ally was a couple of years older than Jenna, had a scathing sense of humor and made the best Bundt cake in the world. It was a happy coincidence that the two of them wore the same size pants and shoes, and that Ally was the reason Jenna and she were next-door neighbors.

Right now, though, Ally was whispering in Jenna's ear all the names she could think of for *penis*. There were so many, although she thought some of them were made up. Like *womb raider* and *clam hammer*. All Jenna had to do was not laugh out loud, but she wasn't sure she could hold on much longer.

Nurse Epperson was talking about adolescent hormones, so nowhere near the end of her talk, when Jenna's cell phone vibrated. Jenna gripped it tightly as she took a step back, not wanting anyone to see her. Of course Ally understood, and she took a strategic position in front of Jenna.

Even with her friend covering for her, Jenna thought about dashing to the ladies' room before she looked at Rick's text, but she couldn't stand it. It had been almost two weeks since she and Rick had said goodbye, and they were still texting and talking every single day.

Busy tomorrow night?

Depends what you have in mind. Phone sex? Weather updates? Sharing recipes?

That first thing. Very much that one. Dammit i'm gong to meeting in five min and nwo I'll have a ahrd on. Thnx.

Jenna giggled, putting her phone in her pocket and her hand over her mouth when she realized how loud she'd been. Eli Stevenson, the history teacher, gave her the stink eye, but she just smiled then tried to look captivated by the estrus talk. When the coast was clear again, she pulled the cell out again and texted:

Why you really do suck at spelling when you're horny. So what did you really want?

You. And your good judgment. Narrowed down to 2 apts. Want to show you.

How? I can't catch the next flight.

Why not? Wouldn't that be...never mind. FaceTime app. I'll show you while we discuss.

I knew there was an app. Just teasing. LOL Sounds great.

"You are not being as subtle as you think," Ally said, scaring the bejesus out of Jenna, who sent a short good-bye before turning off the phone and shoving it into her pocket. All kinds of those hormones the nurse had talked about were coursing through her body, making her shiver in the best way.

She hated that he lived so far away. One thousand, four hundred and sixty-nine miles, to be precise. Thank God it wasn't a real relationship. He was a friend, for sure, but he was not *The One*. If he had been, this long-distance thing would definitely not be enough.

Finally, the lunch bell rang, putting an end to the assembly. Jenna hung back, as did Ally, waiting until there were just a few stragglers left.

"So, how's Rick?"

Of course Ally knew about Rick. That he'd been great after what happened with Payton. Ally was terrifically supportive, even though she'd liked Payton a lot. But when Jenna explained, Ally agreed there was no going back.

"He's fine," Jenna said as the two of them headed for the teachers lounge. "He asked me something time sensitive or I wouldn't have—"

"Hell, I don't care. I'm just jealous," she said, though she'd been seeing someone.

Once inside, Ally got both of their lunches from the fridge. There was a line for the microwave, and since they'd both brought soup, they had to split up, or forget sitting together. Jenna got table duty, using her apple to hold Ally's seat.

A quick look around told her that Chatty Kathy, the one teacher in the school Jenna straight-out didn't like, wasn't in the lounge. Jenna relaxed instantly. The woman really had nothing better to do than gossip and stir up trouble. It was clear to everyone that she hated her job, hated teaching and, most significantly, hated her fellow teachers. She was the first person to notice that Jenna wasn't wearing her ring. Instead of asking what had happened, or better yet, realizing it was none of her business, she'd started a ridiculous rumor.

Of far more importance were the texts Jenna had missed after she'd turned off her phone. There were two. The first was just a few words confirming when he'd call her the following night. The second—he was calling her tonight. Jenna smiled. What a dope. He called her every night.

Ally sat down before Jenna could reply, but that was fine. "Why does your soup always look better than mine?" Ally asked, staring at Jenna's steaming chicken and rice.

"I have no idea," Jenna said. "Except for the fact that you don't use any spices."

"I do so," she said before she swallowed a large spoonful. "But obviously not the right ones."

"Follow a recipe, for heaven's sake."

"You know what's easier than that?" Ally frowned at her lunch. "Eating out. And speaking of going out, how about next Friday night you join me and Craig for dinner at Row 34?"

Jenna knew that coy look. "Just you and Craig?"

"Fine. Craig has this friend… He's a supernice guy. Handsome and wickedly funny. If nothing else, we'll laugh all night."

"I appreciate it, I do, but I really am serious about this break I'm taking from men. I—"

Ally burst out laughing. It was a good thing she had a napkin in her hand.

"What are you laughing about?"

"I'm pretty sure you told me Rick was a man."

Jenna didn't normally let loose with an eye roll, but she did now. "I also told you that we're just friends. That's all. Even if I wasn't taking my time about dating again, I wouldn't date him. He's a storm chaser."

"So, you blushing at his texts and making sure you're finished with your work before seven, that's because he's your buddy?"

Jenna gaped at her. "I don't blush. Not when I read his texts, anyway."

"Right."

"And I've been trying to finish early every night because I have a lot of things to do around the apartment." Damn it, she was pretty sure she was blushing now.

Ally said nothing. Just ate a spoonful of soup, trying to hide a grin.

"I hope you choke on that tasteless crap."

Ally nearly spit the tasteless crap across the table.

RICK WAS AT the International, an apartment complex that was trying hard to be a resort. He wasn't thrilled with the apartment he'd seen, but there was an option with this place he hadn't thought of before.

Considering he was insanely busy at work, he'd managed to pack up a lot of his things, but to find a place and move in before Faith came back would be tricky. He didn't have to be out—she honestly didn't care—but it would make things between them easier.

This apartment complex catered to a younger crowd, although not the college students at nearby University of Oklahoma. The facility had a fantastic gym that came with the place, including one of the best rock walls he'd seen, the most up-to-date machines and a great sauna—lots of ways to ride out the winter and come out the other side in good shape.

The apartment he was looking at was a two-bedroom, two-bath, but it was on the small side and partially furnished. That was a plus because he wasn't going to leave Faith to have to scramble to get a table, or a replacement couch. He still wasn't sure what to do about their shared gym equipment, and signing up at the International could put that decision off for a good while.

It wasn't as if he wanted to settle here for life. Six months was about all he'd be willing to commit to. So, leaving most of the furniture and most of the gym stuff right where it was would help both of them adjust to their new lives.

Another plus was that the place was really new. So he wouldn't be sleeping on a used bed, which was a deal breaker for him. He'd seen the mattress and bedsprings still in their boxes, unopened.

He'd have to make a decision soon. Hopefully by tonight. Which was why he'd made a date with Jenna on FaceTime.

If he thought about the time it was going to take to show her this place—just the apartment, not the grounds or the gym—then hop in his car and show her the other place… it was ridiculous. But he missed her and this was an opportunity to find out some things about what she liked. He was hoping she'd give him a tour of her place once she saw how it was done.

At least he'd narrowed down his choices. Antwan had laughed in his face when Rick had asked if he'd help with the move, but God bless the interns. They'd offered to help. Even though they might just be trying to score points. He needed his stuff moved fast and he couldn't have cared less about their motives. They'd just have to settle for pizza and beer on him.

He looked out at the view from the front of the apartment. It was nice, although it would look better when the snow melted and the pool wasn't covered for the season.

He also liked the way the International made a point of being ecoconscious. For a big place like this, they had their methodology down. Okay, it was time. Even though Jenna had to grade some papers, she'd told him to call at seven. It was now 7:01 p.m. He'd brought his iPad for the tours, so he typed in the necessary info. All Jenna had to do was accept his invite.

And just like that, there she was, smiling at him, her dark hair sitting prettily on her shoulders, her smile broad and her eyes happy. She was wearing the T-shirt she'd kept from their last day. "You taking good care of the jeans you stole?" he asked.

"I did no such thing. I simply didn't tell you I was taking them with me. It really is your fault because who packs without counting their jeans?"

"Okay, you've got me there," he said, lying through his teeth. He definitely counted jeans and T-shirts, and he didn't mind one bit that she'd worn them home underneath that big puffy coat of hers.

"This is exciting," she said. "I've never used this app, or Skype, but that's now on my laptop."

"And we're going to have a conversation about using Skype very soon," he said, enjoying her blush. Yep, Skype sex was on the agenda. "You ready?"

She nodded. Why couldn't she be there with him? The picture might be excellent, but it would never take the place of seeing her in person. Looking into her gaze the way you only could when it was someone you connected with, reaching over to touch her. Pulling her close. Kissing her.

"Uh, you all right there, Rick?"

"Yep. Okay, this is the International," he said, showing her the living room, which, sadly, didn't have a wood-burning fireplace. But it did have an open plan so he could walk her through to the kitchen.

"You don't mind that it's small?" she asked.

"I don't cook much, so no, it's fine."

"Right. Not high on your list. But it's nice. Those aren't granite countertops, are they?"

"Yep. Granite. And there's a dishwasher and everything."

"Fancy," she said. "You really want a lease for only six months?"

"Yeah. My accountant keeps telling me I should buy something. I just don't have the time or energy to look for a place. But I'm missing all kinds of tax benefits by renting."

"That accountant sounds smart. You should listen to him. Especially if you have the means."

"Yeah, I do, and I don't do as much with the money as I should. Work seems to take over my life. Everyone's still in shock that I took off over New Year's. Anyway, now we're heading to the master bedroom."

He brought her into the room and showed her the walk-in closet, the attached bathroom, the new carpet and light green walls.

"I like it," she said. "But do they give you a choice of window treatments?"

He frowned at the windows. "You mean the curtains?"

"Yes."

"I'm not sure. I could ask. Why?"

"I don't know. Maybe you want blinds instead of drapes."

"Yeah, I would prefer blinds. I just didn't think to ask. See? This is why I wanted to show you around before making a final decision."

"Is there enough room for your exercise equipment? Not now, but eventually."

He'd told her about the fitness center, and about waiting to divide up the equipment with Faith.

"Huh. Remember when I said you were a nice man?"

"I'm still wincing from that, yeah." He turned the iPad so he could look into her beautiful dark eyes.

"It's still true," she said.

"I know a number of interns who would disagree, but then again, I don't care much about their opinions."

"But you do about mine?"

He could tell she was only teasing, but oddly, in truth he cared a great deal about what she thought. "It'll take me about twenty minutes to get to the second choice. You okay with that?"

"I'll be here."

And that was the problem. *Here* meant Boston.

And he lived in Oklahoma.

TWENTY-SEVEN MINUTES LATER, Jenna's phone rang. She pushed the FaceTime button and voilà, there was Rick.

"So this place is called the Warwick, and it's another two-bed, two-bath." Something in his tone suggested this was the apartment he truly wanted. She couldn't say why she had that impression, but she wouldn't say anything yet.

"Check out the seating at the counter," he said, and showed her the open-plan kitchen with a raised bar that accommodated five stools. The kitchen appliances had been upgraded to stainless steel, and there was a deep sink, a nice stove. But they weren't in the kitchen for long.

The master suite was upstairs, and much nicer than at the International. It would be a bigger move for him, because the place wasn't furnished, but it had a wood-burning brick fireplace, lots of windows and, therefore, lots of light. Even the second bedroom was roomy, although there was no walk-in closet like in the master bedroom.

There was also a terrific balcony outside the bedroom, French doors that he said overlooked a beautiful grass-and-wooded landscape. But it was too dark for her to actually see for herself.

"You can see my dilemma," he said, taking her to the en suite shower. It was big, built with gorgeous sea-green glass and tile, with a glass enclosure. "It's not like the smart apartment's shower, but…"

"But for real life? It looks great."

"Yeah. So, that's it." He walked her down the stairs, making things a little too wobbly for her to see, but soon they were in the living room.

"I can picture you there," she said. "I liked the International, but I think this place fits you better. And it's a town house, which is cool. There's plenty of room for your stuff so you have the option of working out at home."

He smiled at her. "I can see myself here, too."

"When do you have to make up your mind?"

"I think I already have. I'll call when the management office opens tomorrow."

“Sounds perfect,” she said. “If they have a brochure or something, maybe you can scan one for me.”

“I could,” he said. “Or maybe you can come out here and see it for yourself.”

“Oh. Sure.” She hadn’t expected that, or for her silly heart to start pounding. They’d been planning a Chicago weekend, but they’d never talked about crossing into home turfs before. “Thanks for showing me everything in the meantime.”

“Thanks for your most excellent advice. And since we’re still on FaceTime, feel free to flash me.”

“Hanging up now,” she said, laughing.

After they disconnected, she thought about what he’d said. She couldn’t decide on whether she should be surprised or not. Bottom line, he hadn’t made a big deal out of it, and she shouldn’t, either.

13

Rick took a quick look at the data banks. Nothing serious was happening in the States, but the typhoon in Indonesia was troubling. Ordinarily he would've loved to hang around, watch the progression of the storms. But not tonight. "Okay, all. See you tomorrow."

Twelve heads turned to stare at Rick as he adjusted his backpack over his coat. He knew exactly what they were thinking. Too bad. He'd moved into the new town house three days ago, had worked ungodly late every night since and hadn't taken off so much as an hour to unpack.

Antwan stood up, arms akimbo, his eyes wide with surprise. "Dude. What the hell? We've ordered that disgusting Hawaiian pizza you like, and you're leaving?"

"Yes. I'm leaving. If it's too late to cancel, I'll pay for the pizza."

"But…typhoons."

"Yes, the typhoon is Dave's area. He's in charge and I'd just be hanging around. You don't need me here."

Antwan shook his head. "Something's going on with you, *bredda*. We're going to talk."

"You're right. And I'm late, so, *hasta la vista*, my friends." The moment he turned away, all thoughts vanished, except for the Skype sex he was going to have with Jenna tonight.

She wasn't stupid. She worked with computers every day. Mastered FaceTime in minutes, and had gotten to level ten in Angry Birds. But Skype was making her nuts.

It was also possible that she was freaking out about getting naked and more via the internet. It wasn't that she didn't *want* to try it. Rick had been starring in her X-rated dreams since the night she'd gotten home. But using the camera on her laptop was scary.

Damn it, if she had her own smart apartment, she'd already be lounging with a bottle of wine while she waited for Rick to call and she wouldn't have had to do any of the tech stuff. Her birthday was coming up, and an apartment like that would be the only thing on her wish list.

But right now she was trying to figure out how to make Skype and her laptop work together, which was using up all her grooming time. She'd done some things this morning, like iron her hair and pluck her eyebrows, but for this liaison? She wanted to go bold. Not *Fifty Shades* bold. Just smoky-eyed makeup and matching-underwear bold...but which underwear?

The black lace? The v-tini with the longline push-up? Or should she switch it up and wear the thigh-high stockings she'd bought for a costume... No. There was the peach-colored bra that made her boobs look bigger. But she'd be taking it off, so the illusion would end right there. And he'd already seen her naked so what the hell was wrong with her?

She did the deep-breathing thing that was supposed to instantly relax her, but it didn't work for beans. So she opened a bottle of Moscato and had a pull before she poured it into a glass.

She had enough time to do her makeup and fix Skype, or do her makeup and change but not fix the problem. It was like a nightmarish game of date/screw/marry. Skype first. Makeup next. Underwear...

Oh, hell.

She was supposed to call it lingerie.

THE THING RICK couldn't help noticing as he fixed the sheets on his bed at 8:30 p.m. was that his extreme level of excitement could only be attributed to one of two things: his abstinence since Boston, or the Skype sex that was supposed to happen in thirty minutes.

But it was probably both. Definitely both.

It felt odd, though. His feverish anticipation reminded him of earlier days. He certainly wasn't a kid anymore, or even a horny college student. And while there was no question he liked sex—more than liked it—he hadn't been a big fan of phone sex or any of its offshoots.

Until tonight.

Now that the sheets were nice and tucked instead of just thrown on the bed, he checked the room. Unopened moving boxes lined the right wall, which was fine. But not his coffee mug from this morning, his pants draped over the chair, or the kettlebell in the corner.

There were no pictures on the walls, nothing that said this was his bedroom, but Jenna probably didn't care. He wouldn't give a damn what her place looked like. Still, women noticed stuff. Thankfully, the fact that he'd just moved in should excuse him. This weekend, though, rather than working, he would get every box unpacked, everything put away and all the boxes broken down. No excuses.

It was still too early to call Jenna. Time to get a drink to leave on the nightstand. He wouldn't need anything else but his hand, so should he strip now? Be in bed when he called? Naked?

Yes. Naked. In bed. Under the covers. Definitely.

He stripped very quickly for a man wearing Doc Martens. But just as he dumped all his clothes in the closet and out of view from the newly installed Samsung, he felt a different kind of rush. Adrenaline made his pulse pound and when he got under the covers he spent so much time adjusting his pillows that the next time he checked, it was a couple of minutes to nine.

He got Skype going in two shakes. Luckily, his new TV

came Skype-equipped, complete with a built-in camera above the big screen. He knew Jenna had had to download the program and that he would be her first encounter.

Suddenly, she was there. At least her midsection was. Covered by black material with bright flowers on it.

She stepped back and soon enough he saw her from her knees up. If he'd known this was going to happen, he'd have paid twice the exorbitant price for his huge TV because she looked amazing. The wide angle showed off her legs, especially when she walked back far enough that he could see her high heels.

She tilted her head. "You're undressed."

His gut clenched so tight it took a second to say "Yeah. I thought we were going to..."

She blushed. He watched the pink fill her cheeks bigger than life. He also saw that she was wearing black fuck-me heels, and that did a whole other number on his body, mostly south of the waist. "You wear those shoes to teach in?" he asked.

She looked at him as if he was crazy. "Are you nuts? I wouldn't last past first period."

"It wouldn't matter what you wore. But damn, I wouldn't want to be a boy in your classroom."

"Why not? I have a lot of male students who enjoy my classes."

"Bet they all walk out of the room with their books in front of their flies."

"Actually, I teach mostly eleven- and twelve-year-olds. They're not at the hot-for-teacher stage yet."

"Uh, yeah, they are. Trust me." He couldn't help smiling at what he was watching, but he didn't want to say anything to make her self-conscious. The laptop was clearly at the foot of her bed, and she wasn't using a separate camera. But she obviously didn't know the range of the camera or she'd never have reached under her kimono to move some part of something—he assumed it was underwear.

Well, great, now he was already half-hard. Maybe more.

She smiled at him. "Well, thanks for the implied compliment and the extra worry that my students could be… I'm never wearing anything but oversize mom jeans and sweatshirts again."

Rick laughed. "Sorry. I'm exaggerating because *I* think you're amazingly hot."

"I'm choosing to believe you," she said, sounding a little nervous. "About exaggerating and boys that age…"

He had to step things up before they chickened out. "Okay, I can't stand the suspense. What's under that robe of yours?"

"It's a kimono, but that doesn't matter, I guess. Okay, well…" She didn't move for a minute. Just tilted her head to the side again, but this time she put her hands on her hips. "This is weird."

"What, me wanting to see you in what I imagine is sexy lingerie? Or me already being naked?"

"Both. Because I know you've got nothing on under those covers. And that you're already, um—" she pointed toward the general vicinity of his penis "—participating."

He looked down and, yes, the tenting was really obvious.

"And, I forgot, this is your new bedroom. Congratulations!"

He laughed. "Thanks."

"What?"

He let out a deep breath. "You know we don't have to do this. It's just for fun. So…"

She dropped her kimono.

He lost his ability to speak.

She wore a bra that had some kind of gold hardware

between her uplifted breasts. He'd give anything to be the one who took it off her. Anything.

Then there were her panties. That same lace decorated the peach material above her silk-covered V. There were straps on the sides, too, so maybe it wasn't a thong?

Had to be a thong.

Please, God, he thought. *Let it be a thong.*

Add the high heels?

He'd never once come without some kind of stimulation, but he might just blow if she turned around.

Forcing himself to move his gaze up, past her bra, he saw that she'd just let her hair down, and it fell perfectly over her shoulders. The blush on her cheeks matched her bra. The way she was nibbling on her bottom lip was the last straw.

His tent was now so hard that the head was touching his lower stomach. If he didn't give it a hand soon, he couldn't guarantee his sanity. "You're gorgeous," he said, knowing his whisper would get to her. "I haven't seen anything this beautiful since you were naked in my bed."

"Oh," she said, but it was more of a relieved sigh than a word. "I miss that bedroom."

"Me, too. It's hell having to paint the walls every time my mood changes."

JENNA LAUGHED, LETTING go of all the nerves that she'd been holding so tightly. There wasn't any reason to be nervous, not with Rick. He'd seen her sad and miserable, sobbing until her face was red and puffy. But he'd also seen her happy and laughing so hard she couldn't stop. Mostly because he'd been the one to make her laugh when she'd thought her life was over.

"I was hoping—" Rick's cell phone rang and scowling at it across the room didn't make it stop. "I forgot to turn it off," he said. "No way I'm taking a call. Even if the warning sirens come on."

When he threw his covers off to get up, she moved closer to her laptop screen for a quick peek at his very sizable erection before hurrying back to the bed. Maybe she should move the laptop? Bring it closer to the middle of the… No. She needed all the distance she could get.

"Wait!"

She spun around to face him, unsure whether he was telling her to wait or talking to the person on the phone. Then it rang again, so…

But then she caught on to what Rick was doing and threw her head back with a laugh that would have made her boobs jiggle if they weren't so tightly packed.

He had a pillow held over his penis as he made his way to stop the calls.

"What are you doing?" she said when she could speak again. "I've seen you naked, you absolute nutcase. What, did you get a Prince Albert since Boston? A lurid tattoo? Oh, maybe you shaved." She stopped. "Did you shave?"

He wasn't even in sight anymore, and for all she knew he was in some other room. The ringing had come to an end, so where was he?

"Rick, you know I'm teasing, right?"

He stepped into the frame of her poor little laptop. If a man ever deserved to be on an IMAX screen, it was Rick. He didn't say anything about the teasing, just headed back to his bed, the pillow gripped in his left hand.

"Hey, slow down," she said. "Where's the fire?"

"What? You want me to give you a show?"

"Uh, well, yeah." She crossed her arms and waited. "Extra points if you come at me like you're going to do something unspeakably naughty."

At first, all she noticed was his smile. She'd been joking, but the game evidently had changed because she went all over goose bumps and anticipation.

His cock, which hadn't remained in the upright position, was once again rising to the occasion. When he got to the head of his bed, he turned toward his camera and took himself in his hand. She'd never thought much about penis esthetics, but his was perfect. Not too big to hurt, thick where it should be, and oh, God, he was stroking himself very slowly.

By the time she remembered to look up, they were both breathing hard. He didn't get under the covers again, or, for that matter, in the bed. He just stared through any coquettish teasing right down to the desire that had plagued her since they'd parted.

"Your turn," he said. "But you have to repeat the whole thing. Quid pro quo."

"Uh…no."

"Uh…yes." Rick smiled. "Come on, gorgeous. It's a thong, isn't it? What you're wearing. I doubt any woman wears a thong for any other reason than to be seen wearing a thong."

"For heaven's sake. Observable panty lines?" she said. "No front wedgies? Comfort? Feeling sexier? Should I go on?"

"No. Not unless you're walking toward your screen very slowly. I stopped caring about *why* you were wearing them a while ago."

She sighed. "Fine. Wait. How big is your laptop?"

"Seventeen inches."

The way he looked at her, as if he'd never lied in his life, told her he was hiding something. "Are you watching me on that laptop?"

He hesitated. So that was a no.

"Oh, my God, you're looking at me on your television. Which I know is huge."

"Yes, I am. I was going to teach you how to hook up your laptop to your TV, but I ran out of time with the moving and stuff."

"Hmm. Most people would have their big TV in the living room. But you aren't most people. You would want to see the weather report bigger than big and as clearly as possible. Which means you want to see my naked behind on your, what, sixty-inch, 3-D, supersonic Smart TV from the future?"

He laughed. "It's not that big. Or clear. But you're very astute. That really is why I have big, very high-def TVs in three rooms."

"To see my behind?"

"Now it is. It used to be about weather, and the channel that runs from the lab, and I do not want to talk about my job."

"Oh, come on. Not even you can expect me to willfully show my butt on a huge screen."

"Well, how big is yours?"

"Seventeen inches."

"Well, you need a bigger screen. Jeez. That's like seeing my…me as if I'd just gotten out of a cold shower."

She laughed, really laughed. And then he was laughing, too. When she sat on the bed, honestly not giving a damn about how it made her tummy look, the laughs softened and so did the mood. "I miss you," she said.

He nodded. "It isn't so bad when it's just your voice," he said. "But seeing you? All I can think about is how much I want to touch you. Every inch. I don't need a show. I need you. In person. In my arms."

She sighed, understanding completely. They'd agreed on a weekend to meet but two weeks seemed so far away. "Chicago is just around the corner."

"Definitely not soon enough. But, and I don't mean to be

rude, you're still wearing a lot of things. Any chance you'd show me how you take off that very pretty bra of yours?

Blushing wildly, she almost said no. But it was Rick, and he was holding little Rick, so she could damn well share something of hers. She thought about being flirty about it, but quickly realized it could be flirty or sexy, not both. She unclasped the front hook and flashed him like a stripper. Just wham, bam, here they are, boys.

He liked it. Words weren't needed. The flush on his chest, the pearls of pre-come on his penis. His whole body stiffened into the very picture of want. It was…thrilling. She knew right then she had to go all in.

All in.

She turned around, put her thumbs under the straps on the sides of her panties and pulled them down to the floor, not bending her knees at all.

His groan was pretty damn spectacular. She rose slowly, thanking her years of yoga for the flexibility, and then turned her head toward him. "How's that, sweetie?"

"If you don't get started pretty quickly, this is going to be embarrassing."

"No, it's fine. It's good." She turned her whole body this time, mesmerized by how he was pumping his penis with his right hand and doing a little ball massage with the left. She found it amazingly sexy. "Come for me?" she asked.

"No. You first," he said, but the words were strangled. He must have been very close.

"Uh-uh. Nope. I want to see it. You." She touched her breasts and then pulled at her nipples.

"Shit," he said, but in a good way, because he came.

It made her blush, but it was also very hot, and looking at his face like this…it was more intimate than she ever could have imagined.

She ended up slipping into bed. Arranging the pillows so she could sit up and see her little screen Rick, she wasn't surprised that he was off-camera for a bit. When he came back she said, "Do you mind terribly if I don't do the sexy stuff this time?"

"No. I don't mind." When he got into his bed, it was as close to being with him as they'd ever been. "I vote for leaving our options open."

"Right. We'll just carry on, as usual."

"But maybe once," he said, "before we say good-night, you'll let the covers drop to your lap?"

She smiled at him, and felt something shift in her heart. "I think we can work something out."

14

LOGAN INTERNATIONAL AIRPORT was chock-full of business people trying to get home for the weekend and, for an ordinary Friday, a surprising number of families traveling with children. Jenna switched her carry-on to her other hand just as she spotted the Legal C Bar. Good. She needed a drink. The noisy kids didn't help, but the real reason she was looking for a nice glass of wine had everything to do with the weather.

Not in Boston. Things there were fine. But that wasn't true for the good people of northeast South Dakota. They were facing an unusually strong group of storms. Storms that, according to the National Weather Service, could and would turn into tornadoes. The state had a lot of them, but mostly they were small, and mostly, no one got hurt.

But this storm system was doing strange things. Jenna knew all this because now that she understood more about extreme weather, she was able to guess the times when she wouldn't hear from Rick. Sometimes not for days. Except for the quick texts telling her he was out chasing storms or too busy messing with the data to take breaks, let alone go home.

There was a seat open at the bar, and she ordered a Pinot Gris. Her flight wasn't due to take off for over an hour. She probably shouldn't have gotten to the airport so early, but she was too nervous.

She and Rick were supposed to meet in Chicago in a

few hours. She understood he might have to cancel at the last minute. She hoped with every ounce of her body and soul that he wouldn't. God, how she wanted to see him. On the flat screen in the corner of the bar was a weather map. Her heart thumped as the news showed the destruction of homes and farms in South Dakota. The tornado was the first category-four they'd had in years.

Jenna sighed. She felt awful for all the poor people who'd been affected. And she was willing to admit that she felt awful for her and Rick, too. She'd only allow herself one glass of wine. It was pretty likely she'd be driving back home tonight.

RICK WENT TO the men's room to look at his texts. He'd known they were from Jenna. And he'd also known she'd tell him to take care of business. That they'd reschedule if need be.

Damn it, he didn't want to reschedule. Yes, he was taking more days off this year. But since he'd only taken three vacation days in the previous four years, he had no qualms about getting away for a weekend.

Truthfully, no one gave him any guff about it. Were they surprised? Yes. Teasing? God, yes, and if he had a way to stop it, he would. His text back to her was short: Don't give up on me yet.

The energy of the floor changed the second he walked out of the restroom. Of course they were tracking South Dakota. Rick had personally trained two of the storm chasers out there, and there were lots of good people in the office of climatology. They were using their warning signals properly, and their reporting of data was excellent.

There was no reason he shouldn't leave. The team in the tornado group had it covered. But…this was what he did. He tracked tornadoes. He could count on one hand plus one other finger how many times he'd missed tracking anything above an F2 on the Fujita damage scale. This storm cluster could bring a lot of hell down on Dewey County. And if it picked up enough debris, it could get to be a giant.

His heart was already pumping fast, and they just had supercells forming. He couldn't help it. He remembered those few seconds where he was awake and cogent in that tornado. Every tornado brought excitement and stress, but even if he couldn't be out there himself tracking the big boys, he felt the memory of that rush. That unbelievable feeling of flying. Of unimaginable fear mixed with dazzling wonder.

"What's up with you, man?" Antwan eyed him. "Why aren't you on your way to the airport? You think we can't handle things here?"

"Of course you can. But you know how that adrenaline calls me."

"Rick, you idiot. You want adrenaline? How about you walk into your hotel room to find your Jenna waiting for you?"

Rick grinned as his focus shifted to Jenna, and the dilemma disappeared. *"Mi gaan, mi bredda."*

Antwan laughed, as he always did at Rick's attempt to speak the patois. "I'm never taking you to visit my family. They'd all die laughing and probably disown me, but I'm glad you're going, and that the power has been given to me."

Rick slapped him on the back and headed off to see Jenna. His pace quickened as he reached the parking lot until he was almost running. Before he opened the door to his Jeep, he texted her one line: Board that plane.

Now he needed to stop thinking about tearing off her clothes the second he saw her. It wasn't easy.

THE HILTON GARDEN INN was just three miles from the airport, but because of the snow, Rick took the shuttle. He could have been nicer at the registration desk, but Jenna was just up a floor, and fourteen doors down.

It took two tries to get the green light, and then he opened the door and there she was. He dropped everything where he stood, including his coat and his laptop case. Despite imagining her every day, and sometimes using Skype, he'd forgotten vital things. How she always stood with her shoulders back, her head squarely on her shoulders. Dance lessons, maybe? He could ask. Not text.

It took three seconds for her to reach him.

He put his hands on the side of her neck so he could memorize the shades of brown in her eyes and watch the black of her pupils take over. The dimple on her nose. Damn it. He loved that dimple and he'd forgotten it. Probably because of her lips and the way they stopped him from thinking too much.

Her lips parted and neither one of them shut their eyes until they had to. He wanted to stay right there. Learn every single way it was possible to kiss Jenna, then start again, only rate the kisses in terms of her answering moans.

Someone somewhere laughed, but it didn't concern him. The low voice telling them to get a room got through, though, and he shoved his stuff inside and then kicked the door shut, all without losing a beat.

JENNA FINALLY PULLED BACK, gently, reluctantly. She smiled at Rick and he smiled back as if they shared a secret. Co-conspirators meeting in a hotel for a long weekend of nothing but sex and kissing and cuddling and room service and getting to know each other better. "Hi."

Rick nodded, which was oddly sweet, and whispered, "Hi."

"You came. I wasn't sure until I saw you."

"They'll call me if something drastic happens at work."

"I have no idea what you mean by that. Isn't a tornado drastic by definition?"

"Sort of, depending on where it hits. There are hundreds of small tornadoes that cause no damage to property or people."

She hadn't taken her eyes off him as they stood in the little entryway just inside the room. "Okay. I'll do my best to remember that, although, sorry, don't mean to hurt your feelings or anything, but I don't care. No idea why I brought it up. You're here, and I get to touch you any way I want."

"Yes, you do," he said, right before he pressed his forehead to hers.

It certainly wasn't the touch she'd expected, but after a few seconds it calmed her down, let her come back to the moment. Where had he learned to do that? She'd never have imagined how intimate it would be to connect like this.

Her stomach growled, and they both laughed.

"We should order something. Damn it," he said. "My timing's off. I wanted to slam the door behind me, rip off every stitch of clothing from your body and then ravish you on the bed. I imagined it the whole flight here. It was total caveman stuff."

"I'm not that hungry." She touched the side of his face with her thumb, the feel of him coming back to her in bursts. "You're completely welcome to take—not rip—off my clothes, as long as you get naked, too."

She grabbed the lapels of his jacket and started to walk backward. She'd practiced this, but he didn't know that. He wasn't the only one who'd thought about their first meeting since New Year's weekend.

Stopping when the back of her legs hit the side of the bed, she kissed him before letting him go.

"I don't think I can last another minute without seeing you naked."

Jenna grinned. "You say that as if I'm going to object."

"Okay, then," he said, stripping off her short black sweater in a very smooth move. Then he started on the buttons of her white blouse. She couldn't wait to see what he'd do with her skinny black jeans. Even she had trouble taking them off.

But the real kick for her was what he'd find underneath. A black-and-white polka-dot demi bra and matching thong. He liked thongs.

His breath brushed over her bared shoulder when he removed her blouse. "For me?" he asked.

"I don't think it'll fit, but you can play with it this weekend, if you like."

"I was talking about what was under the bra, but thanks for the offer. And don't think I didn't notice the leopard print on those heels. What are they, six inches? Seven? How in hell did you walk around the airport wearing them?"

"Flats in my suitcase."

"Ah. Of course." Rick kissed her again, and then brought her hand to his fly, to the straining erection behind his jeans. "You'll have to excuse my slow thoughts."

"I think we'd better do something about those jeans," she said.

"First you."

"Go for it. And, um, don't get discouraged. They're not kidding when they say these are skintight."

It took him a while, but he made good use of the time. Without taking off her bra, he managed to lift her nipples over the top of the demi cups, which was very sexy, especially when he was working so hard elsewhere while still flicking and licking her right nipple.

When he had to abandon his duty north to get rid of

her pants, she didn't mind. She just wanted him to hurry. Finally, she stepped out of her jeans.

He moved back to admire his handiwork. Nipples on display, such a tiny thong there was only room for one row of dots and the heels that made her as tall as him.

"Holy shit, you're gorgeous," he said, but the words rode out on a fast breath. He'd worked hard getting her undressed this far. "Now, if you wouldn't mind doing a slow three-sixty, I'll be naked before you get back to the start."

She felt ridiculous as she did it. Really slowly, too. When he nearly fell on his ass as he caught sight of hers, they both started laughing. In another amazing feat, Rick's clothes were off, including his boots.

She thought he was going to go back to teasing her nipples when he walked into her space, but he just gave her a fierce and fast kiss, moved behind her to throw the bedding down, lifted her into his arms and tossed her onto the bed.

She laughed as she caught her breath. "So this is what you meant by caveman?"

"Nope," he said, joining her. "That was just because it was the quickest way I could get you into bed."

Without taking anything else off her, he nestled his knees between her thighs. Her smile was swept away, along with her breath, at the lust in his gaze. When his nostrils flared, her body arched and she no longer gave a damn what he did, as long as he did it now.

"Jenna," he said.

That was all. Just her name. But she felt claimed. Seen. "There are condoms," she said, her voice breathless. "On the bedside table."

"You're brilliant." Balanced as he was on his knees and hands, he went back to her one of her nipples—the one he hadn't tasted—and took it between his teeth. As one hand slipped underneath her back, he flicked her hard and fast with the point of his tongue.

She wasn't sure what she said or did, but when he stopped flicking, and just sucked, she couldn't just lie there and writhe. Once again, she took hold of his hair and urged him to look up.

How desperately she wanted him inside her. Now. "Please," she said, hoping the single word would be enough to get her point across.

He lifted his head and met her gaze. As her heartbeat hammered and her blood flowed so fiercely she could hear it, he leaned over and picked up a condom. She arched up to nip and lick the side of his neck, and then let herself fall back, running her hands up his sides and chest.

His groan was very familiar, and achingly welcome. She watched him tear open the gold packet. "I want to do an awful lot of things," he said, his voice lower, and growly.

"Now? Or in general?"

"Definitely now." He looked down as he sheathed his cock. She followed his gaze, and took in a very deep breath. She'd forgotten how formidable his erection was. Not that she was complaining. They were a great fit, the two of them.

After an epic exhale, she looked up at him again. "First, why don't you remind me what you can do with that."

He smiled and slid his hands underneath her knees. Her stomach and chest tightened as he placed them on his shoulders. "Oh, my God."

"Okay?" he asked.

She nodded, wondering how they'd managed to sync their panting breaths.

He leaned down and forward.

She braced herself. The more forward he moved, the more of her bottom was lifted off the mattress. His gaze was fixed on her tiny thong. "I can't wait to taste you," he said, just before he used one finger to pull the thong down her legs, to the leopard-print heels still on her feet.

Carefully he removed the panties, tossing them behind him. Her legs settled down on his shoulders again, and his smile was awfully smug.

"Think you're smart, don't you?"

"Not particularly, but I know you." He kissed the inside of her ankle. "And I know what you like."

"Yes." Her voice came out as a thread of a whisper. All her muscles were tight and ready. But instead of just plunging into her, the first thing she felt were fingers. Two. All the way.

His eyes drifted closed. "My God, Jenna…you're so…"

She waited for him to finish the sentence, but when his thumb circled her clit, she squeezed his fingers hard enough that he almost lost his balance. She no longer cared what he'd meant to say.

"Now—" he was breathing faster "—or later?"

"What?"

"Do you want to come now, or when I'm inside you?"

"Both," she said, without a hint of hesitation.

She used one shaky elbow to raise herself up and kiss the grin off his face. It was a quickie, no tongue involved at all, but his rhythm broke. The second she fell back again, his fingers slipped out, only to guide his penis to her entrance.

Her entire body quivered. And when he finally thrust into her, it wasn't slow or careful.

It was perfect.

He was thicker than she remembered, maybe longer, but oh, yes, thicker. And he made it very clear he was going to give her all he had. She was primed and ready, not the least bit afraid she couldn't accommodate him. The only fear she had was that she'd rip the sheets.

He almost bent her double just so he could take her mouth in another searing kiss. He was ruthless with his thrusts, his tongue, the way he stared at her as if he was going to wring them both dry.

She loved it. Every second unleashed more of the wild inside her. Greedy and insatiable, she shoved her left hand between them, pushing until he made room for her to find her clit, determined to have the orgasm of her life.

"That's for me," he said, in what she could only call a growl.

"I'm already there."

He filled her with a powerful push, stealing her ability to speak, to think, to breathe.

But when he slowly withdrew, it all came back. "Don't stop," she said between urgent gulps of air.

He obeyed. His lips stretched back, revealing gritted teeth. She was forced to take her hand from the sheets and put it against the headboard so she wouldn't bang her head with every push.

Words were too much for her, and she couldn't control the volume of her cries. Surely the people in the next room must be scandalized, but there again she didn't give one damn.

Her finger was squished on her clit, moving up and down more by him than anything she was doing. It was easy to tell he was getting close when his rhythm changed. She could feel her own tide turning in that place below her belly.

"I'm—"

His head jerked back, his expression feral. Wild. Each thrust was so hard he forced her orgasm. It crashed through her, ending with unbelievably powerful spasms. Her legs wrenched free and wrapped themselves around his waist, but that only lasted a few seconds. Lifting her hand was like moving a boulder. Her legs? No. They dropped.

"Can't take the heat?" he asked.

Her answer was to squeeze the tiniest bit where he was

still inside her, making her pelvis rise just enough that Danger Bond gasped as he slipped out of her and landed with an "umph." Pity his head missed the pillow.

She would have laughed, but with that last move she'd used up all her energy.

"I'll make a scathing retort later," he said.

Jenna nodded, managing half a smile.

Closing her eyes, she thought of the fireworks in the smart apartment. A fantastic innovation, a marvel of ingenuity and glorious to see, to be sure, and yet they were nothing compared to the real fireworks happening inside her.

IN WHAT FELT like the blink of an eye, Rick found himself packing again. He should have been drained dry from making love a truly impressive number of times, but that wasn't the only thing they'd done. They also played chess, talked books and movies, ate a lot of room service—the weekend had gone better than expected, which said a lot. But now it was time to start easing back into the real world.

He didn't want to miss the shuttle. There'd be plenty of places to eat when they got to the airport, and he was as hungry as if he'd just run a 10K. They'd forgotten to order breakfast, but at least they'd had coffee.

Finished with getting his stuff in order, he slipped behind Jenna and put his arms around her. She didn't startle, but she did stop packing to lean into his embrace. "This was good," he whispered.

"Pity about not seeing any of the city, though. I've heard it's a great place to visit."

He kissed her just below her ear where her shoulder met her neck. "Chicago's fine, but visiting all the hot spots on you was more fun."

She groaned. "I really do need to finish packing. Although heaven knows I'd have liked at least another day."

"Well, maybe the next time we get an itch to scratch each other in person, we should make it a longer stay."

Jenna turned around in his arms. "Spring break."

His gaze caught on her damp bottom lip. "What about it?" he murmured, taking a little taste.

Laughing, she drew back. "I get a week off at the end of March."

"I doubt I could take off a whole week, but…" Goddamn it. He was starting to get hard. Hell, not now. He had no self-control when it came to her.

"Maybe I could come to Oklahoma."

"Sure." It seemed she was waiting for him to say something else, but he couldn't remember what they'd been talking about. He glanced at his watch. Even a quickie would be pushing it.

"I know you would be busy and I'm not suggesting I'd stay with you. I'm sure there are hotels in the area. I wouldn't even have brought it up except you mentioned it a few weeks ago—"

He felt like shit. She was flustered all because he'd been too interested in his dick and not listening to her. "Jenna."

"I hear there's a very interesting place called the National Severe Storms Laboratory. I understand they give tours all the time, so I wouldn't be bothering you to show me around."

She was rambling and looking nervous and it was his fault.

"I'd have so much great stuff to teach the kids when school started again."

"Jenna, stop." He hated that she was avoiding his eyes. "Look at me," he said, and waited until she did. "Do you honestly think I'd let you stay anywhere else but with me?"

"Honestly?"

He nodded and tugged her closer.

"I don't know." She bit her lip. "This thing we have—I

mean I know we're just friends. That part's perfectly clear but it's still kind of..."

"Hey...the reason I hesitated was because I hadn't been listening at first. I was too busy thinking about a quickie. I'm sorry."

She gave him one of his favorite smiles. "Seriously?"

He nodded, making sure to meet her gaze. She needed to know he wasn't messing with her.

"So I guess this makes us friends with benefits." She winced. "I never dreamed my name and that phrase could exist in the same sentence."

"Okay, then, let's say we're good friends who happen to like sex with each other."

She nodded. "Who like it very, very much. Except on Skype."

"Yeah," he said, cringing. "No, we won't do that again."

Jenna laughed.

"Spring break sounds good," he said. "We'll talk more about it later. Right now, we have a shuttle to catch."

"Kiss me first?"

He shook his head. "If I kiss you now," he said, bending his head until his lips brushed hers, "we'll miss our flights for sure."

Jenna sighed. "Yes, the real world awaits."

He caught the hint of sadness in her eyes. Was he being a selfish prick? Jenna needed to start dating, find a man like Payton, but someone whom she could trust to be faithful. A man who could fit in to her nine-to-five life and always be there for her.

Rick wasn't that guy. She knew that as well as he did, but sometimes the truth got lost somewhere between the head and the heart. And yeah, he obviously was a selfish prick because he doubted he was capable of letting her go yet.

15

OMG, SHE WAS really doing this.

Jenna followed the crowd, hoping they'd lead her to baggage claim. She was so excited about seeing Rick that she'd forgotten to watch for the signs. They'd talked about her trip to Oklahoma ever since Chicago. She could see how a lot of travel could seriously affect a romantic relationship, but with Rick, everything was simply a matter of mastering expectations.

A perfect example was the fact that she had no problem with Rick having to work three days out of her six-day visit. Because of the active weather season, that was all he could manage. She had a hefty workload herself, and they'd have their nights together. In his town house, which she was incredibly excited to see in real life instead of over her laptop.

Her fellow travelers began to splinter off and she forced herself to stay focused until she spotted the baggage claim sign.

"Jenna!"

She heard his voice, but she couldn't see Rick at first. And then there he was, dodging in and out of the crowd to get to her, and the butterflies in her stomach kicked in again.

To think when he'd told her he would meet her at the airport, she'd told him not to be ridiculous. He had work, and she knew how to get a taxi. But he'd insisted, and now she was ridiculously glad.

When his smile mirrored her own, she revised her theory about long distances being a problem. Reunions were awesome.

"Hi." She barely got the word out before he kissed her right in front of the luggage carousel, ignoring the crowd and holding her as if he feared she'd turn around and leave.

People anxious to get their luggage forced them to move. Jenna saw her own suitcase tumble down onto the carousel, but she didn't have a chance to grab it. Rick had pulled her into a semiprivate kiosk area near the car rentals and swept her into another kiss the moment he could. A kiss that quite possibly could set a record. She refused to let go, and Rick hadn't given up his claim, either.

Would it always be like this? Wanting to climb inside him, to live and breathe this second for an eternity?

A strategic bump against her hip told her he was a little too excited to be in public, and she wondered if her carry-on bag was big enough to hide it for the walk to the car.

Rick eventually leaned back to catch his breath. She hadn't even finished panting when he dived back in, pulling her tightly against him.

"Excuse me."

The voice did not belong to Rick. She knew this because she was kissing him back with equal enthusiasm.

Parting reluctantly, she discovered a nice-looking older gentleman wearing a suit with a badge over his breast pocket.

"If you two wouldn't mind holding off until you're out of the building. Perhaps somewhere outside of the parking lot, it would be greatly appreciated."

Could have been worse. Could have been the police.

As it was, the minute they were in the clear, their eyes met. They both burst out laughing. The hysterical kind, where it was impossible to stop even though her stomach ached and her eye makeup had to be streaming down her cheeks. "Okay, we have to stop," she said.

"Fine." Rick held up his hands. "I'm completely over it."

"Good," she said, but then she looked at him when he looked at her, and they had to go through the entire business again. Luckily, he managed to catch her bag before it made another trip around the carousel.

The long haul out to the parking lot finally cured them, which was good because she hadn't stopped by the bathroom on their way out. God only knew what she looked like. Thankfully, they turned down the final row.

Rick's Jeep was a rugged beast of a Wrangler, a Rubicon, which was interesting. Aside from being an actual river in northern Italy, crossing the Rubicon meant passing the point of no return. If she climbed aboard, would she be irrevocably committed to this odd yet wonderful relationship? She wouldn't mind that a bit.

Rick opened the passenger door. "What's that smile for?"

"Just wondering why this is called a Rubicon." She said the last word in her lowest and most dramatic voice.

"It's one tough son of a bitch," he said, just before he hurried around to the driver's seat. "I've crossed some wicked rivers in this Jeep. So I guess the designers wanted it to represent breaking boundaries and going where no four-wheel drive has gone before. Although, they probably just used the name because it sounded butch."

She was still chuckling as he paid the parking fee, but instead of leaving the lot, he pulled out of the line and parked near a fence.

"You hungry?" he asked. "Jet-lagged? That's almost a six-hour flight."

"I'm fine, actually."

"Would you mind if we went by my office first before we go to my place? Not for too long, I promise."

"No. I'd love it."

"Good, because I have a conference call I'll have to take, but more importantly I want to show you off."

"Oh, great way to not make me nervous."

"No! They'll love you. I didn't mean—I meant to say show you around—"

She put her finger on his lips. "I'm teasing. As long as I can have you to myself tonight, I'm in," she said.

He leaned over to kiss her again, and when he looked into her eyes as if he'd never seen anything more wonderful, her butterflies had butterflies.

ONCE AGAIN, JENNA was amazingly impressed with Rick. The building where he worked was beautiful, designed not just as a laboratory that specialized in studying severe weather, but as an educational facility open to visitors of all ages. She desperately wanted to bring her whole school here, including the teachers. But mostly the kids. They'd love it.

The tour lasted longer than expected since his conference call had been pushed back an hour, but Jenna didn't mind one bit. Watching Rick interact with his colleagues deepened her appreciation for what he did, which was a lot more science than chasing storms, and showed her how important he was to everyone there. She swelled with pride watching how everyone treated him. That they liked him was clear, but they respected him just as much. Even the interns. So much for believing Rick when he talked about how they all must hate him. She had a feeling he encouraged them to rise above what they thought they could do, which was never easy, but almost always worthwhile.

"And this is where I work when I'm not on the floor," Rick said, holding the door for her. "As a rule I don't spend much time in here. Although lately, yeah. When I work late I call you from here."

Jenna grinned. *When* he worked late… That was always.

His office wasn't very big or glamorous: a desk, a computer with a huge monitor, some bookshelves. "Sit," he said, offering her a chair. "You look like you're running out of steam."

Boy, was she ever, and the chair looked inviting. But when her gaze caught on a large framed photo on his wall, she went straight for it.

The picture was grainy, but that didn't matter. Almost the whole frame was filled by a massive tornado, black as night, its funnel a gigantic vacuum, sucking up everything it touched. That was terrifying enough, but in the foreground, looking impossibly small and vulnerable, was a man running for his life. The more she studied it, the more it looked like…

Her heart nearly leaped from her chest. She waited until she knew her voice would work. "Is that you?'

"Yeah, I know. It's embarrassing," Rick said. "That was in Kansas, about ten years ago. When I was still young and stupid."

"You were awfully lucky," she said, astonished she sounded so calm. If she hadn't known better, she would've assumed that person hadn't survived. Not just any person. Rick.

"Extremely lucky. That could easily have gone sideways." Rick came up behind her. He stared idly at the picture while gently rubbing the small of her back, then smiled at her. "I'm sorry about the delay. Hard to predict these conference calls with so many people involved."

She looked into his eyes and could've melted right there. She wondered if he even knew he was touching her. "I'm not sorry," she said. "This has been wonderful. Everyone thinks so highly of you. But that's no surprise."

He just laughed. "I think they're all jealous that I have such a beautiful friend."

"I seriously doubt that, but thank you," she said, while inside, her chest tightened, and not in a good way. It made no sense. He'd given her a compliment, and yet his use of the word *friend* had been like a soft punch to the gut. She'd called him a friend dozens of times. Because that was what he was. So…what the hell? "I hope I get to meet Antwan."

"You will. He's still in the meeting. Covering for me, actually." Rick lowered his hand. "I have to go in a few minutes, after that I promise I won't be long. I can bring you coffee, water, soda. We've got pretty decent vending machines if you want to go to the break room yourself."

"Lead on, Macduff," she said, "or as Shakespeare actually said, 'Lay on, Macduff. And damned be him who first cries, "Hold, enough!"'"

He leaned into her. "God, English teachers are hot." She glanced at the open doorway. Anyone could walk in and see them. He just laughed and said, "Come on, the break room is next door."

He pushed his door open farther, and she completely expected a group of his coworkers to leap out of the way and pretend they weren't eavesdropping. But nope. They were all grown-ups here. In her job it was sometimes hard to tell the difference between the teachers and the students.

As she passed, he whispered, "I'm so glad you're here."

The ache in her gut eased. She was glad, too. Glad she hadn't spooked herself out of coming. It was scary, though. Six whole days. But since he only had three off, it was very much like a long weekend, and they'd already done that, so what could go wrong?

The break room was literally right next door to Rick's office. She stopped at the entrance and scanned the place. "Why can't our teacher's lounge be like this?" The room was bright and cheerful with nice tables, two microwaves and well-stocked vending machines.

Rick poured her a mug—a real mug, not a foam cup—of coffee. "It's not as good as the coffee at the smart apartment."

"Nothing is. I wonder when I'm going to stop comparing."

"Let me know. I think it might have doomed us for life." He checked his watch and frowned. "I've got to go pretty soon. If you need singles…"

He was reaching for his wallet.

"I'm fine," she said. "Thanks. I thought I might check my email while you're gone. Go through all my social media."

"You can use my computer if you don't want to do it on your phone. The password's taped to the inside of the top desk drawer. You'll like using it." He grinned. "You can look at my tornado escapades on my YouTube channel. I won't be gone long enough for you to stream a whole movie, but we do have smoking-fast internet here. Anyway, I've got to go."

"Fine. Don't worry about me. I think I'll accept the offer and wait in your office."

He followed her into the hall, and then all the way into his office.

"What are you doing?" she said, laughing. "Go. I'll be fine."

"I'll miss watching you zip through all those photos and whatever. It's very enlightening, seeing what you like and dislike on Tumblr and Reddit and Instagram and…"

"I'm never telling you anything again," she said, blushing. "I only use Tumblr for work."

"Right. I suppose you can quit whenever you want to."

"I'd watch that smug look if I were you."

He looked at the door, and then moved closer to her.

Close enough that she needed to put her coffee down on his desk.

"I like knowing what matters to you," he said, his voice very soft. "I wish I'd had time to do more with the town house, but the bedroom's all set up."

"I know." She lowered her voice. "Skype sex, remember?"

"I thought we were never to speak of that again." He leaned in, and she could feel his breath on her cheek. "Next time, I'll come see you. Maybe do a presentation for your students."

"Yes. Yes, I was just thinking that. I want it to happen so much."

"I do, too," he said, but it didn't seem as though he was listening anymore. He didn't even hesitate before he kissed her.

The spell broke seconds later when a distinctly Jamaican accent said, "Stop that right now. I've been waiting all day to meet her. Get a room later."

Rick stood aside. "As you may have guessed, this is Antwan Clarke."

"And you're the lovely Jenna," he said. "I'm glad you're here for a few days. Maybe he'll actually leave at six instead of hanging out here every night. It's not good to work so much, even if it's good work."

Antwan was a tall, lean, dark man with shiny black hair, black slacks, a white button-down shirt and a pair of great-looking Converse shoes. His smile was as welcoming as the rapidly cooling coffee waiting for her. "You look different when you're not on Skype," she said. "And leaning at a forty-five-degree angle."

"And you're much more beautiful in person. I'd love to speak to you more, but I have to go to the same conference call as Rick here, so maybe lunch one day before you leave?"

"I'd love it."

Rick turned to her but he didn't kiss her. "See you soon."

The two men left and she finally had the coffee she'd wanted along with a big chocolate-chip cookie she had in her purse. But she was still hungry and after she'd finished checking email, she gave in to temptation. Taking her wallet with her, she stopped just before entering the break room. Was it possible she'd actually heard her name?

"She's the one he met in Boston, right?"

"I don't know but she's hot," another man said. Someone Jenna immediately liked.

"He's taken a hell of a lot of time off. According to Bev, he's got like weeks of vacation built up. He never went anywhere with Faith."

"Damn, she was hot, too," the first man said. "Rick's getting up there. Maybe he's looking to get serious."

"Who knows? I was a year younger than him when I got married."

"If I had a woman like what's-her-name, I'd think about getting married, too."

The men started talking about a fantasy football league, so Jenna scurried back into Rick's office, closing the door behind her. She sat down again in front of his computer, but the screen was dark, acting like a big mirror. She needed to chill. Relax. Any other time, she'd have been preening about those men calling her hot. And thrilled they'd thought Rick was lucky to have her. She just couldn't muster the energy.

She took her phone out of her purse and tried reading on her Kindle app. It was a great story that had made the last half of her flight go by quickly. But now she couldn't concentrate. She kept looking up at the picture of Rick on the wall and thinking how cold his office was. She put down her phone, rubbed her arms and then turned on the computer.

Instead of going right to Tumblr, she typed *storm* but she froze before she got to the second word. Instead, she shut the machine down, and went back to the break room, grateful to find it empty and that the coffee was fresh. She took her cup and a Danish back to his office to wait, although she wasn't sure why she'd paid for a pastry. She had no appetite at all.

EVEN THOUGH RICK lived close to work, he was grateful to finally pull in to his garage after a quick stop at the store. Jenna had caught a chill back at the office, and he wanted everything to be perfect when she saw his place for the first time.

Relatively perfect, if you ignored the alarming number of unpacked boxes in every room.

"Your own garage?" Jenna looked at him, then at the boxes near the door that led into his kitchen. "I can't think of a single apartment building in South Shore that offers a private garage."

"This is Norman. The cost of living is low. Very low. But on the plus side, it's unbearably humid in summer and freezing cold in winter. Not to mention that when it comes to tornadoes, the odds are ever in our favor."

The sound of her laughter did something to his chest. Opened it, made it easier to breathe. "Come on. I'll give you the grand tour."

He got her suitcase and carry-on from the back of the Jeep while she grabbed a heavy-looking briefcase. She'd said she had a lot of work to do, and he was glad of it. He hated the idea of leaving her, but if that was the price he had to pay for having her here, he'd take it.

"It's unlocked," he said, then followed her inside.

"This kitchen's great. The open floor plan, stainless steel appliances, granite countertops. Even the cupboards are beautiful."

"And mostly empty. Sorry about that. But I guess we'll manage."

"I'm a huge fan of open plans like this," she said, barely pausing as she moved into the living room. "My apartment is just a bunch of square rooms pushed together in the most unimaginative way possible. Thank God I've got the balcony to play with."

"I've still got furniture to buy, some gym equipment to replace the things Faith kept. That's a new couch and coffee table."

"They're great," she said. "I like the leather, and the clean lines. The coffee table goes well with everything. Pity the walls are all just white." She turned in the direction of the fireplace.

"Yeah, for a six-month lease, they don't let you paint. At least I've got that," he said, nodding at his gigantic television above the mantel. "But I don't play with it much. I mostly watch the weather. And *Game of Thrones*. But mostly the weather."

"That makes perfect sense. Weather changed the trajectory of your life. It was the single biggest motivating force you had."

"I'm going to write that down, and show it to people who think I'm a nerd."

"Oh, no. You're definitely a nerd."

"Thanks so much."

"Where should I put this?" she asked, lifting the briefcase. "I've got my laptop, so I can work anywhere."

"I've got a desk upstairs so you can spread out a bit. Why don't I show you and drop off all this stuff so we can relax."

Rick led her up the stairs. Once again he wished he'd taken the time to make the place look more lived in. Less like a storage locker. But there was an excellent desk in the spare room that he hadn't even touched yet.

"Isn't this your desk?"

"Technically. But I haven't used it much."

"Ah, right. Well, it's terrific. I love library lamps. I've got one at home."

"Look in the top drawer."

She sat first, and kind of swooned at the chair, which had cost him a fortune. But when she opened the drawer she burst out laughing.

He'd been so sure she'd like that. Well, shit. Guess he didn't know her as well as he'd—

"Oh, my God, it's like you walked inside my head and took an inventory of all the things that I love. You've got all the great colors of Post-its, and the tabs, and the colored paper clips."

"You like?"

She looked up at him, and he could tell from her eyes she did. And when she closed the drawer and stood up again, he knew she was about to show him how pleased she was.

He let the bags fall from his hands so he could pull her close. She wrapped her arms around his neck and they met with the kiss he'd been dying to give her in his office. Right now, she was all that mattered. Kissing her was like coming home. He liked how she held him as she moved her head by inches, treating each kiss like an experiment.

If it hadn't been five thirty, and she hadn't been exhausted and starving, he would have walked her right over to his bed. In fact…

No, she hadn't eaten anything but coffee and junk food. Not a good way to start what he hoped would be an epic night. The grumbling of her stomach signaled that the kisses were over for now.

"Wait," she said, her hands still on him. "I want to remember which kiss we were on."

"You have a list?"

"It's too small, though. I'll need so many more to fill out the whole dance card."

"I have no objections to that plan."

"Good. I wish I weren't so hungry, but your forearm is starting to look appealing, so…"

"Off we go. You like Mexican, right?"

"I do."

Downstairs, he headed for the kitchen but Jenna wasn't behind him. Odd. He found her at the window that looked out at the back.

"You have a yard."

"It came with."

"It'll mean mowing and with those trees, some raking in the fall."

He slipped behind her and pulled her against his chest. "I know, right? I'm crazy for getting this place. I don't know how long I'll be here, but I've already bought furniture…"

"You said your accountant advised you to buy a house."

He nodded. Kissed her temple. "I think this is something in the middle. I was really tired of living like a frat boy. The old apartment was mostly an excuse for a gym. But I saw this place and thought, why not? Give living like a grown-up a try."

"Well, that's good, I suppose. As long as it's really what you want."

He nodded again. "Who knows. I might even start doing some planting this summer."

She smiled and let herself relax against his chest. He wouldn't be doing any planting, and he'd end up hiring someone to cut the grass and rake. Rick lived and breathed his work and had little time in his life for anything else.

16

"OH, FOR…" RICK WENT to the window, shoved it open and yelled, "I'll be right down. Hold on."

"It's your own fault," Jenna said. "You were the one—"

"I know exactly why I'm late, and I'd do it again in a minute. In fact, I'm going to just cancel my appointments for today," he said, trying to climb back into bed. "I'll tell the director I had an emergenc—"

"Stop," she said, laughing and pushing him away. He was already dressed and she wasn't going to be responsible for him missing work. "After impressing upon me how important today's meeting is? No, you're not going to have an emergency. Unless Antwan comes up here and drags you out by your… You're not wearing a tie."

Jenna was still naked and after a night of debauchery, she planned to go straight back to sleep when Rick left. But not for too long. She had a lot to do today.

The week was flying by. Every night had been different. Twice they'd gone out to eat, twice they'd had food delivered. She'd never expected to find such great Indian food in Norman. She'd worked when Rick did. She'd met him and Antwan for lunch her second day, and they'd gone to the movies on his day off.

But a good deal of their time together had been spent in bed. Going through condoms like tissues during flu season.

Damn if he wasn't the most amazing lover she'd ever

had. Last night, they'd done it twice. It was his night to call it, so the first was him in back of her, and the second was her on top. Rick's favorite. Hers, too, now.

No wonder the honking horn had scared the crap out of her this morning. Rick jumping up to take the fastest shower in the northern hemisphere hadn't helped her settle down again. Now he'd donned not just clothes but a suit. A really sharp three-piece that made him look sexy as hell. The deep charcoal-gray with his sky-blue eyes? Please. He could have any woman on the planet, and probably some from other galaxies.

He kissed her, huffed his displeasure, then went to the closet. A few seconds later he held out his hands, each one holding a tie. There was no contest. "The one on the right. It's the color of your eyes."

He tossed the loser into the closet as if it was now dead to him. "Coffee. I'll have to stop because—"

"It's made. I programmed it last night."

"Colombian?"

"Seriously?"

He shook his head then came to her again, although this time on the side of the bed, not in it. She looked up at his slightly stubbled face. "You forgot to shave."

"I'll tell him I'm growing a beard."

"Kiss me already. And go."

He did exactly that, tasting very minty. When he was at the bedroom door she said, "Is it okay if I open some kitchen boxes?"

"Open any box you want, do anything you like," he said, as he walked out of the room. But two seconds later he stuck his head back in. "You have to split the money with me if you sell anything on eBay."

"Have a great meeting," she yelled after him, but she doubted he'd heard because he was racing down the stairs. The front door closed with a bang a few seconds later, and she smiled as she snuggled under the sheets. Being in his house had helped her build a profile of sorts of Rick Sinclair.

He was a hedonist when it came to things that touched his skin. The sheets, for example, were decadent, as were the pillows. On the other hand, his dishes were…usable. She might discover a great set of Wedgwood dinnerware as she searched for wineglasses, but she doubted it. After Faith's return from Mexico, they'd amicably divided up things. But since neither one of them had ever cared about kitchen items, Rick had warned Jenna not to expect much.

That he'd called his previous apartment a frat house lifted her spirits and made the prospect of her day too exciting to go back to sleep. Not that she was going to redecorate or anything, but she could certainly unpack a box or two. Maybe pick up something fun at the mall, something homey.

She really wanted to surprise him. Having done all her *teacher's homework*, she planned to make dinner for the two of them since it was their last night before she had to leave—something she could barely stand to think about. But first, she had to make sure he had the right pans and things for cooking her signature lasagna.

After her shower, she put on some jeans, a T-shirt and her favorite red sweater, then went to look through every box that was labeled "Kitchen." And some that weren't.

By 1:00 p.m., she'd discovered that his plates were unique in that none of them matched anything else. He did, however, have a cake stand and two expensive stand mixers, of all things. It made her laugh picturing him trying his hand at baking a cake.

Thankfully, she found a roasting pan that would do the job. Now, armed with a map and the GPS in his Jeep, she was off to the mall. Getting into the Rubicon was easy enough, but she had to move the seat forward quite a bit.

She didn't rush to the mall, not when she hadn't driven a stick shift in ages. So she practiced in the quiet residential area. It all came back quickly, and she made her way out to the busy streets. It was fun being in the biggest, baddest vehicle on the road.

Not literally, but it felt like it. At home, she drove a nice small sedan. It was a perfect car for her commutes to school, the market, the movies. In this leviathan, it felt as if she didn't stop for lights—the lights stopped for her.

Still riding on her high from last night, she found a great parking spot. Inside the mall everything felt familiar—she could have been back home with the big department stores near every exit. She found exactly what she was looking for in Macy's and then bought a few other things she liked. That she hoped he'd like.

After the mall, she hit up Whole Foods, then made it back to Rick's by 2:34 p.m.

"IT SMELLS FANTASTIC in here. Am I in the right house?"

Jenna's smile was a mixture of coyness and pleasure, and as always, the sight of her made his chest tighten in a great way. As he entered the kitchen, he understood both. She hadn't just opened a few boxes. There were all sorts of things on the counters and even in the cupboards. There was also a lasagna the size of a small country on the stovetop and an opened bottle of red wine sitting next to a pair of his wineglasses.

On the other side of the stove there were colorful nested bowls he didn't recognize. It was a lot. She'd worked hard doing what he should've done long before she got here. "Wow. You were busy." He'd never imagined her being so domestic and wasn't quite sure what to say. "What's all this?"

Hesitating, she searched his face. "I thought I'd make something that we could eat tonight with enough left over to freeze in portions, so you could have some another time." She wasn't looking at him as she went to the new bowls. "And these are a housewarming gift. Because this is your new house and I noticed you didn't have any. Bowls, I mean. They all have lids. One's in the fridge, though, because of the salad. And the big one would work really well for popcorn."

"They're great. It's really nice of you. I mean, you had a lot of work to do for your classes, and it looks as if you've spent all day on me."

The smile she gave him was off. "Not all day."

He lifted her chin, and even then she didn't seem to want to meet his gaze. "Thank you. Again. Really. You've done more in a day than I've done since I moved in. It feels very homey."

"Well, I, uh… Happy housewarming." She took a deep breath and slipped away. "Are you at all hungry? I can serve up dinner now, if you want."

"Tell you what, let me get washed up and changed, then I can't wait to taste that lasagna."

"Okay," she said. "I'll just pour some wine, then."

Rick wasn't really sure why seeing all the plates and things in the cupboard made him uncomfortable. He'd never expected Jenna to go to so much trouble for him. His head was spinning. He hadn't decided about how to arrange the cupboards yet. Well, guess he didn't have to worry about that anymore.

It was so different from anything he'd done with Faith. That didn't make it wrong, just…weird. No, that wasn't the right word. Hell, at his old place, the most used items in the kitchen were takeout menus. Faith never cared about cooking, and neither did he. He wasn't sure what he'd do with those bowls, except the popcorn one. But still, Jenna had gone out of her way to make his apartment feel like a home.

He wasn't comfortable going upstairs quite yet. Near the wine, Jenna was messing with something, he couldn't tell what, but she was right by a long stretch of empty countertop. When Jenna turned to him, he picked her up and sat her down right there.

"Hey," she said. "What the…? What are you doing?"

"I want to kiss you."

"And on the countertop is important because…?"

He looked into her eyes as he made his way between her thighs, then leaned down and held her steady as he laid one on her. When her arms went around his neck, he could feel her relax. He pulled back just a bit so he could nibble on her earlobe before he whispered, "Thank you. But you're the housewarming gift I like the best."

"If I overstepped, I apologize."

"No, you didn't. I told you to do anything you wanted. It's me," he said. "I feel guilty and, yeah, a little embarrassed. I should've had these boxes unpacked and things put away long before you got here."

"Please don't." Jenna touched his face. "I don't care about that. I was so glad I could help in some small way."

"And I appreciate it but that doesn't excuse my obtuseness." He frowned. "Is that a word?"

That made her laugh. "Have I told you how hot you look in this suit?" She caught his lapels and held on to him. "How was your meeting?"

"It went great. Got what we wanted."

Her smile was soft, her gaze open and hiding nothing. Then she pulled him into another kiss.

"Okay," he said finally. "I'll be back shortly."

"I'll hold you to it," she said and hopped down.

He left, but halfway up the stairs, he caught a motion in his peripheral vision. Jenna, at the other counter, the one where they ate, took two candles away. They weren't his. But they were very nice.

Damn it, he thought he'd fixed things. Mostly it was that she'd surprised him. He thought she'd been doing what she called her teacher's homework.

Evidently her uneasiness was contagious. He was still feeling a little off, himself. He hadn't lied. He did feel guilty. But not just because he hadn't unpacked. Back in Chicago, he'd wondered if he was being a selfish prick for staying involved with her. He had no doubts about it now. *Selfish prick* might be an understatement.

He was crazy about her, there was no getting around that, but that didn't change anything. She had her life in Boston. He had his here. The work he was doing was making a difference. Literally, people's lives had been changed for the better. But chasing storms? Chasing the rush when the earth showed her incredible power? Hell, yeah, it was dangerous, but so was driving on the freeway.

In one way he wished she'd never seen that picture of him in his office. He knew it had gotten to her because of some of the questions she'd been asking him about exit strategies during a storm. On the other hand, she needed to understand exactly what he did. He doubted she'd ever be able to see his life in any other terms but unpredictable and dangerous. Everything she didn't want in a partner.

He wouldn't say anything tonight. It was just...he should've thought more about what keeping this friendship of theirs alive would mean to her down the road. Good God, her ideal man had been Payton. The steadiest guy in the world. A real nine-to-fiver, who would have fit nicely into the 1950s.

Rick was nothing like that.

She thought a suit made him look hot. He'd rather have a root canal than wear one. And that summed up a lot of the differences between them.

He changed back into his real wardrobe. Worn jeans

and a thick sweater made complete by a pair of his trusty Nikes.

Damn it, the guilt wasn't easing but he didn't want to ruin their last night together.

What if all this—the phone calls, flying to Chicago, her coming here—was holding Jenna back from finding someone she could build a life with? They didn't talk about it, really. So far the physical distance between them had made it easy to overlook problems that would torpedo most relationships.

The phenomenal sex didn't help. It was the best, most adventurous and just plain hot sex he'd ever had. But the idea of not talking to her, not flying wherever he needed to go, not being inside her, made him ache in a way he'd never once felt even watching Faith kiss another man.

He'd always known that he and Jenna could only ever be friends. Well, no, that wasn't accurate. In the beginning, yes, their relationship had been very clear to him. But to be honest, it had turned to gray very quickly. Tonight he'd had a taste of what it would be like with Jenna. To really be with her.

He liked it. A hell of a lot. But the phone could ring any minute, and he'd have to rush out the door straight into an oncoming storm.

She'd told him the kind of man she wanted for the long run. She'd never been coy about it. Being with him… It would make both of them miserable. He wasn't going to do that to Jenna.

He just needed to be more careful, that was all. More aware. After this trip, maybe they shouldn't talk every night. He should give her some space to start dating again. Even if he had no desire to date, she might.

Jesus. He squeezed his eyes shut. He couldn't stand to think about her seeing someone else. It would kill him to know. But he'd have to know eventually. Because it could mean the end of their...whatever it was they had.

Of course it would end them. Shit. He needed to get real. Because he cared too much about her to stand in the way of her moving on.

Well, goddamn it. This was a hell of a way to discover that he was in love.

JENNA WAS STILL futzing with the big bowl of popcorn, making sure the top didn't close all the way so the steam wouldn't make the popcorn soggy, when Rick asked, "How did you like driving the Jeep? Have any trouble?"

The popcorn instantly forgotten, she spun to face him, her eyes huge and excited. "It was awesome. The Rubicon totally rocks. I love it so, so much, I can't even describe it."

Surprised, Rick laughed. Definitely not the reaction he'd expected. "Just like that," he said, snapping his fingers. "I've been replaced by a Jeep."

"Sorry, but yeah. I felt like king of the road in that thing. You know how terrible traffic is in Boston. If I drove that baby in the city, there'd be semis and Hummers and me. Everyone else had better get the hell out of the way."

Rick really laughed. "This is a whole side of you I haven't seen." He needed this comic relief. He'd tried to lighten up over dinner, and for the most part he believed he'd pulled it off. But seeing her like this...this was great. He'd worried about her driving the Jeep for nothing. Maybe their differences weren't so great after all.

"Puts my little Camry to shame," she said, turning back to the popcorn. "Maybe I'll trade it in."

"You don't want a Rubicon where you live." Rick watched her put things on a tray. "I don't know about watching a movie. Or the popcorn, since I just ate my weight's worth of the best lasagna ever."

"Let's just start a movie." Jenna used her I'm-completely-unaware-of-subtext smile. "Then we can maybe do something else."

"Look," he said. "I'm all in favor of bribing me with sex. Works for me, every time. But, and I may be wrong, using it to watch a movie? What could you possibly want to see that would be worth throwing down bribes?"

"I think *Ladyhawke* is on tonight, and I haven't seen it in years. It's one of my favorites. Although, I should have checked the time and channel. But here," she said, giving him the popcorn bowl and then grabbing them drinks.

"Uh, Rutger Hauer?"

"And Michelle Pfeiffer," she said, wiggling her eyebrows, and then leading him to the stairs.

"And now you're enticing me with pretty women? Does she get naked in this movie?"

"No."

"Does she mention me by name?"

Jenna laughed. "Several times."

"Oh, okay, then. Let's give it a go. But first, I must insist that we take off all our clothes."

Entering the bedroom, Jenna pulled off her red sweater. "Nope."

"Why not?"

"I'll agree to wearing one of your T-shirts and my panties."

"Ah," Rick said. "The classics. Good choice."

It didn't take them long to settle into the TV-watching position. Pillows behind them, popcorn between them, lots of napkins on either side. He barely remembered *Ladyhawke*. It wasn't exactly his kind of movie. If memory served, the ending of this film was really, really—no kidding—really schmaltzy.

"It started twenty minutes ago." Jenna sounded so sad, he wanted to kiss her. Help her feel better.

Instead he told her, "I don't mind. I think I remember

someone escaping from some medieval prison or something, by using the *Shawshank* maneuver."

"Close enough." She leaned over and kissed him very sweetly. "Thank you."

"Do I have your word that even if I fall asleep, you'll wake me for sex?"

She tipped her head to the right. "On my last night here? What do you think?"

Her last night. Rick tried to smile, for Jenna's sake. But he wasn't feeling it.

JENNA HADN'T SEEN the film in ages. When she'd seen it for the first time, she'd fallen deeply in lust with Rutger Hauer and the wondrously happy ending. Matthew Broderick had been a revelation, and, well, she'd been young. Watching it now with Rick, she wasn't sure how she felt.

"You really think of this as a romance?" Rick asked, his hand steadily moving from the popcorn bowl to his mouth. Despite all his protestations that he was far too full.

"Of course it is. True love, a wicked curse that keeps them apart, the fight to find a way back to each other. What film are you watching?"

"I don't really see it that way. By all rights, they shouldn't have been able to break the curse. It's a tragic love story with a cheat at the end."

"But the cheat at the end isn't that outrageous. People knew what eclipses were. And the priest felt guilty, so..."

"Well," he said, shaking his head. "The beauty of the film is that the two of them can never have what they desire. They're destined to just miss each other every sunrise and every sunset."

"Well, that's romance, too. If they never give up."

"Then neither of them can ever be happy. Which is basically a tragedy."

Jenna sighed. "No. Because loving someone despite

the odds is *every* romance. And Navarre still had to win her at the end."

"See, I think they had to add that. Take a film like, um, *Witness.* They can never be together. Their worlds are so far apart. It's still a love story, but there was no magic trick in the end to give them a happily-ever-after. He had to leave her if either of them were ever going to find happiness."

"Fine," she said. "But here comes the part where Michelle runs into his arms, so shhh. Eat your popcorn quietly, please."

"Yes, ma'am," he said.

She watched the rest of the film, but he'd ruined it for her. Not intentionally. She was certain for him it was simply a discussion about the film. For her, though…all she could think about was their own impending tragedy.

Being here had been so great. With the exception of that little blip when he'd gotten home, when she'd realized she had gone a little overboard, it had been a perfect week. Waking up to his smile, laughing together, going out to dinner and making love without a care in the world.

Knowing he'd be there at the end of the day.

There was this line on a TV show she loved. The main characters said it to each other. *I love you and I like you.* She'd been thinking about that for a couple of days now, but she couldn't figure out a way to get there. Not with Rick. As much as she…who was she kidding? As much as she loved him, they were destined to be friends until one of them met the right person.

When the movie ended, she took away the popcorn bowl so there was nothing between them. All it took was one kiss, and yes, her hand going around his cock, to wash away any lingering thoughts about endings and things that could never be.

She didn't rush things. Once he was hard, she skimmed

her palm over his dark thatch of hair, then above it, carefully, slowly, memorizing.

It felt like he'd had the same idea. It was a slow burn, where every inch of him had a place in her memory, one she could pull out when she needed to. Even as she stroked him, his hands had touched her in the same way. Wanting to pause the world for an hour while they touched each other everywhere.

"I don't want to go home," she whispered, her mouth very close to his ear. "I'm going to miss you so much."

"Me, too," he whispered back, and she thought she heard a break in his voice.

He had to move to do it, but he found a way that both of them could keep exploring. Now, they could kiss.

Perfect. Talking was overrated. And she couldn't quite trust herself not to cry.

17

RICK'S CELL PHONE rang at 3:45 a.m. He tried to grab it quickly and quietly, but Jenna had awakened at the first ring.

"Okay," he said. "No, it's fine. "

He was leaving. Jenna wasn't groggy anymore. The most likely reason for him to get a call at this hour was a tornado.

"Yeah," he said, his voice almost free of the postsleep slurring. "Except for Gordo. Maybe Elizabeth? And if she can't, try Jonah. Yeah. Okay. Thirty." He hung up and looked at her. "Rotten timing but duty calls."

"A tornado? Is it close?"

"Nope. About four hours away, heading for Topeka, but it's not even a tornado yet. The projection is high for a cluster event, so my team will drive up with a new kind of mobile radar and see what we see. The bad part is I doubt I'll be able to get back before you have to leave. I wanted to take you to the airport."

"But a cluster event. You must be excited about that, yes?"

He turned to her, moving close enough to kiss. "Yeah. There's a lot we need to learn about them. But what's way more important is that I wanted to make out here before we made out in the car before we went to the airport."

"Well, if there's going to be a tornado, maybe I won't be able to go tonight?"

He shook his head. "You don't have to worry about a thing. Your flight might see a bit of rain, but not much, so, the worst you'll have to put up with is snoring neighbors. Are you able to sleep on a red-eye?"

She knew he was changing the subject, and she let him. There wasn't much she could do to stop him from driving four hours straight into danger. She doubted she'd sleep until Rick was home safe. "Yeah," she said, hoping the lie didn't show. "I'm out the minute we take off."

His smile was so tender it made her whole chest constrict, and that was a precursor to crying, which she absolutely refused to do. He did this all the time. It was part of his job, for heaven's sake.

"I've got to go," he said, touching her cheek. "I'll be able to text you during the drive, although there's no telling what kind of communication we'll have when we're in the thick of things. But I'll definitely let you know when it's over, okay?"

She nodded again and then kissed him, hugging him so tightly she'd probably leave a bruise.

Why in hell had she been so excited to see *Ladyhawke*? She hadn't slept well because of it. The disagreement she'd had with Rick hadn't been about the movie. It had been about them. About their future together. Even if he did come home safe and sound, new tornadoes would form, tearing apart lives like a scythe cutting wheat. She wished she hadn't learned so much about them. Like what the enhanced Fujita scale actually meant, and how there wasn't anything a person could do when the roof of a barn was swept up and smashed your truck to a tin can.

But what she could do was be an adult, and not make him feel any guilt at all.

"Thank you for my housewarming gift," he said when they ended the kiss. "You're right. It was a perfect popcorn bowl. And man, that lasagna? You should go into business for yourself. Seriously, best lasagna ever."

Jenna couldn't help smiling. "Well, look at that. To absolutely no one's surprise you're still, above all, a very nice man."

He winced. "I try."

"It makes all the difference. Now leave, because if you think I'm staying awake at this hour you're nuts. Oh, wait. I can get the coffee going. You must have a thermos somewhere, right?"

"I'll get coffee at the lab. And I'll text you. Damn it, I miss you already."

She sniffed, but smiled right up until he walked into the master bath. And was left with nothing but his scent clinging to his pillow.

It was amazing how quickly he was dressed. Another quick kiss on her temple, a hand over her hair, then he and his heavy Doc Martens clomped downstairs. She heard him drop something in the kitchen. It didn't sound as if it broke.

After that? Silence. Sadness.

Endings.

OF COURSE, HIS TEAM had rushed in after getting the call. They were students from the University of Oklahoma, each of them very excited about what was to come. They'd hit the road quickly—after all, this is what they'd been trained for—and they all knew what to do. Now, in the truck, when they weren't trying to get comfortable, they were telling jokes, mostly about him. Standard protocol on these excursions, but only if they liked the boss. He wasn't complaining, just groaning and rolling his eyes. He was also texting Jenna like a seventh grader because he had seen the fear in her eyes. She really was a terrible liar.

He texted her a bit about the group. Three of the six had been on a tornado run with him before, and the other three had attended classes at U of O, including some he taught. The closer they got to the storms, the higher the tension rose. But each of them understood that they were going to make a difference. The data they collected was ultimately going to save lives. Hell, he was excited, too.

And while he couldn't do much to assuage Jenna now, once he was clear of the storm he'd call her. Let her know he was still in one piece. And some time in the future she might be interested in listening to what he did on these expeditions. Rick recorded everything once the action started, and explained every observation. Jonah would be filming, too, which was even better, because she'd see that it was safety first, always. And that his equipment and his team were never closer than a mile to any active core.

In his whole career, no one on any of his teams had ever been hurt. He wished he could say that across the board, but sometimes, shit happened and weather, despite all they knew, was fickle. Not that anyone had died, but in 2008, one of the teams had been banged up something fierce. A freak vortex, something they didn't understand too well back then, had caught them by surprise.

The science had blossomed in the last ten years. Thrilling stuff. He loved what he did. Where he worked, at the center of everything tornado.

"Come on, boss. It's your turn."

"What? It isn't my turn if I didn't know you were playing."

"Haven't you been listening?"

"No."

Elizabeth, a promising grad student who'd be working at the lab next year, pulled out Rick's thermos of coffee. "We're talking about why we got into climatology. And it's your turn."

"Well, who went before me?"

The kids laughed. "You're first."

"Hell, no. Ask Jonah and his group to go first, and then

if we don't like it we can shut off the walkie-talkies, say it was a glitch."

"Uh, boss." Aja, who worked on the Mesoscale Predictability Experiment, held up her two-way radio. "They're already on."

There was a lot of grumbling from the truck in front of them. Rick made the "gimme" motion to Aja and she handed him the walkie-talkie. "All you have to do is be interesting. It's not too much to ask."

"Then you go first," came a voice he didn't immediately recog— No, it was hipster James, with his weird goatee and too-short tight pants.

"Fine," Rick said, speaking into the stupid device. For all he knew, this was all going to be recorded. "Okay, when I was just a year old and first learning to talk—"

Elizabeth snatched the walkie-talkie out of his hand. "Okay, Dr. Sinclair, if you don't want to tell us, fine. We'd rather hear about your girlfriend, anyway."

"My what?"

"The beautiful Jenna."

"What the hell?" Rick shook his head. "I thought this was supposed to be about how we came to climatology."

"Well, now it's about you and Jenna," Aja said. "Much more interesting."

He sighed. There wasn't one person in either vehicle that had less than a 4.0 GPA, and this was what they wanted to hear. "You're all fired. Each one of you. When we get back, you can collect your last paycheck."

"Fine," Elizabeth said. "Tell us about when you were learning to talk."

"It's a mind-boggling story. Which I'm certainly not going to tell now. You guys ruined it."

"But she is pretty," Aja said. "I saw her in the break room."

He couldn't hold back his smile. "Yes, she's a beauty. Smart as hell. Funny. Teaches English. Makes the best lasagna I've ever had." He played with his cell phone, waiting to hear the ding of her reply. "She's great. In every way but one."

"Well," Elizabeth said. "You can't just stop there."

He thought about doing just that, but what the hell. "She lives in Boston, And as you very nosy students know, I live here in Oklahoma."

"Oh. Bummer."

Rick had no idea who said that, but… "Yeah," he said. "Bummer."

JENNA WAS PACKED and nervous. She'd checked her luggage four times so far. Cleaned the kitchen, the bedroom and part of the bathroom. There were boxes that needed unpacking but after yesterday's misunderstanding, she decided to leave them alone.

The Topeka tornadoes were on the news already. The regular news. She was watching The Weather Channel of course, but they kept talking about the goddamn weather of the world when all she cared about was Topeka. Two smaller funnels had touched ground, but then had been swallowed by the monster in the middle, which was tearing a path through Kansas.

She sat and watched, playing a vicious game of "Where's Rick?" but she couldn't spot him anywhere. The camera people were keeping their distance, and the regular news stations kept going back to radar screens, which showed the data Rick cared about. Why hadn't she asked him more questions? Like what he actually did when he caught a tornado?

They hadn't finished the wine from last night, but she was getting close to the end of it now. Her plane didn't leave until midnight, it wasn't a full flight and the taxi wouldn't be at Rick's until 10:15 p.m.

She muted the TV, grabbed her cell phone and hit speed

dial. Ally picked up instantly. "I was beginning to think we needed to send out a search party. You've only texted twice this whole week."

"I'm sorry. Every minute that I had free I was working on lesson plans and those worksheets from hell."

Ally moaned. "Don't talk to me about those if you have any sense of self-preservation."

"Oh," she said, glued to the TV, peering into yet another shot of a huge funnel cloud only to realize she'd seen that shot before. "Tonight proves beyond a shadow of a doubt that I don't. I'm going out of my mind with worry."

"What? Why?"

"There's a tornado in Topeka. A big one. They're expecting it to be a family of tornadoes, actually, with multiple vortices. Or maybe not. That's a bunch of separate tornadoes following in quick succession. Either way, hugely dangerous. And Rick is right in the middle of it."

"Holy crap. I was just listening to that on the news. I figured you guys were too far away."

"He left at four this morning. You know how I get about this stuff. I couldn't stand it when Payton had to fly to Florida. But he was just traveling and Rick is there to collect data. I could save him the hassle and tell him the important data right now—it's a huge, crazy tornado and he could die."

"Jenna? Hun? Take a deep breath, okay?

She did. Two deep breaths. "All right," Jenna said. "That helped. It did. But frankly, a full bottle of wine and a few Xanax would help more. Sadly, I only have a little wine, and I can't even get drunk because that would be a fun plane ride home in the same sky as a family of tornadoes."

"Wait a minute. The same sky? Not kidding here—are you sure you shouldn't postpone?"

"No, I was exaggerating. Again. Because I turn into a ridiculous child when someone I care about is spitting in the eye of a damn tornado. As if my freaking out accomplishes anything except to make everyone around me anxious. I'm going to call Rick's friend at the Weather Center. He'll tell me if it's safe or not.

"But really, I'm not worried about me. It's just that I haven't heard from Rick. I have no idea how long tornadoes last. Or what he has to do when he gets there. He texted me a lot on the drive. Then he warned me that he'd be swamped. I thought that meant he'd cut back, but he hasn't texted in hours."

"Jenna, call his friend. I can hear your breathing, and if you don't slow down you're going to hyperventilate."

Jenna closed her eyes and focused all her attention on Ally's voice. The instructions were so clear even an overstimulated idiot like herself could understand them. Except now she could see that picture of Rick in his office. Good God, she couldn't think about it. Or let the panic overtake her.

"You got that, sweetie?"

Jenna nodded, really trying to act like a grown-up even if she didn't feel like one. "Yes. I do. Thank you." She wouldn't talk about or think about the picture.

"He's going to be fine."

"Is he?" Jenna asked. "You know, storm chasers aren't invulnerable. They can die. It doesn't matter that they practice safety, that the work they do is incredibly important. I know it doesn't do me any good to think like this, but… you know what? I need to call the guy he works with."

"Okay. Then sip the wine, my friend. Call me. Breathe, breathe, breathe. I'll be here, and I won't give a damn what the time is. If you need me, call."

"I promise. I will."

"Good," Ally said. "Can I ask you something, though? Not storm-related?"

"Of course."

"How has it been? With you two? Your texts left a lot to be desired."

"It's been wonderful. He's wonderful. I enjoy him so much, Ally, I can't tell you. But it's been horrible, too."

"What do you mean? Jenna?"

"It's touched down." Jenna stood up, her heart pounding like mad as she watched streets being ripped up and houses being torn apart. "I have to go. But just so you know, you were right."

"About?"

"I'm in love with him. It's… He's the one for me. I know it, I feel it. I love him. The man who chases danger like I go to the library. And this? Watching. Waiting to see if he's alive? I can't. I'm not that kind of person."

"Let's get through tonight. I'm not turning off my phone."

"Thank you." Jenna hung up and called Antwan's direct line.

He picked up quickly. "You watching this?"

"Yes, I'm watching, and I'm terrified. Where is he? Have you heard from him? I'm going crazy here. It's been hours since he last texted me. I'm supposed to be going home on the red-eye tonight, but I can't if he's still in the middle of this—"

"Whoa, whoa, hold up. He's fine. Busy as hell, but fine. Do you have an Android or an iPhone?"

"Yes."

"Good, download the scanner radio weather app. You'll actually hear him. He's broadcasting live. I don't know why he didn't tell you. Just don't forget that tornadoes are louder than you can possibly imagine, so don't let the noise upset you. If you still need me, I'll be here long after the tornadoes are gone."

"Thank you. I'll go get that app. Oh, but I'm supposed to fly to Boston at midnight. Safe? Not safe?"

"Hold on two seconds."

She was shaking she wanted to download that app so badly. And why bother asking about flying tonight? She wasn't going anywhere. Not until she saw Rick, in the flesh, for herself, and counted all of his fingers and toes.

"Safe as houses," Antwan said. She didn't miss the irony. "Don't worry. He'll be fine, you'll be fine."

"Thank you," she said, even though too many people were so sure things would be fine, they made her more afraid than she had been.

Once she was disconnected from Antwan, she found the app. With shaking fingers, she somehow managed to get it working and then…

Rick's voice.

Yelling at the top of his lungs. Thank goodness Antwan had reminded her of the noise, because it was the stuff of nightmares. But Rick was shouting above it all, so he was okay. For now.

She poured the last of the wine, parked herself once more on the couch, where she could watch his gigantic television, and listened to the sound of his voice.

Her heart began to settle back to non-heart-attack levels, and she honestly couldn't tell if his words were garbled or if she just didn't understand what he was saying. Either way, it was okay.

Until it wasn't.

"Get the hell in the truck. Now, now, now! We are pulling out, people. Leave that, it's fine, just g—"

She waited for him to come back online. Checked that the app was still working.

It was.

She bent over and put her head between her knees.

18

JENNA SWEPT HER gaze over the twenty kids eating their lunches before they toured the Salem Witch Museum. Most of them were great kids who earned the trip with their grades, but there were four really bright students who were more interested in anarchy than history. At least according to Sylvia, the teacher whom Jenna was helping out on this field trip.

But everything was calm at the common across the street from the museum. Everyone, including the two volunteer parent chaperones, was eating from their boxed lunches while Sylvia had run to the office to check on the time for the guided tour.

Jenna wasn't hungry. In the three weeks since her Oklahoma trip, she and Rick weren't speaking as often as they had before spring break. There were valid reasons for the change in routine. Rick hadn't needed to explain. She'd been watching The Weather Channel compulsively and seen for herself the extreme weather events that were stacked like dominoes. At least three of them were in Rick's territory, so of course, those were the ones she listened to, using her weather app. He'd always come home safely, but during the events she'd been a wreck.

And her last night in Oklahoma, when she'd completely freaked out while waiting to hear from him? He'd been nothing but understanding and suggested strongly that she take the app off her phone.

She didn't think it was possible for someone like him to really understand the bone-chilling terror of knowing someone they loved had willingly run into danger, and he didn't need to know. He'd been running after storms since he was fourteen. Nothing she said was going to change him.

But that Topeka tornado had put up a wall between them. She hated that they didn't talk every day. Hell, they barely spoke twice a week. They still texted, though, but it wasn't the same.

She missed him like crazy.

Four months was a long run when she considered the two of them were as different as black and white. The way they'd met. That damn apartment. Her foolish heart.

Truth was, she needed to step off this speeding train wreck. Let it go. Let him go. God, she was trying, but first, she had to stop thinking about him so much. Everything reminded her of Rick.

"Ms. Delaney?"

"Yes." She turned to find one of the ninth graders—Toni—putting her empty box into one of the bins.

"Are we going to have time to go to the shop in the museum? They have these really cute earrings."

"No, sorry, Toni. No shopping today."

"But—"

Jenna's phone rang. She saw who it was and her pulse quickened. "Can we talk about this in a few minutes?"

Toni nodded, but she wasn't happy.

Jenna did a quick check of her student charges, all accounted for, and then answered. "Hi."

"Hey," Rick said, just as his invitation to join him on FaceTime came through.

She couldn't swallow. This was a first since spring break. She pressed Yes, of course, making sure no one was too close as she sat on the far end of the gazebo.

"What's going on?" she asked, noting he looked tired. No wonder. He was probably eating terribly, not getting enough sleep. Although she had no room to call the kettle black.

"I was hoping you'd be home tonight."

Using every lesson she'd learned when facing irrational, horrible parents, she let her expression remain neutral. Let her smile look real. "What's up?"

"Just watching *The Godfather* on Cinemax. No commercials. I thought we could watch it. Together."

They'd done that once before with *The Cabin in the Woods*, right after Chicago. It had been a ball. She almost told him yes before she remembered. "Oh, no. I won't be home tonight. I've got this dinner thing."

His expression changed, and she understood right away what he was thinking. She could admit she had plans with Ally, but that wouldn't help her step back. Step away.

"Anyone I know?"

"A friend of a friend. So, I noticed you have a window of downtime before that arctic front comes down."

"Listen to you," he said. "I never imagined you being a weather junkie."

"Believe me. I didn't, either."

His pause was heavy, and even though she wanted to fill the space with chatter, she didn't. "Anyway," he said finally, and she could tell he was trying to sound chipper and failing badly. "I'll call you another time."

"That'd be great." She smiled at him, and that was when she had to hold back a sob, blink back tears. Stop herself from telling him she was more confused than she'd ever been in her whole life. How much she missed him.

Of course, he'd already disconnected. She wanted to call him right back—

"Ms. Delaney?"

Sitting up straight, Jenna tried to look normal. "I'm

sorry, Toni, but we don't have time to shop. We have the tour in a few minutes."

"Yeah, I wasn't… I was just looking for Shoshanna. Did she go to the bathroom?"

Jenna had no idea. She'd been so focused on her own problems she hadn't looked up once. "Did you ask Mrs. Wagner?"

"She told me to ask you."

Oh, God, that was right. Sylvia had run to the office. She'd left Jenna in charge.

Jenna stood and glanced around. "Did you check the bathroom?"

"No, but I can."

"Wait. I'll go. Stay with Mrs. Wagner and the rest of the group." Jenna felt sick. She just might end up needing the bathroom herself.

If Shoshanna, one of the most clever of the anarchists, had disappeared, it was all Jenna's fault. And God only knew where the girl was. Last time she'd pulled a stunt like this, she was caught smoking with a tattooed biker.

A hot fist twisted inside her chest. Jenna could hardly take a breath. Shoshanna could be hurt, could have run off with a stranger and put herself in terrible danger. It wasn't likely, but if she had, it would be Jenna's fault.

What was the matter with her? She'd never done anything like this before. Never shirked her duty, never let her students out of her sight. And for what? To feel this horror every time he went out after a storm?

Damn it, why had she let things go so far? She'd been delusional. From day two, she'd known Rick was not for her. He blew wherever the wind would take him. Literally. And what, was she supposed to pretend he wasn't risking his life? That she would never know if he'd come home at all?

No.

Thankfully, she spotted Shoshanna coming from the museum. Jenna could breathe again. Think more clearly. Yes, Rick had been slowly pulling away. He'd probably seen this thing between them had gone too far. It didn't matter that he'd woken up first. Now it was her turn to let go.

RICK TORE THE tape off the box in one furious pull, then rolled it into a ball and threw it at the goddamn television set. *The Godfather* was one of his favorite films, and right now, he couldn't bear it. He found the remote and shut it off, not even tempted to turn on The Weather Channel. This whole night could have been great, but no, Jenna was out with a "friend of a friend." He'd have to be a moron to mistake that for anything but a date.

He'd already unpacked everything in his bedroom. His drawers were full, so was the closet. The kettlebells were back in the spare room, where they belonged.

Now he was working his way through the living room. He had one pile going for donations, one pile for trash and the rest had to be put away before he went to bed. Or, at this rate, before he went to bed tomorrow night.

The box he'd just stripped open was full of bathroom things, and the moment he saw the gift-wrapped boxes inside, his heart sank.

Goddamn it.

Hermès body wash. Guerlain body milk. Bond No. 9 shower gel.

He'd ordered those before they'd left the smart apartment. And he'd forgotten all about them. It had been so busy—

Bullshit. He didn't slow down because that was what he did. Worked. Thought about work. Worked some more. Never slowing down. Just pushing, racing, chasing the rush.

She would have been so jazzed to see that body milk in his shower. But he hadn't slowed down. No, that wasn't quite true. He'd been calm with Jenna. Patient. Not something that happened very often. Yet he still hadn't remembered the gifts he'd bought her even as he'd made her feel bad for doing the same thing.

He'd bought them because she'd loved them. And he wanted her to remember that time they had together. He'd had them wrapped because he'd wanted to see the look on her face when she opened them.

She deserved so much more.

The rest of the stuff in the box was all junk. Half-finished shampoo, bar soaps he'd never opened, a cologne that he'd liked, but rarely used. The only things he gave a damn about were the things that made him think of Jenna. He put those on the coffee table, and then took the box out to the big Dumpsters near the garage. It made a satisfying crash when it landed.

Before he got all the way inside, the doorbell rang. He wasn't expecting anyone.

Antwan was on his doorstep, a six pack of Killian's Irish Red in hand. "Are you going to let me in anytime soon?"

Rick stepped back. "So you couldn't be bothered to help me pack, but now you want to help unpack?"

"No, not here to work. Jesus, man, you've got two and a half months left on your lease, and now you're unpacking?"

"Yeah, well, I'm trying to— You know what? I don't have to explain myself to you. Is that beer cold, or do you want one from the fridge?"

"Colder the better." Antwan handed him the six-pack. "And you'd better start explaining yourself to me. You've been an asshole for days. You left early because of what Walt said, and you never give a damn about anything that *bagga* mouth has to say. I know it's because of Jenna, and I'm betting you've done something stupid."

"Stupid?" He popped the top on Antwan's beer and put it on the counter. "I'm not. I'm doing the right thing for once. It just sucks, that's all."

"Explain to me what the right thing is."

"Letting her get on with her life. The life she deserves with someone who isn't me."

"You do know she likes you, yes? A lot?"

"That's not good enough. I told you who she wants. A suit. Who works five days a week, and isn't called in the middle of the night to go chasing tornadoes. And I'm still pissed as hell that you told her about that weather-scan app. She didn't need to know it existed."

"Why not? It's your job."

"It scared her."

Antwan was walking down the line of boxes, reading the contents' lists. "That makes sense. It's dangerous work. Why wouldn't she be scared?"

"Stop it. You know as well as I do that she would never be happy with me. And I'd be so worried about her, I'd probably end up getting myself killed. It was easy with Faith. She didn't make a big deal out of the storm chasing."

Antwan smiled, and if it wasn't the most condescending smile in the world, it was close. "Faith didn't love you."

"Neither does Jenna."

"Oh?"

"Come on, Antwan. Don't. I like her too much to play games now. She's never been shy about what she's looking for in a husband, and I don't cut it."

"A husband? That's very optimistic."

"Does optimistic mean something else in Jamaica? I just said, I'm not—"

"I heard what you said. Now hear me. I saw exactly what Jenna wants every time she looked at you. She thought she wanted that other man. The one who kissed Faith. But that didn't turn out the way she planned. So maybe what she thinks she wants isn't what she needs."

"What the hell are you talking about? She told me she wants someone who loves her. Who couldn't stop thinking about her. Who wouldn't shut up about her."

"Is that all?"

"No. She wants someone steady. Someone she can always count on. Who knows to run from the storms, not toward them."

Antwan nodded. "Right. Look, I don't know. I'm not married. I'm not good at my own relationships, but *bredda*, I can see with both eyes. Faith was a nice girl, but not for you. Jenna. She's for you, Rick."

"Yeah, well, she might be, but we'll never know. She's on a date right now with her perfect man."

Antwan laughed. "The stories you tell yourself are gold, my friend. Nothing to do with reality, but that's never stopped you."

"If you're going to help me unpack, great. If not? Go home."

Antwan put his half-finished beer on the counter, smiled and left.

Rick got back to work. He was glad that self-righteous dick he worked with had gone. Thought again about how he was doing the right thing by letting Jenna go. About ten minutes to midnight, it occurred to him that she'd be spitting mad at him for making decisions for her.

About ten minutes after midnight, he made one decision for himself. But it was one hell of a decision.

FOR THE FIRST time since she'd started teaching, Jenna was counting down the days for school to end. It was the end of April. Another three weeks to go before she could store her briefcase for a couple of months. And while it was still too soon to plant, she could start preparing for the garden.

She slid open the glass door and stepped out onto her balcony. Of course it immediately reminded her of Rick's town house and his little backyard, and that she hadn't heard from him in two days. Not even a text. She'd almost had to sit on her hands not to send one herself.

Staring down at the raised box, she realized she'd come out without her work gloves. She stooped down, anyway, and shoved her fingers through the soil. The dirt was cold and so was she. This wouldn't be the soothing experience she'd been hoping for.

Truth was, she was exhausted from her tangled thoughts. Every time she knew without a doubt she needed to break things off with Rick, she immediately knew without a doubt that she loved him and was willing to do whatever it took to make it work with him.

Back inside, she thought about cleaning out the fridge, but that wouldn't help get her mind off Rick.

Although, the pros were definitely ahead of the cons, and maybe if she wrote them down, it would help her see—

Her doorbell rang. Couldn't be Ally. She looked through the peephole. Blinked. Then looked through it again. With a pulse of about three thousand beats per second, she opened the door. The door in Boston, where she lived, far, far away from Norman, Oklahoma.

"Hey," Rick said.

He was in jeans and a T-shirt, wearing the leather jacket she liked so much, and of course, his Nikes. A carry-on bag was next to him.

"What are you doing here? Is Boston going to have a tornado?"

He grinned. Shook his head. "No, Boston's safe. I hope I'm not intruding, showing up like this. I would have called, but I was afraid I'd chicken out."

"Well, then, you'd better come in."

He picked up his case and walked inside, doing a full sweep of her tiny, boxlike apartment.

"Do you want something to eat? Or drink?"

"Not yet, but thanks."

"Want to sit down?" she asked, and she could hear the tremor in her voice. This could be monumentally bad. Or something else, but she'd better be prepared for monumentally bad.

"Sorry I didn't bring chocolates. I should have. Knowing how much you like them."

Jenna blinked again. Wondered if she should sit. Probably. Because she could barely breathe.

"First of all," he said, looking more uncomfortable than she'd ever seen him, "I wanted you to know that I finished unpacking. Every last box."

"Congratulations," she said, starting to think this might be a dream. A weird one at that.

"But I also want to tell you that I remember a lot of things you said. Like how you wanted someone who loved you. Who couldn't shut up about you. Who, damn it, what was the third—"

"Who couldn't stop thinking about me."

He grinned. "Yeah, that's the one. But you also want someone who's steady. Who you can count on."

"Rick, are you—"

"Please, wait. I need to get this out before… Anyway. You also wanted to have the upper hand. And you do. You really do. Because I love you so much. It's actually kind of scary. You remember when you asked how was I going to top being swept away by a tornado? The answer is you, Jenna."

"What?"

He took her hand and walked her over to her couch, where they both sat down. "I've been looking in the rearview mirror for twenty years. Watching that old tornado.

I don't want to anymore. Not when I can look ahead and see a future with you."

"But—"

"Nope, not done yet. That picture of me running from that EF 5? I don't keep it there because I'm proud of it. It embarrasses me that I was so stupid, but I keep it there as a reminder that I was really lucky. By all rights, I should have been killed by that monster. And I'm finally listening to my own advice.

"I can't promise I'll never go out chasing again, but the reason would have to be damn good. I've trained too many people to think I'm the only one who can storm-chase right. And I can't promise I won't get home late during the season, but I'll try not to. Because, damn it, Jenna. I love you. I can't stop thinking about you. I can't shut up about you."

Bewildered by his confession, and shaking from head to toe, she said, "My turn?"

He nodded, looking so scared that she had to let him know the truth right off. "I love you, too. And the man I fell in love with is a storm chaser, among other things. I can't ask you to give that up for me. I don't want you to resent me or anything. I'll bear it. I'll be scared to death, but you can't help who you love, and for me, that's you."

"Thank God," he said. "Not the part about me chasing storms. I want you much more than that. I— Shit. I mean, wait."

He hurried over to his carry-on and opened it up. He took two wrapped boxes from on top of his clothes and gave them to her.

Jenna unwrapped the first one. Guerlain body milk. The second one was the Hermès. "The smart apartment."

He nodded. "I changed my mind about *Ladyhawke*. It was totally a romance. Even with the magic at the end. We had ours in the beginning, that's all."

She pretty much climbed into his lap, she wanted to kiss him so much. He kissed her back, held her so tight, she'd never fall. He was almost right. Their magic wasn't *just* in the beginning.

* * * * *

Gage Ringer: Powerful, fierce, unforgettable...
and temporarily sidelined from his MMA career
with an injury. Back home, he has one month
to win over the woman he could never forget...

Read on for New York Times *bestselling author*
Lori Foster's

HARD KNOCKS

The stunning prequel novella for her Ultimate series!

HARD KNOCKS

Lori Foster

CHAPTER ONE

GAGE RINGER, better known as Savage in the fight world, prowled the interior of the rec center. His stride was long, his thoughts dark, but he kept his expression enigmatic to hide his turmoil from onlookers. He didn't want to be here tonight. He'd rather be home, suffering his bad mood alone instead of covering up his regret, forced to pretend it didn't matter. His disappointment was private, damn it, and he didn't want to advertise it to the world. Shit happened.

It had happened to him. So what?

Life went on. There would be other fights, other opportunities. Only a real wimp would sit around bellyaching about what could have been, but wasn't. Not him. Not publicly anyway.

Tonight the rec center would overflow with bodies of all shapes, sizes and ages—all there for different reasons.

Cannon Coulter owned the rec center. It was a part of Cannon's life, a philanthropic endeavor that, no matter how big Cannon got, how well-known he became in the Supreme Battle Championship fight world, would always be important to him.

Armie Jacobson, another fighter who helped run the rec center whenever Cannon had to travel for his career, had planned a long night of fun. Yay.

Not.

At least, not for Gage.

Earlier they'd had a party for the kids too young to stick around and watch the pay-per-view event that night on the big screen. One of Cannon's sponsors had contributed the massive wall-mounted TV to the center.

So that they wouldn't feel left out, Armie had organized fun activities for the younger kids that had included food, games and some one-on-one play with the fighters who frequented the rec center, using it as a gym.

With the kiddie party now wrapping up, the more mature crowd would soon arrive, mixing and mingling while watching the fights.

The rec center had originally opened with very little. Cannon and some of his friends had volunteered to work with at-risk youths from the neighborhood to give them an outlet. They started with a speed bag, a heavy bag, some mats and a whole lot of donated time and energy.

But as Cannon's success had grown, so too had the rec center. Not only had Cannon added improvements, but his sponsors loved to donate anything and everything that carried their brand so that now the size of the place had doubled, and they had all the equipment they needed to accommodate not only a training camp for skilled fighters, but also dozens of boys, and a smattering of girls, of all ages.

Gage heard a distinctly female laugh and his gaze automatically went to Harper Gates.

So she had arrived.

Without meaning to, he inhaled more deeply, drawing in a calming breath. Yeah, Harper did that to him.

He watched as Harper assisted Armie in opening up folding chairs around the mats. Together they filled up every available speck of floor space. She stepped around a few of the youths who were still underfoot, racing around, wrestling—basically letting off steam with adult supervision, which beat the hell out of them hanging on street corners, susceptible to the thugs who crawled out of the shadows as the sun went down.

Gage caught one boy as he recklessly raced past. He twirled him into the air, then held him upside down. The kid squealed with laughter, making Gage smile, too.

"You're moving awfully fast," Gage told him.

Bragging, the boy said, "I'm the fastest one here!"

"And humble, too," he teased.

The boy blinked big owl eyes at him while grinning, showing two missing teeth. He was six years old, rambunctious and considered the rec center a second home.

"I need you to take it easy, okay? If you're going to roughhouse, keep it on the mats."

"'Kay, Savage."

Gage glanced at a clock on the wall. The younger crowd would be heading out in a few more minutes. Still holding the boy suspended, he asked, "Who's taking you home?"

"My gram is comin' in her van and takin' all of us."

"Good." Luckily the grandmother was reliable, because the parents sure as hell weren't. And no way did Gage want the boys walking home. The rec center was in a decent enough area, but where the boys lived…

The kid laughed as Gage flipped him around and put him back on his feet.

Like a shot, he took off toward Miles, who was already surrounded by boys as he rounded them up.

Grandma would arrive soon. She'd probably appreciate how the kids had been exercised in the guise of play, schooled on control and manners, and fed. The boys always ate like they were starving. But then, Gage remembered being that age and how he could pack it away.

Briefly, his gaze met Harper's, and damn it, he felt it, that charged connection that had always existed between them. She wore a silly smile that, despite his dark mood, made him want to smile, too.

But as they looked at each other, she deliberately wiped

the smile away. Pretending she hadn't seen him at all, she got back to work.

Gage grunted. He had no idea what had gotten into her, but in his current frame of mind, better that he just let it go for now.

Very shortly, the most dedicated fight fans would arrive to catch the prelims. By the time the main card started, drawing a few high school seniors, some interested neighbors and the other fighters, there'd be bodies in all the chairs, sprawled on the mats and leaning up against the concrete walls. Equipment had been either moved out of the way or stored for the night.

This was a big deal. One of their own was competing tonight.

The high school guys were looking forward to a special night where they'd get to mingle more with their favorite fighters.

A dozen or more women were anxious to do some mingling of their own.

Armie, the twisted hedonist, had been judicious in handing out the invites: some very hot babes would be in attendance, women who'd already proven their "devotion" to fighters.

Gage couldn't have cared less. If he hadn't been fucked by karma, he'd be there in Japan, too. He didn't feel like celebrating, damn it. He didn't want to expose anyone to his nasty disposition.

The very last thing he wanted was a female groupie invading his space.

Actually, he'd been so caught up in training, he'd been away from female company for some time now. You'd think he'd be anxious to let off steam in the best way known to man.

But whenever he thought of sex…

Harper laughed again, and Gage set his back teeth even

while sneaking a peek to see what she found so funny. Armie said something to her, and she swatted at him while smiling widely.

Gage did a little more teeth grinding.

Like most of the fighters, Armie understood Gage's preoccupation and ignored him. Now if he would just ignore Harper, too, Gage could get back to brooding.

Instead, he was busy thinking of female company—but there was only one woman who crowded his brain.

And for some reason, she seemed irritated with him.

His dark scowl made the stitches above his eye pull and pinch, drawing his thoughts from one problem and back to another.

One stupid mistake, one botched move during practice, and he had an injury that got him kicked out of the competition.

Damn it all, he didn't want to be here tonight, but if he hadn't shown up, he'd have looked sad and pathetic.

"Stop pacing," Harper said from right behind him. "It makes you look sad and pathetic."

Hearing his concern thrown right back at him, Gage's left eye twitched. Leave it to Harper to know his exact thoughts and to use them as provocation. But then, he had to admit, she provoked him so well....

He'd missed the fights. And he'd missed Harper.

The only upside to heading home had been getting to see her. But since his return three days ago, she'd given him his space—space he wanted, damn it, just maybe not from her. At the very least, she could have *wanted* to see him, instead of treating him like one of the guys.

Relishing a new focus, Gage paused, planning what he'd say to her.

She didn't give him a chance to say anything.

With a hard whop to his ass, she walked on by and sashayed down the hall to the back.

Gage stood there, the sting of her swat ramping up his temper…and something else. Staring after her, he suffered the sizzling clench of emotions that always surfaced whenever Harper got close—which, since he'd returned home with his injury, had been rare.

He'd known her for years—grown up with her, in fact—and had always enjoyed her. Her wit. Her conversation. Her knowledge of mixed martial arts competition.

Her cute bod.

They'd recently taken their friendship to the next level, dating, spending more private time together. He'd enjoyed the closeness…

But he'd yet to enjoy her naked.

Time and circumstances had conspired against him on that one. Just when things had been heating up with Harper, just when it seemed she was ready to say "yes" instead of "not yet," he'd been offered the fight on the main card in Japan. He'd fought with the SBC before. He wasn't a newbie.

But always in the prelims, never on the highly publicized, more important main card. Never with such an anticipated event.

In a whirlwind, he'd gone off to a different camp to train with Cannon, getting swept up in the publicity and interviews that went with a main card bout…

Until, just a few lousy days ago—*so fucking close*—he'd miscalculated in practice and sustained a deep cut from his sparring partner's elbow.

A cut very near his eye that required fifteen stitches.

It made him sick to think of how quickly he'd been pronounced medically ineligible. Before he'd even caught his breath the SBC had picked his replacement.

That lucky bastard was now in Japan, ready to compete.

And Gage was left in Ohio. Instead of fighting for

recognition, he fought his demons—*and got tweaked by Harper.*

He went after her, calling down the empty hallway, "I am not pathetic."

From inside a storage room, he heard her loud "Ha!" of disagreement.

Needing a target for his turbulent emotions and deciding Harper was perfect—in every way—he strode into the room.

And promptly froze.

Bent at the waist, Harper had her sexy ass in the air while she pulled disposable cups off the bottom shelf.

His heart skipped a beat. Damn, she was so hot. Except for bad timing, he'd be more familiar with that particular, *very perfect* part of her anatomy.

Not sleeping with her was yet another missed opportunity, one that plagued him more now that he didn't have the draining distraction of an upcoming fight. His heart started punching a little too hard. Anger at his circumstances began to morph into red-hot lust as he considered the possibilities.

But then, whenever he thought of Harper, lust was the least confusing of his emotions.

Now that he was home, he'd hoped to pick up where they'd left off. Only Harper had antagonism mixed with her other more welcoming signals, so he had to proceed with caution.

"What are you doing?" he asked, because that sounded better than saying, *"Damn, girl, I love your ass."*

Still in that tantalizing position, she peeked back at him, her brown hair swinging around her face, her enormous blue eyes direct. With her head down that way, blood rushed to her face and made her freckles more noticeable.

There were nights he couldn't sleep for wondering about

all the places she might have freckles. Many times he'd imagined stripping those clothes off her, piece by piece, so he could investigate all her more secret places.

Like him, she was a conservative dresser. Despite working at a secondhand boutique clothing store she always looked casual and comfortable. Her jeans and T-shirts gave an overview of sweet curves, but he'd love to get lost in the details if he could ever get her naked.

She straightened with two big boxes in her hands. "Armie had small juice containers out for the kids, but of course adults are going to want something different to drink. Same with the snacks. So I'm changing up the food spread."

Due to her schedule at the boutique, Harper had been unable to attend the party with the youngsters, but she'd sent in snacks ahead of time. She had a knack for creating healthy treats that looked fun and got gobbled up. Some of the options had looked really tasty, but if she wanted to switch them out, he could at least help her.

She glanced at the slim watch on her wrist. "Lots to do before everyone shows up for the prelims."

Since pride kept him at the rec center anyway…

"What can I do to help?"

Her smile came slow and teasing. "All kinds of things, actually. Or—wait—do you mean with the setup?"

"I… What?" Was that a come-on? He couldn't tell for sure—nothing new with Harper. Clearly she'd been pissed at him about something, but now, at her provocative words, his dick perked up with hopes of reconciliation.

Snickering, she walked up to him, gave him a hip bump, then headed out of the room. "Come on, big boy. You can give me a hand with the folding tables."

As confusion warred with disgruntlement, he trailed after her. "All right, fine." Then he thought to remind her, "But I'm not pathetic."

Turning to face him, she walked backward. "Hit home with that one, did I?"

"No." *Yes.*

"I can help you to fake it if you want."

Despite the offhand way she tossed that out, it still sounded suggestive as hell. "Watch where you're going." Gage reached out, caught her arm and kept her from tripping over the edge of a mat.

Now that he had ahold of her, he decided to hang on. Where his fingers wrapped around her arm just above her elbow, she was soft and sleek and he couldn't stop his thumb from playing over the warm silk of her skin.

"Thanks," she said a little breathlessly, facing forward again and treading on.

"So." Though he walked right beside her, Gage couldn't resist leaning back a bit to watch the sway of her behind. "How would we fake it? Not that I need to fake shit, but you've got me curious."

Laughing, she leaned into him, smiled up at him, and damn it, he wanted her. *Bad.*

Always had, probably always would.

He'd had his chance before he left for the new camp. Even with the demands of training, he'd wanted her while he was away. Now he was back and the wanting boiled over.

Her head perfectly reached his shoulder. He stood six-three, nine inches taller than her, and he outweighed her by more than a hundred pounds.

But for a slim woman, she packed one hell of a punch. "Harper," he chided. She was the only person he knew who seemed to take maniacal delight in tormenting him.

Rolling her eyes, she said, "You are such a grouch when you're being pathetic." She stepped away to arrange the cups on a long table placed up against the wall. "Everyone feels terrible for you. And why not? We all know you'd have won. Maybe even with a first-round knockout."

Did she really believe that? Or was she just placating him? "Darvey isn't a slouch." Gage wouldn't want an easy fight. What the hell would that prove?

"No," she agreed, "but you'd have creamed him."

"That was the plan." So many times he'd played it out in his head, the strategy he'd use, how he'd push the fight, how his cardio would carry him through if it went all three rounds. Darvey wasn't known for his gas tank. He liked to use submissions, manipulating an arm or leg joint to get his opponent to tap before something broke. His plan was always to end things fast. But Gage knew how to defend against submissions, how to make it *his* fight, not anyone else's.

"Sucks that you have to sit this one out," Harper continued. "But since you do, I know you'd rather be brimming with confidence, instead of moping around like a sad sack."

Folding his arms over his chest, he glared down at her. "I don't mope."

She eyed his biceps, inhaled slowly, blew the breath out even slower.

"Harper."

Brows raised, she brought those big blue eyes up to focus on his face. "What?"

He dropped his arms and stepped closer, crowding her, getting near enough to breathe in her unique scent. "How do you figure we'd fake things?"

"Oh, yeah." She glanced to one side, then the other. "People are looking at us."

"Yeah?" Currently the only people in the gym were the guys helping to set it up for the party. Armie, Stack, Denver, a few others. "So?"

"So..." She licked her lips, hesitated only a second, then

came up against him. In a slow tease, her hands crawled up and over his chest. Fitted against him, she went on tiptoe, giving him a full-body rub.

Without even thinking about it, Gage caught her waist, keeping her right there. Confusion at this abrupt turnaround of hers stopped him from doing what came naturally.

Didn't bother her, though.

With her gaze locked on his, she curled her hands around his neck, drew him down to meet her halfway and put that soft, lush, taunting mouth against his.

Hell, yeah.

Her lips played over his, teasing, again provoking. They shared breath. Her thighs shifted against his. Her cool fingers moved over his nape and then into his hair. The kiss stayed light, slow and excruciating.

Until he took over.

Tilting his head, he fit his mouth more firmly against her, nudged her lips apart, licked in, deeper, hotter…

"Get a room already."

Gasping at the interruption, Harper pulled away. Embarrassed, she pressed her face against his chest before rearing back and glaring at Armie.

Gage just watched her. He didn't care what his dipshit friends said.

But he'd love to know what Harper was up to.

"Don't give me that look," Armie told her. "We have high school boys coming over tonight."

"The biggest kids are already here!"

"Now, I know you don't mean me," Armie continued, always up for ribbing her. "You're the one having a tantrum."

Gage stood there while they fussed at each other. Harper was like that with all the guys. She helped out, gave as good as she got, and treated them all like pesky brothers that she both adored and endured.

Except for Gage.

From the get-go she'd been different with him. Not shy, because seriously, Harper didn't have a shy bone in her hot little body. But maybe more demonstrative. Or rather, demonstrative in a different way.

He didn't think she'd smack any of the other fighters on the ass.

But he wasn't stupid. Encouraged or not, he knew guys were guys, period. They'd tease her, respect her boundaries, but every damn one of them had probably thought about sleeping with her.

For damn sure, they'd all pictured her naked.

Those vivid visuals were part of a man's basic DNA. Attractive babe equaled fantasies. While Harper hustled around the rec center helping out in a dozen different ways, she'd probably been mentally stripped a million times.

Hell, even while she sniped back and forth with Armie, Gage pictured her buck-ass, wondering how it'd feel to kiss her like that again, but without the barrier of clothes in the way.

"You need a swift kick to your butt," Harper declared.

"From you?" Armie laughed.

Fighting a smile, she said, "Don't think I won't."

"You wanna go?" Armie egged her on, using his fingertips to call her forward. "C'mon then, little girl. Let's see what you've got."

For a second there, Harper looked ready to accept, so Gage interceded. "Children, play nice."

"Armie doesn't like *nice*." She curled her lip in a taunt. "He likes *kinky*."

In reply, Armie took a bow.

True enough, if ever a man liked a little freak thrown

into the mix, it was Armie. He'd once been dropped off by a motorcycle-driving chick dressed in leather pants and a low-cut vest, her arms circled with snake tattoos. She'd sported more piercings than Gage could count—a dozen or so in her ears, a few in her eyebrows, lip, nose. The whole day, Armie had limped around as if the woman had ridden him raw. He'd also smiled a lot, proof that whatever had happened, he'd enjoyed himself.

Unlike Gage, Armie saw no reason to skip sex, ever. Not even prior to a fight. The only women he turned down were the ones, as Harper had said, that were too nice.

"Come on." She took Gage's hand and started dragging him toward the back.

"Hey, don't leave my storage closet smelling like sex," Armie called after them. "If you're going to knock boots, take it elsewhere!"

Harper flipped him the bird, but she was grinning. "He is so outrageous."

"That's the pot calling the kettle black." Just where was she leading him?

"Eh, maybe." She winked up at him. "But I just act outrageous. I have a feeling it's a mind-set for Armie."

Ignoring what Armie had said, she dragged him back into the storage closet—and shut the door.

Gage stood there watching her, thinking things he shouldn't and getting hard because of it. Heart beating slow and steady, he asked, "Now what?"

CHAPTER TWO

COULD A MAN look sexier? No. Dumb question. Harper sighed. At twenty-five, she knew what she wanted. Whether or not she could have it, that was the big question.

Or rather, could she have it for the long haul.

"Is that for me?" She nodded at the rise in his jeans.

Without changing expressions, Gage nodded. "Yeah." And then, "After that kiss, you have to ask?"

Sweet. "So you like my plan?"

Looking far too serious, his mellow brown gaze held hers. "If your plan is to turn me on, yeah, I like it."

As part of her plan, she forced a laugh. She had to keep Gage from knowing how badly he'd broken her heart.

Talk about pathetic.

Gage was two years older, which, while they'd been in school, had made him the older, awesome star athlete and popular guy that *every* girl had wanted. Her included.

Back then, she hadn't stood a chance. He'd dated prom queen, cheerleader, class president material, not collect-for-the-homeless Goody Two-shoes material.

So she'd wrapped herself in her pride and whenever they'd crossed paths, she'd treated him like any other jock—meaning she'd been nice but uninterested.

And damn him, he'd been A-OK with that, the big jerk.

They lived in the same small neighborhood. Not like Warfield, Ohio, left a lot of room for anonymity. Everyone knew everyone, especially those who went through school together.

It wasn't until they both started hanging out in the rec center, her to help out, him to train, that he seemed to really tune in to her. Course, she hadn't been real subtle with him, so not noticing her would have required a deliberate snub.

She was comfortable with guys. Actually, she was comfortable with everyone. Her best friend claimed she was one of those nauseatingly happy people who enjoyed life a little too much. But whatever. She believed in making the most of every day.

That is, when big, badass alpha fighters cooperated.

Unfortunately, Gage didn't. Not always.

Not that long ago they'd been dating, getting closer. Getting steamier.

She'd fallen a little more in love with him every day.

She adored his quiet confidence. His motivation and dedication. The gentle way he treated the little kids who hung out at the center, how he coached the older boys who revered him, and the respect he got—and gave—to other fighters.

She especially loved his big, rock-solid body. Just thinking about it made her all twitchy in private places.

Things had seemed to be progressing nicely.

Until the SBC called and put him on the main card for freaking other-side-of-the-world Japan, and boom, just like that, it seemed she'd lost all the ground she'd gained. Three months before the fight, Gage had packed up and moved to Harmony, Kentucky, to join Cannon in a different camp where he could hone his considerable skills with a fresh set of experienced fighters.

He'd kissed her goodbye first, but making any promises about what to expect on his return hadn't been on his mind. Nope. He'd been one big obsessed puppy, his thoughts only on fighting and winning.

Maybe he'd figured that once he won, his life would get too busy for her to fit into it.

And maybe, she reminded herself, she was jumping ahead at Mach speed. They hadn't even slept together yet.

But that was something she could remedy.

Never, not in a million years, would she have wished the injury on him. He'd fought, and won, for the SBC before. But never on the main card. Knowing what that big chance had meant to him, she'd been devastated on his behalf.

Yet she'd also still been hurt that the entire time he was gone, he hadn't called. For all she knew, he hadn't even thought about her. Ignoring him had seemed her best bet—until she realized she couldn't. Loving him made that impossible.

And so she decided not to waste an opportunity.

Gage leaned against the wall. "I give up. How long are you going to stand there staring at me?"

"I like looking at you, that's all." She turned her back on him before she blew the game too soon. "You're terrific eye candy."

He went so silent, she could hear the ticking of the wall clock. "What are you up to, Harper?"

"No good." She grinned back at him. "Definitely, one hundred percent no good." Locating napkins and paper plates on the shelf, she put them into an empty box. Searching more shelves, she asked, "Do you see the coffeemaker anywhere?"

His big hands settled on her waist. "Forget the coffeemaker," he murmured from right behind her. Leaning down, he kissed the side of her neck. "Let's talk about these no-good plans of yours."

Wow, oh, wow. She could feel his erection against her tush and it was so tantalizing she had to fight not to wiggle. "Okay."

He nuzzled against her, his soft breath in her ear, his hands sliding around to her belly. Such incredibly large hands that covered so much ground. The thumb of his right hand nudged the bottom of her breast. The pinkie on his left hovered just over the fly of her jeans.

Temptation was a terrible thing, eating away at her common sense and obscuring the larger purpose.

He opened his mouth on her throat and she felt his tongue on her skin. When he took a soft, wet love bite, she forgot she had knees. Her legs just sort of went rubbery.

To keep her upright, he hugged her tighter and rested his chin on top of her head. "Tell me what we're doing, honey."

Took her a second to catch her breath. "You don't know?" She twisted to face him, one hand knotted in his shirt to hang on, just in case. "Because, seriously, Gage, you seemed to know exactly what you were doing."

His smile went lazy—and more relaxed than it had been since he'd found out he wouldn't fight. He slipped a hand into her hair, cupping the back of her head, rubbing a little. "I know I was making myself horny. I know you were liking it. I'm just not sure why we're doing this here and now."

"Oh." She dropped against him so she could suck in some air. "Yeah." Unfortunately, every breath filled her head with the hot scent of his powerful body. "Mmm, you are so delicious."

A strained laugh rumbled in his chest. "Harper."

"Right." To give herself some room to think, she stepped back from him. So that he'd know this wasn't just about sex, she admitted, "I care about you. You know that."

Those gorgeous brown eyes narrowed on her face. "Ditto."

That kicked her heart into such a fast rhythm, she almost gasped. *He cared about her.* "And I know you, Gage. Probably better than you think."

His smile softened, and he said all dark and sensuous-like, "Ditto again, honey."

Damn the man, even his murmurs made her hot and bothered. "Yeah, so…" Collecting her thoughts wasn't easy, not with a big hunk of sexiness right there in front of her, within reach, ready and waiting. "I know you're hammered over the lost opportunity."

"The opportunity to have sex with you?"

Her jaw loosened at his misunderstanding. "No, I meant…" Hoping sex was still an option, she cleared her throat. "I meant the fight."

"Yeah." He stared at her mouth. "That, too."

Had he somehow moved closer without her knowing it? Her back now rested against the shelving and Gage stood only an inch from touching her. "So…" she said again. "It's understandable that you'd be stomping around in a bad mood."

He chided her with a shake of his head. "I was not stomping."

"Close enough." Damn it, now she couldn't stop staring at his mouth. "But I know you want to blow it off like you're not that upset."

"I'm not *upset.*" He scoffed over her word choice. "I'm disappointed. A little pissed off." His feet touched hers. "I take it you have something in mind?"

She shifted without thinking about it, and suddenly he moved one foot between hers. His hard muscled thigh pressed at the apex of her legs and every thought she had, every bit of her concentration, went to where they touched.

Casual as you please, he braced a hand on the shelf beside her head.

Gage was so good at this, at stalking an opponent, at gaining the advantage before anyone realized his intent.

But she wasn't his opponent. Keeping that in mind, she gathered her thoughts, shored up her backbone and made a proposal. "I think we should fool around." Before he could reply to that one way or the other, she added, "Out there. Where they can all see." *And hopefully you'll like that enough to want to continue in private.*

He lifted one brow, the corner of his mouth quirking. "And you called Armie kinky."

Heat rushed into her face. "No, I don't mean anything really explicit." But that was a lie, so she amended, "Well, I mean, I do. But not with an audience."

Again his eyes narrowed—and his other hand lifted to the shelving. He effectively confined her, not that she wanted freedom. With him so close, she had to tip her head back to look up at him. Her heart tried to punch out of her chest, and the sweetest little ache coiled inside her.

"I'm with you so far," he whispered, and leaned down to kiss the corner of her mouth.

"I figured, you know…" How did he expect her to think while he did that? "We could act all cozy, like you had other things on your mind. Then no one would know how distressed you are over missing the fight."

"First off, I'm not acting." His forehead touched hers. "Second, I am *not* distressed. Stop making me sound so damned weak."

Not acting? What did that mean? She licked her lips—and he noticed. "I know you're not weak." Wasn't that her point? "So…you don't like my plan?"

"I like it fine." His mouth brushed her temple, his tongue touched the inside of her ear—*Wow, that curled her toes!*—then he nibbled his way along her jaw, under her chin. "Playing with you will make for a long night."

"Yes." A long night where she'd have a chance to show him how perfect they were for each other. And if he didn't see things the same as she did, they could still end up sharing a very special evening together. If she didn't have him forever, she'd at least have that memory to carry her through.

But before she settled for only a memory, she hoped to—

A sharp rap on the door made her jump.

Gage just groaned.

Through the closed door, Armie asked, "You two naked?"

Puffing up with resentment at the intrusion, Harper started around Gage.

Before she got far, he caught her. Softly, he said, "Don't encourage him," before walking to the door and opening it. "What do you want, Armie?"

"Refreshments for everyone." Armie peeked around him, ran his gaze over Harper, and frowned. "Damn, fully clothed. And here I was all geared up for a peep show."

Harper threw a roll of paper towels at him.

When Armie ducked, they went right past him and out into the hall.

Stack said, "Hey!"

And they all grinned.

Getting back to business, she finished filling the box with prepackaged cookies, chips and pretzels, then shoved it all into Armie's arms, making him stumble back a foot.

He just laughed at her, the jerk.

"Where did you hide the coffeemaker?" Harper asked, trying to sound normal instead of primed.

"I'll get it." Armie looked at each of them. "Plan to join us anytime soon?"

Unruffled by the interruption, Gage said, "Be right there."

"Not to be a spoilsport, but a group of the high school boys have arrived, so, seriously, you might want to put a lid on the hanky-panky for a bit."

"People are here already?" She'd thought she had an hour yet. "They're early."

Armie shrugged. "Everyone is excited to watch Cannon fight again." He clapped Gage on the shoulder. "Sucks you're not out there, man."

"Next time," Gage said easily with no inflection at all.

Harper couldn't help but glance at him with sympathy.

"If you insist on molesting him," Armie said, "better get on with it real quick."

She reached for him, but he ducked out laughing.

She watched Armie go down the hall.

Gage studied her. "You going to molest me, honey?"

Did he want her to? Because, seriously, she'd be willing. "Let's see how it goes."

His eyes widened a little over that.

She dragged out a case of cola. Gage shook off his surprise and took it from her, and together they headed back out.

A half hour later they had everything set up. The colas were in the cooler under ice, sandwiches had been cut and laid out. A variety of chips filled one entire table. More people arrived. The boys, ranging in ages from fifteen to eighteen, were hyped up, talking loudly and gobbling down the food in record time. The women spent their time sidling up to the guys.

The guys spent their time enjoying it.

"Is there more food in the back room?"

Harper smiled at Stack Hannigan, one of the few fighters who hadn't yet staked out a woman. "Yeah, but I can get it as soon as I finish tidying up here." Every ten minutes she needed to reorganize the food. Once the fights started, things would settle down, but until then it was pure chaos.

Stack tugged on a lock of her hair. "No worries, doll. Be right back." And off he went.

Harper watched him walk away, as always enjoying the show. Long-legged with a rangy stride, Stack looked impressive whether he was coming or going—as all of them did.

In some ways, the guys were all different.

Stack's blond hair was darker and straighter than Armie's. Denver's brown hair was so long he often contained it in a ponytail. Cannon's was pitch-black with a little curl on the ends.

She preferred Gage's trimmed brown hair, and she absolutely loved his golden-brown eyes.

All of the fighters were good-looking. Solid, muscular, capable. But where Stack, Armie and Cannon were light heavyweights, her Gage was a big boy, a shredded heavyweight with fists the size of hams. They were all friends, but with different fighting styles and different levels of expertise.

When Stack returned with another platter of food, he had two high school wrestlers beside him, talking a mile a minute. She loved seeing how the older boys emulated the fighters, learning discipline, self-control and confidence.

With the younger kids, it sometimes broke her heart to see how desperate they were for attention. And then when one or more of the guys made a kid feel special, her heart expanded so much it choked her.

"You're not on your period, are you?" Armie asked from beside her.

Using the back of her hand to quickly dash away a tear, Harper asked him, "What are you talking about?"

"You're all fired up one minute, hot and bothered the next, now standing here glassy-eyed." Leaning down to better see her, he searched her face and scowled. "What the hell, woman? Are you *crying?*"

She slugged him in the shoulder—which meant she hurt her hand more than she hurt him. Softly, because it wasn't a teasing subject, she said, "I was thinking how nice this is for the younger boys."

"Yeah." He tugged at his ear and his smile went crooked. "Makes me weepy sometimes, too."

Harper laughed at that. "You are so full of it."

He grinned with her, then leveled her by saying, "How come you're letting those other gals climb all over Gage?"

She jerked around so fast she threw herself off balance. Trapped by the reception desk, Gage stood there while two women fawned over him. Harper felt mean. More than mean. "What is he doing now?"

"Greeting people, that's all. Not that the ladies aren't giving it the old college try." He leaned closer, his voice low. "I approve of your methods, by the way."

"Meaning what?"

"Guys have to man up and all that. Be tough. But I know he'd rather be in the arena than here with us."

Than here—with her. She sighed.

Armie tweaked her chin. "Don't be like that."

"Like what?"

"All 'poor little me, I'm not a priority.' You're smarter than that, Harper. You know he's worked years for this."

She did know it, and that's why it hurt so much. If it wasn't so important to him, she might stand a chance.

"Oh, gawd," Armie drawled, managing to look both disgusted and mocking. "You're deeper down in the dumps than he is." He tipped up her chin. "You know, it took a hell of a lot of discipline for him to walk away from everyone, including you, so he could train with another camp."

She gave him a droll look rife with skepticism.

Armie wasn't finished. "It's not like he said goodbye to you and then indulged any other women. Nope. It was celibacy all the way."

"That's a myth." She knew because she'd looked it up. "Guys do not have to do without in order to compete."

"Without sex, no. Without distractions, yeah. And you, Harper Gates, are one hell of a distraction."

Was she? She just couldn't tell.

Armie leaned in closer, keeping his voice low. "The thing is, if you were serving it up regular-like, it'd probably be okay."

She shoved him. "Armie!" Her face went hot. Did everyone know her damn business? Had Gage talked? Complained?

Holding up his hands in surrender, Armie said, "It's true. Sex, especially good sex with someone important, works wonders for clearing the mind of turmoil. But when the lady is holding out—"

She locked her jaw. "Just where did you get this info?"

That made him laugh. "No one told me, if that's what you're thinking. Anyone with eyes can see that you two haven't sealed the deal yet."

Curious, eyes narrowed in skepticism, she asked, "How?"

"For one thing, the way Gage looks at you, like he's waiting to unwrap a special present."

More heat surfaced, coloring not only her face, but her throat and chest, too.

"Anyway," Armie said, after taking in her blush with a brow raised in interest, "you want to wait, he cares enough not to push, so he did without. It's admirable, not a reason to drag around like your puppy died or something. Not every guy has that much heart." He held out his arms. "Why do you think I only do local fighting?"

"You have the heart," Harper defended. But she added, "I have no idea what motivates you, I just know it must be something big."

Pleased by her reasoning, he admitted, "You could be right." Before she could jump on that, he continued. "My point is that Gage is a fighter all the way. He'll be a champion one day. That means he has to make certain sacrifices, some at really inconvenient times."

Oddly enough, she felt better about things, and decided to tease him back a little. "So I was a sacrifice?"

"Giving up sex is always a sacrifice." He slung an arm around her shoulders and hauled her into his side. "Especially the sex you haven't had yet."

"Armie!" She enjoyed his insights, but he was so cavalier about it, so bold, she couldn't help but continue blushing.

"Now, Harper, you know..." Suddenly Armie went quiet. "Damn, for such a calm bastard, he has the deadliest stare."

Harper looked up to find Gage scrutinizing them. And he did look rather hot under the collar. Even as the two attractive women did their best to regain his attention, Gage stayed focused on her.

She tried smiling at him. He just transferred his piercing gaze to Armie.

"You could go save him from them," Harper suggested.

"Sorry, honey, not my type."

"What?" she asked as if she didn't already know. "The lack of a Mohawk bothers you?"

He laughed, surprised her with a loud kiss right on her mouth and a firm swat on her butt, then he sauntered away.

CHAPTER THREE

GAGE LOOKED READY to self-combust, so Harper headed over to him. He tracked her progress, and even when she reached him, he still looked far too intent and serious.

"Hey," she said.

"Hey, yourself."

She eyed the other ladies. "See those guys over there?" She pointed to where Denver and Stack loitered by the food, stuffing their faces. "They're shy, but they're really hoping you'll come by to say hi."

It didn't take much more than that for the women to depart.

Gage reached out and tucked her hair behind her ear. "Now why didn't I think of that?"

"Maybe you were enjoying the admiration a little too much."

"No." He touched her cheek, trailed his fingertips down to her chin. "You and Armie had your heads together long enough. Care to share what you two talked about?"

She shrugged. "You."

"Huh." His hand curved around her nape, pulling her in. "That's why he kissed you and played patty-cake with your ass?"

She couldn't be this close to him without touching. Her hands opened on his chest, smoothing over the prominent muscles. What his chest did for a T-shirt should be illegal. "Now, Gage, I know you're not jealous."

His other hand covered hers, flattening her palm over his heart. "Do I have reason to be?"

"Over *Armie?*" She gave a very unladylike snort. "Get real."

He continued to study her.

Sighing, she said, "If you want to know—"

"I do."

Why not tell him? she thought. It'd be interesting to see his reaction. "Actually, it's kind of funny. See, Armie was encouraging me to have sex with you."

Gage's expression went still, first with a hint of surprise, then with the heat of annoyance. "What the hell does it have to do with him?"

No way could she admit that Armie thought they were both sad sacks. "Nothing. You know Armie."

"Yeah." He scowled darker. "I know him."

Laughing, she rolled her eyes. "He's lacking discretion, says whatever he thinks and enjoys butting in." She snuggled in closer to him, leaning on him. Loving him. "He wants you happy."

"I'm happy, damn it."

She didn't bother telling him how *un*happy he sounded just then. "And he wants me happy."

Smoothing a hand down her back, pressing her closer still, he asked, "Sex will make you happy?"

Instead of saying, *I love you so much, sex with you would make me ecstatic,* she quipped, "It'd sure be better than a stinging butt, which is all Armie offered."

"Want me to kiss it and make it better?"

She opened her mouth, but nothing came out.

With a small smile of satisfaction, Gage palmed her cheek, gently caressing. "I'll take that as a yes."

She gave a short nod.

He used his hand on her butt to snug her in closer. "Armie kissed you, too."

Making a face, she told him, "Believe me, the swat was far more memorable."

"Good thing for Armie."

So he *was* jealous?

"Hey," Stack called over to them. "We're ready to get things started. Kill the overhead lights, will you?"

Still looking down at her, Gage slowly nodded. "Sure thing." Taking Harper with him, he went to the front desk and retrieved the barrel key for the locking switches.

The big TV, along with a security lamp in the hallway, would provide all the light they needed. When Gage inserted the key and turned it, the overhead florescent lights clicked off. Given that they stood well away from the others, heavy shadows enveloped them.

Rather than head over to the crowd, Gage aligned her body with his in a tantalizing way. His hand returned to her bottom, ensuring she stayed pressed to him. "Maybe," he whispered, "I can be more memorable."

As he moved his hand lower on her behind—his long fingers seeking inward—she went on tiptoe and squeaked, "*Definitely.*"

Smiling, he took her mouth in a consuming kiss. Combined with the way those talented fingers did such incredible things to her, rational thought proved impossible.

Finally, easing up with smaller kisses and teasing nibbles, he whispered, "We can't do this here."

Her fingers curled in against him, barely making a dent in his rock-solid muscles. "I know," she groaned.

He stroked restless hands up and down her back. "Want to grab a seat with me?"

He asked the question almost as if a big *or* hung at the end. Like... *Or should we just leave? Or should we find an empty room?*

Or would you prefer to go anywhere private so we can both get naked and finish what we started?

She waited, hopeful, but when he said nothing more, she blew out a disappointed breath. "Sure."

And of course she felt like a jerk.

He and Cannon were close friends. Everyone knew he wanted to watch the fights. Despite his own disappointment over medical ineligibility, he was excited for Cannon's competition.

Her eyes were adjusting and she could see Gage better now, the way he searched her face, how he…waited.

For her to understand? Was Armie right? Maybe more than anything she needed to show him that she not only loved him, but she loved his sport, that she supported him and was as excited by his success as he was.

"Yes, let's sit." She took his hand. "Toward the back, though, so we can sneak away later if we decide to." Eyes flaring at that naughty promise, he didn't budge.

"Sneak away to where?"

"The way I feel right now, any empty room might do." Hiding her smile, Harper stretched up to give him a very simple kiss. "That is, between fights. We don't want to miss anything."

His hand tightened on hers, and she couldn't help thinking that maybe Armie's suggestion had merit after all.

GAGE GOT SO caught up in the prefights that he almost—*almost*—forgot about Harper's endless foreplay. Damn, she had him primed. Her closeness, the warmth of her body, the sweet scent of her hair and the warmer scent of her skin, were enough to make him edgy with need. But every so often her hand drifted to his thigh, lingered, stroked. Each time he held his breath, unsure how far she'd go.

How far he wanted her to go.

So far, all he knew was that it wasn't far enough.

Once, she'd run her hand up his back, just sort of feeling

him, her fingers spread as she traced muscles, his shoulder blades, down his spine…

If he gave his dick permission, it would stand at attention right now. But he concentrated on keeping control of things—himself and, when possible, Harper, too.

It wasn't easy. Though she appeared to be as into the fights as everyone else, she still had very busy hands.

It wasn't just the sexual teasing that got to him. It was emotional, too. He hated that he wasn't in Japan with Cannon, walking to the cage for his own big battle. He'd had prelim fights; he'd built his name and recognition.

He'd finally gotten that main event—and it pissed him off more than he wanted to admit that he was left sitting behind.

But sitting behind with Harper sure made it easier. Especially when he seemed so attuned to her.

If her mood shifted, he freaking felt it, deep down inside himself. At one point she hugged his arm, her head on his shoulder, and something about the embrace had felt so damn melancholy that he'd wanted to lift her into his lap and hold her close and make some heavy-duty spur-of-the-moment promises.

Holding her wouldn't have been a big deal; Miles had a chick in his lap. Denver, too.

With Harper, though, it'd be different. Everyone knew a hookup when they saw one, and no way did Gage want others to see her that way. Harper was like family at the rec center. She was part of the inner circle. He would never do anything to belittle her importance.

Beyond that, he wanted more than a hookup. He cared about her well beyond getting laid a single time, well beyond any mere friendship.

Still, as soon as possible, he planned to get her alone and, God willing, get her under him.

Or over him.

However she liked it, as long as he got her. Not just for tonight, but for a whole lot more.

Everyone grimaced when the last prelim fight ended with a grappling match—that turned into an arm bar. The dominant fighter trapped the arm, extended it to the breaking point while the other guy tried everything he could to free himself.

Squeezed up close to his side, peeking through her fingers, Harper pleaded, "Tap, tap, tap," all but begging his opponent to admit defeat before he suffered more damage. And when he did, she cheered with everyone else. "Good fight. Wow. That was intense."

It was so cute how involved she got while watching, that Gage had to tip up her chin so he could kiss her.

Her enthusiasm for the fight waned as she melted against him, saying, "Mmm…"

He smiled against her mouth. "You're making me a little nuts."

"Look who's talking." She glanced around with exaggerated drama. "If only we were alone."

Hoping she meant it, he used his thumb to brush her bottom lip. "We can be." His place. Her place. Either worked for him. "It'll be late when the fights end, but—"

"I really have to wait that long?"

Yep, she meant it. Her blue eyes were heavy, her face flushed. She breathed deeper. He glanced down at her breasts and saw her nipples were tight against the material of her T-shirt.

Okay, much more of that and he wouldn't be able to keep it under wraps.

A roar sounded around them and they both looked up to see Cannon on the screen. Gage couldn't help but grin. Yeah, he wanted to be there, too, but at the same time, he was so damn proud of Cannon.

In such a short time, Cannon had become one of the

most beloved fighters in the sport. The fans adored him. His peers respected him. And the Powers That Be saw him as a big draw moneymaker. After he won tonight, Gage predicted that Cannon would be fighting for the belt.

He'd win it, too.

They showed footage of Cannon before the fight, his knit hat pulled low on his head, bundled under a big sweatshirt. Keeping his muscles warm.

He looked as calm and determined as ever while answering questions.

Harper squeezed his hand and when she spoke, Gage realized it was with nervousness.

"He'll do okay."

Touched by her concern, he smiled. "I'd put money on it."

She nodded, but didn't look away from the screen. "He's been something of a phenomenon, hasn't he?"

"With Cannon, making an impact comes naturally."

"After he wins this one," she mused, "they'll start hyping him for a title shot."

Since her thoughts mirrored his own, he hugged her. Her uncanny insight never ceased to amaze him. Then again, she was a regular at the rec center, interacted often with fighters and enjoyed the sport. It made sense that she'd have the same understanding as him.

"Cannon's earned it." Few guys took as many fights as he did, sometimes on really short notice. If a fighter got sick—or suffered an injury, as Gage had—Cannon was there, always ready, always in shape, always kicking ass. They called him the Saint, and no wonder.

Gage glanced around at the young men who, just a few years ago, would have been hanging on the street corner looking for trouble. Now they had some direction in their lives, the attention they craved, decent role models and a good way to expend energy. But the rec center was just a small part of Cannon's goodwill.

Whenever he got back to town, he continued his efforts to protect the neighborhood. Gage had enjoyed joining their group, going on night strolls to police the corruption, to let thugs know that others were looking out for the hardworking owners of local family businesses. Actual physical conflicts were rare; overall, it was enough to show that someone was paying attention.

It didn't hurt that Cannon was friends with a tough-as-nails police lieutenant and two detectives. And then there was his buddy at the local bar, a place where Cannon used to work before he got his big break in the SBC fight organization. The owner of the bar had more contacts than the entire police department. He influenced a lot of the other businesses with his stance for integrity.

Yeah, Cannon had some colorful, capable acquaintances—which included a diverse group of MMA fighters.

Saint suited him—not that Cannon liked the moniker. It wasn't nearly as harsh as Gage's own fight name.

Thinking about that brought his attention back to Harper. She watched the TV so he saw her in profile, her long lashes, her turned up nose, her firm chin.

That soft, sexy mouth.

He liked the freckles on her cheekbones. He liked everything about her—how she looked, who she was, the way she treated others.

He smoothed Harper's hair and said, "Most women like to call me Savage."

She snorted. "It's a stupid nickname."

Pretending great insult, he leaned away. "It's a fight name, not a nickname. And it's badass."

She disagreed. "There's nothing savage about you. You should have been named Methodical or Accurate or something."

Grinning, he shook his head. "Thanks, but no thanks."

"Well," she muttered, "you're not savage. That's all I'm saying."

He'd gotten the name early on when, despite absorbing several severe blows from a more experienced fighter, he'd kept going. In the end, he'd beaten the guy with some heavy ground and pound, mostly because he'd still been fresh when the other man gassed out.

The commentator had shouted, *He's a damn savage*, and the description stuck.

To keep himself from thinking about just how savage Harper made him—with lust—he asked, "Want something to eat?"

She wrinkled her nose. "After those past few fights? Bleh."

Two of the prelim fights were bloody messes, one because of a busted nose, but the other due to a cut similar to what Gage had. Head wounds bled like a mother. During a fight, as long as the fighter wasn't hurt that badly, they wouldn't stop things over a little spilled blood. Luckily for the contender, the cut was off to the side and so the blood didn't run into his eyes.

For Gage, it hadn't mattered. If only the cut hadn't been so deep. If it hadn't needed stitches. If it would have been somewhere other than right over his eye. If—

Harper's hand trailed over his thigh again. "So, *Savage*," she teased, and damned if she didn't get close to his fly. "Want to help me bring out more drinks before the main event starts?"

Anything to keep him from ruminating on lost opportunities, which he was pretty sure had been Harper's intent.

"Why not?" He stood and hauled her up with him.

They had to go past Armie who stood with two very edgy women and several teenagers, munching on popcorn and comparing biceps.

Armie winked at Harper.

She smiled at him. "We'll only be a minute."

The idiot clutched his chest. "You've just destroyed all my illusions and damaged Savage's reputation beyond repair."

Gage rolled his eyes, more than willing to ignore Armie's nonsense, but he didn't get far before one of the boys asked him about his cut. Next thing he knew, he was surrounded by wide eyes and ripe curiosity. Because it was a good opportunity to show the boys how to handle disappointment, he lingered, letting them ask one question after another.

Harper didn't complain. If anything, she watched him with something that looked a lot like pride. Not exactly what he wanted from her at this particular moment, but it felt good all the same.

He didn't realize she'd gone about getting the drinks without him until Armie relieved her of two large cartons of soft drinks. Together they began putting the cans in the cooler over ice. They laughed together, and even though it looked innocent enough, it made Gage tense with—

"You two hooking up finally?"

Thoughts disrupted, Gage turned to Denver. Hard to believe he hadn't noticed the approach of a two-hundred-and-twenty-pound man. "What?"

"You and Harper," Denver said, while perusing the food that remained. "Finally going to make it official?"

"Make what official?"

"That you're an item." Denver chose half a cold cut sandwich and devoured the majority of it in one bite.

Gage's gaze sought Harper out again. Whatever Armie said to her got him a shove in return. Armie pulled an exaggerated fighter's stance, fists up, as if he thought he'd have to defend himself.

Harper pretended a low shot, Armie dropped his hands

to cover the family jewels, and she smacked him on top of the head.

The way the two of them carried on, almost like siblings, made Gage feel left out.

Were he and Harper an item? He knew how he felt, but Harper could be such a mystery.

Denver shouldered him to the side so he could grab some cake. "Gotta say, man, I hope so. She was so glum while you were away, it depressed the hell out of everyone."

Hard to imagine a woman as vibrant as Harper ever down in the dumps. When he'd left for the camp in Kentucky, she'd understood, wishing him luck, telling him how thrilled she was for him.

But since his return a few days ago, things had been off. He hadn't immediately sought her out, determined to get his head together first. He didn't want pity from anyone, but the way he'd felt had been pretty damned pitiful. He'd waffled between rage at the circumstances and mind-numbing regret. No way did he want others to suffer him like that, most especially Harper.

He knew he'd see her at the rec center and had half expected her to gush over him, to fret over his injury, to sympathize.

She hadn't done any of that. Mostly she'd treated him the same as she did the rest of the guys, leaving him confused and wallowing in his own misery.

Until tonight.

Tonight she was all about making him insane with the need to get her alone and naked.

"You listening to me, Gage?"

Rarely did another fighter call him by his given name. That Denver did so now almost felt like a reprimand from his mom. "Yeah, *Denver,* I'm listening."

"Good." Denver folded massive arms over his massive chest, puffing up like a turkey. "So what's it to be?"

If Denver expected a challenge, too bad. Gage again sought out Harper with his gaze. "She was really miserable?"

Denver deflated enough to slap him on the back. "Yeah. It was awful. Made me sad as shit, I don't mind telling you."

"What was she miserable about?"

"Dude, are you that fucking obtuse?"

Stack stepped into the conversation. "Hell, yeah, he is." Then changing the subject, Stack asked, "Did Rissy go to Japan with Cannon?"

Denver answered, saying, "Yeah, he took her and her roommate along."

Merissa, better known as Rissy, was Cannon's little sis. A roommate was news to Gage, though. "If you have ideas about his sister, you're an idiot."

Stack drew back. "No. Hell, no. Damn man, don't start rumors."

Everyone knew Cannon as a nice guy. More than nice. But he was crazy-particular when it came to Merissa. For that reason, the guys all looked past her, through her or when forced to it, with nothing more than respect. "Who's the roommate?"

"Sweet Cherry Pie," Denver rumbled low and with feeling.

Stack grinned at him.

Gage totally missed the joke. "What?"

"Cherry Payton," Denver said, and damn if he didn't almost sigh. "Long blond hair, big chocolate-brown eyes, extra fine body…"

"Another one bites the dust," Stack said with a laugh.

"Another one?"

"Obtuse," Denver lamented.

Stack nodded toward Harper. "You being the first, dumb ass."

"We all expect you to make her feel better about things."

Confusion kicked his temper up a notch. "What *things*?"

Slapping a hand over his heart, Stack said, "How you feel."

Striking a similar pose, Denver leaned into Stack. "What you want."

Heads together, they intoned, *"Love."*

"You're both morons." But damn it, he realized that he did love her. Probably had for a long time. How could he not? Priorities could be a bitch and he hated the idea that he'd maybe made Harper unhappy by not understanding his feelings sooner.

He chewed his upper lip while wondering how to correct things.

"Honesty," Stack advised him. "Tell her how the schedule goes, what to expect and leave the rest up to her."

"Harper's smart," Denver agreed. "She'll understand."

It irked Gage big-time to have everyone butting into his personal business. "Don't you guys have something better to do than harass me?"

"I have some*one* better to do," Stack told him, nodding toward one of the women who'd hit on Gage earlier. "Butting in to your business was just my goodwill gesture of the day." And with that he sauntered off.

Denver leaned back on the table of food. "We all like Harper, you know."

Gage was starting to think they liked her a little too much. "Yeah, I get that."

"So quit dicking around, will you?" He grabbed up another sandwich and he, too, joined a woman.

Gage stewed for half a minute, turned—and almost ran into Harper.

CHAPTER FOUR

GAGE CAUGHT HER ARMS, steadying them both. "Why does everyone keep sneaking up on me?"

She brushed off his hands. "If you hadn't been ogling the single ladies, maybe you'd be more aware."

She absolutely had to know better than to think that, but just in case… "How could I notice any other woman with you around?"

She eyed him. "Do you notice other women when I'm not around?"

Damn, he thought, did she really *not* know how much he cared? Worse, had she been sad while he was away?

The possibility chewed on his conscience. "No, I don't." He drew her up to kiss her sweetly, and then, because this was Harper, not so sweetly.

To give her back a little, he shared his own complaint. "You spend way too much time horsing around with Armie."

Shrugging, she reached for a few chips. "I was trying not to crowd you."

"What does that mean?"

While munching, she gestured around the interior of the rec center. "This is a fight night. You're hanging with your buds. When I see you guys talking, I don't want to horn in."

Whoa. Those were some serious misconceptions. To help clear things up, he cupped her face. "You can't."

"Can't what?"

"Horn in. Ever."

Brows pinching in disgruntlement, she shoved away from him. "I just told you I wouldn't."

He hauled her right back. "I'm not saying you shouldn't, honey, I'm saying you can't because there's never a bad time for you to talk to me. Remember that, okay?"

Astonished, she blinked up at him, and he wanted to declare himself right then. Luckily the first fight on the main card started and everyone went back to their seats, saving him from rushing her.

This time, Gage had a hard time concentrating. He saw the fight, he cheered, but more of his attention veered to Harper, to how quiet she was now.

Thinking about him?

The fight ended in the first round with a knockout.

Instead of reacting with everyone else, Harper turned her face up to his. As if no time had passed at all, she said, "That's not entirely true."

Damn, but it was getting more difficult by the second to keep his hands off her. He contented himself by opening his hand on her waist, stroking up to her ribs then down to her hip. "What's that?"

"There are plenty of times when I can't intrude."

She was still stewing about that? "No."

Like a thundercloud, she darkened. Turning to more fully face him, she said low, *"Yes."* Before he could correct her, she insisted, "But I want you to know that I understand."

Apparently she didn't. "How so?"

Leaning around him, she glanced at one and all to ensure there were no eavesdroppers. As if uncertain, she puckered her brows while trying to find the right words. "I know when you're in training—"

"I'm pretty much always in training."

She looked like she wanted to smack him. "There's training and then there's *training.*"

True enough. "You mean when I go away to another camp."

"That, and when you're close to a fight."

Should he tell her how much he'd enjoy coming home to her—every night, not just between fights? Would she ever be willing to travel with him? Or to wait for him when she couldn't?

He had a feeling Harper would fit seamlessly into his life no matter what he had going on.

Being as honest as he could, Gage nodded. "There will be times when my thoughts are distracted, when I have to focus on other stuff. But that doesn't mean I don't care. It sure as hell doesn't mean you have to keep your distance."

The next fight started and though a few muted conversations continued, most in attendance kept their comments limited to the competition. Beside him, Harper fell silent. Gage could almost feel her struggling to sort out everything he'd said.

Again, he found himself studying her profile; not just her face, but her body, too. Her breasts weren't large, but they fit her frame, especially with her small waist and the sexy flare of her hips. She kept her long legs crossed, one foot nervously rocking. She drew in several deep breaths. A pulse tripped in her throat.

By the second the sexual tension between them grew.

The end of the night started to feel like too many hours away. They had at least three more fights on the main card. Cannon's fight would be last. It wasn't a title fight, but it'd still go five rounds.

The current match went all three rounds and came down to a split decision. Gage no longer cared; hell, he'd missed more of the fight than he'd seen.

Around him, voices rose in good-natured debate about how the judges had gotten it right or wrong.

"What do you think?" Gage asked Harper.

She shrugged. "Depends on how the judges scored things. The guy from Brazil really pushed the fight, but the other one landed more blows. Still, he didn't cause that much damage, and the Brazilian got those two take-downs—"

Gage put a finger to her mouth. "I meant about us."

Her wide-eyed gaze swung to his. "Oh." She gulped, considered him, then whispered, "I like it."

"It?"

"There being an 'us.'"

Yeah, he liked it, too, maybe more than he'd realized before now. "I missed you while I was away."

She scoffed. "You were way too busy for that."

"I worked hard, no denying it. But it wasn't 24/7. I found myself alone with my thoughts far too often."

She forced a smile. "I'm sure at those times you were obsessed about the SBC, about the competition, about winning."

"All that—plus you." When it came to priorities, she was at the top. He'd just made too many assumptions for her to realize it.

She looked tortured for a moment before her hand knotted in his shirt and she pulled him closer. With pained accusation, she said, "You didn't call."

Hot with regret, Gage covered her hand with his own. "I was trying to focus." Saying it out loud, he felt like an ass.

But Harper nodded. "That's what I'm saying. There will be times when I need to stay out of your way so I don't mess with that focus."

He hated the idea of her avoiding him.

Almost as much as he hated the thought of ever leaving her again. Yet that was a reality. He was a fighter; he would go to other camps to train, travel around the country, around the world.

He'd go where the SBC sent him.

"You have to know, Gage. I'd never get in your way, not on purpose."

He almost groaned.

"I'm serious! I know how important your career is and I know what a nuisance it can be to—"

Suddenly starved for the taste of her, for the feel of her, Gage took her mouth in a firm kiss.

But that wasn't enough, so he turned his head and nibbled her bottom lip until she opened. When he licked inside her warm, damp mouth, her breath hitched. Mindful of where they were, he nonetheless had a hell of time tempering his lust.

Damn it.

The next fight started. Cannon would be after that.

In a sudden desperate rush, Gage left his chair, pulling her up and along with him as he headed toward the dimly lit hallway. He couldn't wait a second more. But for what he had to say, had to explain, he needed the relative privacy of a back room.

Luckily she'd seated them at the end of the back row. In only a few steps, and without a lot of attention, he had them on their way.

Tripping along with him, Harper whispered, *"Gage."*

"There are high school boys out there," he told her. He glanced in the storage room, but no, that was too close to the main room and the activity of the group.

"I know. So?"

He brought her up and alongside him so he could slip an arm around her. "So they don't need to see me losing my head over you."

She stopped suddenly, which forced him to stop.

Looking far too shy for the ballsy woman he knew her to be, she whispered, "Are you?"

This time he understood her question. "Losing my head over you?" Gently, he said, "No."

Her shoulders bunched as if she might slug him.

Damn, but he adored her. "I lost it a long time ago. I just forgot to tell you."

Suspicious, she narrowed her eyes. "What does that mean exactly?"

Not about to declare himself in a freaking hallway, he took her hands and started backing up toward the office. "Come along with me and I'll explain everything." This particular talk was long overdue.

She didn't resist, but she did say, "The fight you should have been in is next. And Cannon will be fighting soon after that."

"I know." At the moment, seeing the fight he'd missed was the furthest thing from his mind. As to Cannon, well, he'd be in a lot of fights. This wasn't his first, wouldn't be his last. If all went well, Gage would get her commitment to spend the night, and more, before Cannon entered the cage. "The thing is, I need you."

She searched his face. "Need me…how?"

In every way imaginable. "Let me show you."

Her gaze went over his body. "Sounds to me like you're talking about sex."

Did lust taint his brain, or did she sound hopeful? They reached the office door and he tried the handle. Locked, of course. Trying not to think about how the night would end, he said, "Seriously, Harper, much as I love that idea, we're at the rec center."

"So?"

Damn, she knew how to throw him. He sucked in air and forged on. "I thought we'd talk." Digging in his pocket, he found the keys he'd picked up earlier when he shut off the lights.

Sarcasm added a wicked light to her beautiful blue eyes. "Talk? That's what you want to do? Seriously?"

"Yeah. See, I need to explain a few things to you and

it's better done in private." The door opened and he drew her in.

Typical of Harper, she took the initiative, shutting and locking the door, then grabbing him. "We're alone." Her mouth brushed his chin, his jaw, his throat. "Say what you need to say."

"I love you."

She went so still, it felt like he held a statue. Ignoring her lack of a response, Gage cupped her face. "I love you, Harper Gates. Have for a while now. I'm sorry I didn't realize it sooner. I'm especially sorry I didn't figure it out before I took off for Kentucky."

Confused, but also defending him, she whispered, "You were excited about the opportunity."

She made him sound like a kid, when at the moment he felt very much like a man. "True." Slowly, he leaned into her, pinning her up against the door, arranging her so that they fit together perfectly. She was so slight, so soft and feminine—when she wasn't giving him or one of the other fighters hell. "I thought it'd be best for me to concentrate only on the upcoming fight, but that was asinine."

"No," she said, again defending him. "It made sense."

"Loving you makes sense." He took her mouth, and never wanted to stop kissing her. Hot and deep. Soft and sweet. With Harper it didn't matter. However she kissed him, it blew his mind and pushed all his buttons.

He brushed damp kisses over to the side of her neck, up to her ear.

On a soft wail, Harper said, "How can you love me? We haven't even had sex yet."

"Believe me, I know." He covered her breast with his hand, gently kneading her, loving the weight of her, how her nipple tightened. He wanted to see her, wanted to take her in his mouth. "We can change that later tonight."

"I'll never last that long." She stretched up along his

body, both hands tangled in his hair, anchoring him so she could feast off his mouth.

No way would he argue with her.

Everything went hot and urgent between them.

He coasted a hand down her side, caught her thigh and lifted her leg up alongside his. Nudging in against her, knowing he could take her this way, right here, against the door, pushed him over the edge.

Not what he would have planned for their first time, but with Harper so insistent, he couldn't find the brain cells to offer up an alternative.

"Are you sure?" he asked, while praying that she was.

"Yes. Now, Gage." She moved against him. "Right now."

HARPER GRABBED FOR his T-shirt and shoved it up so she could get her hands on his hot flesh, so she could explore all those amazing muscles. Unlike some of the guys, he didn't shave his chest and she loved—*loved, loved, loved*—his body hair.

God, how could any man be so perfect?

She got the shirt above his pecs and leaned in to brush her nose over his chest hair, to deeply inhale his incredible scent. It filled her head, making her dazed with need.

When she took a soft love bite, he shuddered. "Take it easy."

No, she wouldn't.

"We have to slow down or I'm a goner."

But she couldn't. Never in her life had she known she'd miss someone as much as she'd missed him when he'd left. Now he was back, and whether he really loved her or was just caught up in the moment, she'd worry about it later.

She needed him. All of him.

She cupped him through his jeans and heard him groan. He was thick and hard and throbbing.

He sucked in a breath. "Harper, baby, seriously, we have to slow down." Taking her wrist, he lifted her hand away. "You need to catch up a little."

"I'm there already." She'd been there since first deciding on her course of action for the night.

"Not quite." Gage carried both her hands to his shoulders before kissing her senseless, giving her his tongue, drawing hers into his mouth.

She couldn't get enough air into her starving lungs but didn't care. Against her belly she felt his heavy erection, and she wanted to touch him again, to explore him in more detail.

He caught the hem of her T-shirt, drawing it up and over her head. Barely a heartbeat passed before he flipped open the front closure on her bra and the cups parted.

Taking her mouth again, he groaned as his big hands gently molded over her, his thumbs teasing her nipples until she couldn't stop squirming. She wasn't one of the overly stacked groupies who dogged his heels, but she didn't dislike her body, either.

She'd always considered herself not big, but big enough.

Now, with his enormous hands on her, she felt delicate—even more so when he scooped an arm under her behind and easily lifted her up so he could draw one nipple into his hot mouth.

Harper wrapped her legs around his waist, her arms around his neck. He took his time, drawing on her for what felt like forever, until she couldn't keep still, couldn't contain the soft cries of desperate need.

From one breast to the other, he tasted, teased, sucked, nibbled.

"Gage…" Even saying his name took an effort. "Please."

"Please what?" he asked, all full of masculine satisfaction and a fighter's control. He licked her, circling, teasing. "Please more?"

"Yes."

Back on her feet, she dropped against the door. He opened her jeans and a second later shoved them, and her panties, down to her knees.

Anticipation kept her still, kept her breath rushing and her heart pounding. But he just stood there, sucking air and waiting for God knew what.

"Gage?" she whispered with uncertainty.

One hand flattened on the wall beside her head, but he kept his arm locked out, his body from touching hers. "I should take you to my place," he rasped, sounding tortured. "I should take you someplace with more time, more privacy, more—"

Panic tried to set in. "Don't you even *think* about stopping now." No way could he leave her like this.

His mouth touched her cheek, the corner of her lips, her jaw, her temple. "No, I won't. I can't."

A loud roar sounded from the main part of the room. Knowing what that meant, that Cannon's fight was about to start, guilt nearly leveled Harper. "I forgot," she admitted miserably.

"Doesn't matter," he assured her.

But of course it did. He was here to watch Cannon compete, to join in with his fight community to celebrate a close friend.

She was here to show him she wouldn't interfere and yet, that's exactly what she'd done. "We could—"

"No, baby." Need made his short laugh gravelly. "Believe me when I say that I *can't*."

"Oh." Her heart started punching again—with excitement. "We'll miss the fight."

"We'll catch the highlights later. Together." He stroked her hair with his free hand, over her shoulder, down the side of her body.

"You're sure?"

Against her mouth, he whispered, "Give or take a bed for convenience, I'm right where I want to be." His kiss scorched her, and he added, "With you."

Aww. Hearing him say it was nice, but knowing he meant it multiplied everything she felt, and suddenly she couldn't wait. She took his hand and guided it across her body.

And between her legs.

They both groaned.

At first he just cupped her, his palm hot, his hand covering so much of her. They breathed together, taut with expectation.

"It seems like I've wanted you forever," he murmured at the same time as his fingers searched over her, touching carefully. His forehead to hers, he added, "Mmm. You're wet."

Speaking wasn't easy, but he deserved the truth. "Because I *have* wanted you forever."

"I'm glad, Harper." His fingers parted her swollen lips, stroked gently over her, delved. "Widen your legs a little more."

That husky, take-charge, turned-on tone nearly put her over the edge. Holding on to his shoulders, her face tucked into his throat, she widened her stance. Using two fingers, he glided over her, once, twice, testing her readiness—and he pressed both fingers deep.

Legs stiffening, Harper braced against the door.

"Stay with me," Gage said before kissing her throat.

She felt his teeth on her skin, his hot breath, those oh-so-talented fingers.

"Damn, you feel good. Tight and wet and perfect." He worked her, using his hand to get her close to climax. "Relax just a little."

"Can't." Her fingernails bit into his shoulders. "Oh, God."

"If we were on a bed," he growled against her throat, "I could get to your nipples. But you're so short—"

"I'm not," she gasped, unsure whether she'd be able to take that much excitement. "You're just so damn big."

"Soon as you come for me," he promised, "I'll show you how big I am."

Such a braggart. Of course, she'd already had a good idea, given she often saw him in nothing more than athletic shorts. And she'd already had her hands on him. Not long enough to do all the exploring she wanted to do, but enough to—

He brought his thumb up to her clitoris, and she clenched all over.

"Nice," he told her. "I can feel you getting closer."

Shut up, Gage. She thought it but didn't say it, because words right now, at this particular moment, would be far too difficult.

He cupped her breast and, in keeping with the accelerated tempo of the fingers between her legs, he tugged at her nipple.

The first shimmer of approaching release took her to her tiptoes. *"Gage."*

"I've got you."

The next wave, stronger, hotter, made her groan in harsh pleasure.

"I love you, Harper."

Luckily, at that propitious moment, something happened in the fight because everyone shouted and cheered—and that helped to drown out the harsh groans of Harper's release.

CHAPTER FIVE

GAGE BADLY WANTED to turn on lights, to strip Harper naked and then shuck out of his own clothes. He wanted to touch her all over, taste her everywhere, count her every freckle while feeling her against him, skin on skin, with no barriers.

Even with her T-shirt shoved up above her breasts and her jeans down around her knees, holding Harper in his arms was nice. Her scent had intensified, her body now a warm, very soft weight limp against him. He kept one hand tangled in her hair, the other cupping her sexy ass.

He let her rest while she caught her breath.

If he'd found a better time and place for this, he could stretch her out on a bed, or the floor or a table—didn't matter as long as he could look at every inch of her, kiss her all over.

Devour her slowly, at his leisure.

But they were in an office, at the rec center, with a small crowd of fighters and fans only a hallway away.

He kissed her temple, hugged her protectively.

His cock throbbed against her belly. He badly wanted to be inside her, driving them both toward joint release.

But this, having Harper sated and cuddling so sweetly… yeah, that was pretty damn special.

"Mmm," she murmured. "I lost my bones somewhere."

"I have one you can borrow."

He felt her grin against his throat, then her full-body

rub as she wiggled against him. "Yes," she teased. "Yes, you do."

"I like hearing you come, Harper." With small pecks, he nudged up her face so he could get to her mouth. "Whatever you do, you do it well."

That made her laugh, so the kiss was a little silly, tickling.

She drew in a deep breath, shored up her muscles, and somewhat stood on her own. "The fight is still going on?"

"Sounds like."

"So all that excitement before—"

"You coming?"

She bit his chest, inciting his lust even more. "No, I meant with everyone screaming."

"Probably a near submission. Cannon is good on the ground, good with submissions." Good with every facet of fighting. "But let's not talk about Cannon right now."

"You really don't mind missing his fight?"

"Jesus, woman, I'm about to bust my jeans. Cannon is the furthest thing from my mind."

Happy with his answer, she said, "Okay, then, let's talk about you." She nibbled her way up to his throat. "There is just so much of you to enjoy."

"You could start here," he said, taking one of her small, soft hands down to press against his fly.

"I think I will." With her forehead to his sternum, she watched her hands as she opened the snap to his jeans, slowly eased down the zipper. "I wish we had more light in here."

Because that mirrored his earlier thought, he nodded. "You can just sort of feel your way around."

"Is that what you did?" Using both hands, she held him, so no way could he reply. She stroked his length, squeezed him. "You are so hard."

"Yup." He couldn't manage anything more detailed than that.

"You have a condom?"

"Wallet."

Still touching him, she clarified, "You have a condom in your wallet?"

"Yup."

She tipped her face up to see him, and he could hear the humor in her voice. "A little turned on?"

"A *lot* turned on." He covered her hand with his own and got her started on a stroking rhythm he loved. *"Damn."*

Harper whispered, "Kiss me."

And he did, taking her mouth hard, twining his tongue with hers, making himself crazy by again exploring her, the silky skin of her bottom, the dampness between her thighs, her firm breasts and stiffened nipples.

Harper released him just long enough to say, "Shirt off, big boy." She tried shoving it up, but Gage took over, reaching over his back for a fistful of cotton and jerking the material away. Anticipating her hands, her mouth, on his hot skin, he dropped the shirt.

She didn't disappoint. Hooking her fingers in the waistband of his jeans, she shoved down the denim and his boxers, too, then started feeling him all over. His shoulders to his hips. His pecs to his abs. She grazed her palms over his nipples, then went back to his now throbbing cock.

"You are so impressive in so many ways."

He tried to think up a witty reply, but with her small, soft hands on him, he could barely breathe, much less banter.

"I've thought about something so many times…" And with no more warning than that, she sank to her knees.

Oh, God. Gage locked his muscles, one hand settling on top of her head.

Holding him tight, Harper skimmed her lips over the sensitive head, licked down the length of his shaft.

Never one for half measures, she drew her tongue back up and slid her mouth over him.

A harsh groan reverberated out of his chest. "Harper."

Her clever tongue swirled over and around him—and she took him deep again.

Too much. Way too much. He clasped her shoulder. "Sorry, honey, but I can't take it."

She continued anyway.

"Harper," he warned.

She reached around him, clasping his ass as if she thought she could control him.

But control of any kind quickly spiraled away. Later, he thought to himself, he'd enjoy doing this again, letting her have her way, giving her all the time she wanted.

Just not now, not when he so desperately wanted to be inside her.

"Sorry, honey." He caught her under the arms and lifted her to her feet, then set her away from him while he gasped for breath. As soon as he could, he dug out his wallet and fumbled for the condom.

Sounding breathless and hot, she whispered, "You taste so good."

He'd never last. "Shh." He rolled on the condom with trembling hands. Stepping up to her in a rush, he stripped away her shirt and bra, shoved her jeans lower. "Hold on to me."

Hooking her right knee with his elbow, he lifted her leg, opening her as much as he could with her jeans still on, his still on. He moved closer still, kissing her until they were both on the ragged edge.

"Now," Harper demanded.

He nudged against her, found his way, and sank deep in one strong thrust.

More cheers sounded in the outer room, but neither of

them paid much attention. Already rocking against her, Gage admitted, "I'm not going to last."

She matched the rhythm he set. "I don't need you to… *Gage!*"

Kissing her, he muffled her loud cries as she came, holding him tight, squeezing him tighter, her entire body shimmering in hot release. Seconds later he pinned her to the door, pressed his face into her throat, and let himself go.

For several minutes he was deaf and blind to everything except the feel of Harper in his arms where she belonged.

Little aftershocks continued to tease her intimate muscles, and since he remained joined with her, he felt each one. Their heartbeats danced together.

Gradually he became aware of people talking in the outer room. They sounded happy and satisfied, telling him the fight had ended.

Harper came to the same realization. "Oh, no. We missed everything?"

"Not everything." After a nudge against her to remind what they hadn't missed, he disengaged their bodies. Slowly he eased her leg down, staying close to support her—which was sort of a joke, given how shaky he felt, too.

"Do you think Cannon won?"

"I know he did."

Her fingers moved over his face, up to the corner of his eye near his stitches. "You're sure?"

"Absolutely." He brought her hand to his mouth and kissed her palm. "I was sure even before the fight started."

Letting out a long breath, she dropped her head. "I'm sorry we missed it."

"I don't have any regrets."

She thought about that for a second, then worried aloud, "They'll all know what we were doing."

"Yeah." There was barely enough light to see, but he

located paper in the printer, stole a sheet, and used it to wrap up the spent condom. He pitched it into the metal waste can.

"I hope they didn't hear us."

Gage tucked himself away and zipped his jeans. "Even if they did—"

She groaned over the possibility. "No, no, no."

Pulling her back into his arms, he teased, "They won't ask for too many details."

Her fisted hands pressed against his chest. "I swear, if Armie says a single word, I'll—"

Gage kissed her. Then touched her breasts. And her belly. And lower.

"Gage," she whispered, all broken up. "We can't. Not now."

"Not here," he agreed, while paying homage to her perfect behind. "Come home with me."

"Okay."

He'd told her that he loved her. She hadn't yet said how she felt. But while she was being agreeable… "I'll fight again in two months."

Gasping with accusation, she glared at him. "You knew you'd fight again—"

"Of course I will." He snorted. "I got injured. I didn't quit."

"Yeah, I know. But…" Her confusion washed over him. "I didn't realize things were already set. Why didn't you tell me?"

"Didn't come up." He kissed the end of her nose. "And honestly, I was too busy raging about the fight I'd miss to talk about the next one."

He felt her stillness. "You're not raging anymore?"

"Mellow as a newborn kitten," he promised. "Thank you for that."

Thinking things through, she ran her hands up his chest to his collarbone. "Where?"

"Canada."

Gage felt her putting her shoulders back, straightening her spine, shoring herself up. "So when you leave again—"

Before she could finish that thought, he took her mouth, stepping her back into the door again, unable to keep his hands off her ass. When he came up for air, he said, "If you can, I'd love it if you came with me."

She was still all soft and sweet from his kiss. "To Canada?"

"To wherever I go, whenever I go. For training. For fighting." He tucked her hair behind her ear, gave her a soft and quick kiss. "For today and tomorrow and the year after that."

Her eyes widened and her lips parted. "Gage?"

"I told you I love you. Did you think I made it up?"

In a heartbeat, excitement stripped away the uncertainty and she threw herself against him, squeezing tight. With her shirt still gone, her jeans still down, it was an awesome embrace.

A knock sounded on the door, and Armie called, "Just about everyone is gone if you two want to wrap it up."

"He loves me," Harper told him.

Armie laughed. "Well, duh, doofus. Everyone could see that plain as day."

Gage cupped her head in his hands, but spoke to Armie. "Any predictions on how she feels about me?"

"Wow." The door jumped, meaning Armie had probably just propped his shoulder against it. "Hasn't told you yet, huh?"

"No."

"Cruel, Harper," he chastised her. "Really cruel. And here I thought you were one of those *nice* girls."

Lips quivering, eyes big and liquid, she stared up at him. "I love you," she whispered.

"Me or Gage?" Armie asked with facetious good humor.

Harper kicked the door hard with her heel, and Armie

said, "Ow, damn it. Fine. I'm leaving. But Gage, you have the keys so I can't lock up until—"

"Five minutes."

"And there go my illusions again."

The quiet settled around them. They watched each other. Gage did some touching, too. But what the hell, Harper was mostly naked, looking at him with a wealth of emotion.

"I should get dressed."

"You should tell me again that you love me."

"I do. *So much,*" Harper added with feeling. "I have for such a long time."

Nice. "The things you do to me…" He fumbled around along the wall beside the door and finally located the light switch.

She flinched away at first, but Harper wasn't shy. God knew she had no reason to be.

Putting her shoulders back, her chin up, she let him look. And what a sight she made with her jeans down below her knees and her shirt gone. He cupped her right breast and saw a light sprinkling of freckles decorating her fair skin.

"Let's go," he whispered. "I want to take you home and look for more freckles."

That made her snicker. As she pulled up her jeans, she said, "I don't really have that many."

"Don't ruin it for me. I'll find out for myself."

By the time they left the room, only Armie, Stack and Denver were still hanging around.

With his arm around Harper, Gage asked, "You guys didn't hook up?"

"Meeting her in an hour," Stack said.

"She's pulling her car around," Denver told him.

Armie shrugged toward the front door. "Those two are waiting for me."

Two? Everyone glanced at the front door where a couple of women hugged up to each other. One blonde, one raven-haired.

"Why does she have a whip in her belt?" Harper asked.

"I'm not sure," Armie murmured as he, too, watched the women. "But I'm intrigued."

"Are they fondling each other?" Gage asked.

"Could be." Armie drew his gaze back to Harper and Gage, then grinned shamelessly. "But I don't mind being the voyeuristic third wheel."

The guys all grinned with amusement. They were well used to Armie's excesses.

A little shocked, Harper shook her head. "One of these days a nice girl will make an honest man of you. That is, if some crazy woman doesn't do you in first."

"At least I'd die happy." Leaning against the table, arms folded over his chest, Armie studied them both. "So. You curious about how your match went?"

"Wasn't my match," Gage said.

"Should have been. And just so you know, Darvey annihilated your replacement."

"How many rounds?"

"Two. Referee stoppage."

Gage nodded as if it didn't matter all that much. Darvey had gotten off easy because Gage knew he'd have won the match.

Then Armie dropped a bombshell. "Cannon damn near lost."

Because he'd been expecting something very different, Gage blinked. "No way."

Armie blew out a breath. "He was all but gone from a vicious kick to the ribs."

"Ouch." Gage winced just thinking of it. If the kick nearly took Cannon out, it must have been a liver kick, and those hurt like a mother, stole your wind and made breathing—or fighting—impossible.

Stack picked up the story. "But you know Cannon. On his way down he threw one last punch—"

"And knocked Moeller out cold," Denver finished with enthusiasm. "It was truly something to see. Everyone was on their feet, not only here but at the event. The commentators went nuts. It was crazy."

"Everyone waited to see who would get back on his feet first," Stack finished.

And obviously that was Cannon. Gage half smiled. Every fighter knew flukes happened. Given a fluke injury had taken him out of the competition, he knew it better than most. "I'm glad he pulled it off."

"That he did," Armie said. "And if you don't mind locking up, I think I'll go pull off a few submissions of my own."

Harper scowled in disapproval, then flapped her hand, sending him on his way.

A minute later, Denver and Stack took off, too.

Left alone finally, Gage put his arm around Harper. "Ready to go home?"

"My place or yours?"

"Where doesn't matter—as long as you're with me."

She gave him a look that said *"Awww!"* and hugged him tight. Still squeezed up close, she whispered with worry, "I can't believe Cannon almost lost."

Gage smoothed his hand down her back. "Don't worry about it. We fighters know how to turn bad situations to our advantage."

"We?" She leaned back in his arms to see him. "How's that?"

"For Cannon, the near miss will only hype up the crowd for his next fight." He bent to kiss the end of her freckled nose. "As for me, I might have missed a competition, but

I got the girl. There'll be other fights, but honest to God, Harper, there's only one *you.* All in all, I'd say I'm the big winner tonight."

"I'd say you're *mine.*" With a trembling, emotional smile, Harper touched his face, then his shoulders, and his chest. As her hand dipped lower, she whispered, "And that means we're both winners. Tonight, tomorrow and always."

* * * * *

Want more sizzling romance from
New York Times *bestselling author Lori Foster?*
Pick up every title in her Ultimate series:

HARD KNOCKS
NO LIMITS
HOLDING STRONG
TOUGH LOVE

Available now from HQN Books!

COMING NEXT MONTH FROM

HARLEQUIN® Blaze®

Available September 15, 2015

#863 TEASING HER SEAL

Uniformly Hot!

by Anne Marsh

SEAL team leader Gray Jackson needs to convince Laney Parker to leave an island resort before she gets hurt—and before his cover is blown. But as his mission heats up, so do their nights...

#864 IF SHE DARES

by Tanya Michaels

Still timid months after being robbed at gunpoint, Riley Kendrick wants to rediscover her fun, daring side, and Jack Reed, her sexy new neighbor, has some wicked ideas about how to help.

#865 NAKED THRILL

The Wrong Bed

by Jill Monroe

They wake up in bed together. Naked. And with no memory. So Tony and Hayden follow a trail of clues to piece together what—or *who*—they did on the craziest night of their lives.

#866 KISS AND MAKEUP

by Taryn Leigh Taylor

Falling into bed with a sexy guy she met on a plane is impulsive even for Chloe. But when Ben's client catches them together, she does something even more impulsive: she pretends to be his wife!

SPECIAL EXCERPT FROM

US Navy SEAL Gray Jackson is undercover...posing as a massage therapist at a sultry Caribbean resort. But when he gets his hands on Dr. Laney Parker, can he keep his mind on his mission?

Read on for a sneak preview of
TEASING HER SEAL,
Anne Marsh's *latest story*
about supremely sexy SEALs in the
UNIFORMLY HOT! *miniseries*

Gray had magic hands. Laney should have gone for sixty or even the full ninety minutes instead of the paltry thirty minutes she'd ponied up for. He was that good.

"You're tight here." He pressed a particularly tense spot on her back, and she stopped caring that she was stretched out, bare-ass naked and vulnerable. God, he was good.

"Trigger point." Not, apparently, that she needed to tell him. The man knew what he was doing.

"Are you a doctor?"

"Trauma surgeon." Was that sultry whisper her voice? Because, if so, Gray was definitely a miracle worker. She felt herself melting under his touch and, wow, how long had it been since she'd done that?

He found and pressed against another knot. "So I should call you Dr. Parker."

He moved around to the front of the massage bed. The bed had one of those circle doughnut things that she'd always thought were awkward. She opened her eyes as Gray's feet moved into view. She'd never had a foot fetish before, but he was barefoot, and his feet were sun-bronzed and strong-looking. Those few inches of bare skin made her want to see more. She'd bet the rest of him was every bit as spectacular.

It was probably bad she found his feet sexy. He was just doing a job.

Really, really well.

He gently pulled her ponytail free before running his hands through her hair, pressing his fingertips against her scalp. Maybe she'd been a cat in a former life, because she'd always loved having her hair played with. For long minutes, Gray rubbed small sensual circles against her scalp. She bit back a moan. *Just lie here. Keep still.* She probably wasn't supposed to arch off the table, screaming *more, more, more*. Although she could. She definitely could.

He moved closer, his thighs brushing against the bed. If she lifted her head, the situation could get awkward fast. Thinking about that made her stiffen up again, but then he cupped the back of her neck, pressing and rotating. And oh, she could feel the tension melting away. The small tugs on her hair sent a prickle of excitement through her entire body.

"Should I call you *Doctor*?" he prompted.